CAVANILA'S
CHOICES

A Novel of the Minoan Cataclysm

JESSE SISKEN

Parthenos Publishing
Lexington, KY.

ISBN: 0615940277
ISBN 13: 9780615940274
Library of Congress Control Number: 2013957972
Parthenos Publishing, Lexington, KY.

Cavanila's Choices is a novel. Though based upon actual historical events and
locations, all names, places and incidents are drawn from the author's imagi-
nation or are used in a fictitious manner.

DEDICATION

To my wife, with love and many thanks

ACKNOWLEDGMENTS

Special thanks to: John Younger who accepted this nontraditional student into his wonderfully enjoyable and edifying course in Ancient Greek Archaeology during the summer of 2002; the many scholars of the Aegean Bronze Age, including those who share their expertise on Dr. Younger's list serve, *Ageanet;* Anaya Sarpaki for her encouragement, suggestions and critique that helped make this tale far better and richer than it might otherwise have been. All errors, exaggerations or distortions, intended or otherwise, are totally of my own doing.

My thanks to Evangelos Levas for introducing me to the Greek language; Giannis and Maria Genezakis for graciously welcoming me into their home in Archanes. It was Giannis who took me up to Mt. Juktas and their son, George, who piqued my interest in the Stavromyti cave. My thanks also to Methodius Psomas who guided me up the western approach to Karphi, and to Phaneromeni and Agia Forteini as well.

I owe much to Dr. Ross Scaife (now deceased) for his instruction, help and friendship, both within and outside his stimulating classes in Greek and Roman Art, and to Kim Edwards who taught me much about creative writing in her course at the University of Kentucky.

I also wish to acknowledge several welcoming and helpful groups. They include: the Carnegie Center for Learning and Literacy in Lexington, KY, a unique and wonderful institution under the direction of Jan Eisenhour and more recently Neil Chethic who mentored me early on in this writing process; The Bard's Corner Writers Group of Elizabethtown, KY; the Eagle Creek Writer's group of Lexington and the Novels in Progress Workshop at Spalding University sponsored by the Green River Writers Group. I am particularly indebted to Robert Louis Ebert and Elaine Palencia for their encouragement and very much appreciated critiques of this manuscript, and to many others who read parts or all of the manuscript and offered constructive criticism and encouragement. In alphabetical order they include Shelly Adams, Sue Ballard, Christine Ciringione, Bobbi Florio Graham, Judy Higgins, Elsbeth Johnson, Diana Sisken Lockridge, Karin Nilausen, Leatha Kendrick, Lynn Pruett, Dorothy Herd Sisken, Anna St. Clair and Jerrold Woodward. To all, my heartfelt thanks.

TABLE OF CONTENTS

Acknowledgments   v

Preface   xiii

PART I HARBINGER

1. Akrotiri, a Seaside Town on Thera, an Island in the Aegean Sea
   Early spring, ~ 1625 B. C. E.   3

2. But this Was No Festive Occasion   13

3. We Need Your Help   21

4. The Exodus Begins   29

5. Minos's Throne Room   33

6. They Are All Our People   43

7. If the Gods Are Willing   49

8. Something About the Boy Caused Him to Worry about His
   Son's Virility   55

9. A Golden Bull   59

10. Condemnation and Dreams   65

11. Jenora   73

12. Manganari   79

13. You Will Have Your Jewels   87

14. The Dedication   93

15. I Am Not Just another Woman   103

16. "Wait," she whispered.   113

17. Minos's Countenance Suddenly Changed   121

18. Our Problems Have Become Unmanageable   129

19. Unthinkable   137

20. What Will Happen to Minoa Now?   147

21. We Can't Ignore Those Injustices   153

PART II CATACLYSM

22. Return to Akrotiri   165

23. A Man Who Suddenly Understood He Had Been Sentenced
    to Death   175

24. The Second Blast   183

25. The Greatest Wave   187

26. We Need That Food   193

27. I Have Spoken   199

PART III CHOICES

28. Let the Sun Shine   207

29. I Will Not Tolerate Disobedience   217

30. A Broad Smile on His Face   223

31. He Knows   229

32. There Is Something Else I Need to Tell You   235

33. You Call Me a Failure?   241

34. I Will Make You a Trade   249

35. Please, Not Again   259

36. The Baby...Boy or Girl?   269

37. I Have Made My Decision   277

MAPS

Thera   2

Aegean Region   19

Central Kephtor   92

PREFACE

Cavanila's Choices was born in the fall of the year 2000, when I saw some of the amazing artistic and architectural accomplishments of the Minoan culture that flourished in Crete (Kephtor) thirty-five hundred years ago. Though it is unknown exactly why or when that marvelous civilization met its demise, many believe it occurred within a generation or two after the eruption in the seventeenth century BCE of the volcano at what is now the Greek island of Thera (Santorini), sixty miles north of Crete. That eruptive event, one of the greatest natural disasters on earth in the last ten thousand years, devastated Thera and covered it with many meters of ash and pumice. Yet, unlike Pompeii, no bodies or precious belongings have so far been unearthed from beneath that volcanic blanket. It has been suggested that a precatastrophic event may have warned the inhabitants, perhaps as many as twenty thousand people, to leave that island before the final disaster occurred.

This is a fictional account of what it might have been like on those islands, from the first warning to the eruption's immediate aftermath, as seen and lived by my wholly imagined characters. Though I have used some names from Greek mythology, I have ignored much of the legendry surrounding them. But as *Cavanila's Choices* matured, I could not avoid dealing with real-life questions such as how so many people might have escaped and what might have happened if they sought refuge with a another population that was already under stress. In all, situations not restricted to the ancients.

A common problem writers of historical novels face is the choice of place names. And the earlier the period, the more difficult the problem. The sites described in this book have had multiple names through history and we know little about what they were actually called by those who lived there in the 17th century B. C. E. In this book, I chose to be inconsistent, to use some older names, like Kephtor for Crete, to help provide a flavor of the ancient world, but also more modern names to make it easier for the reader to identify with the setting of the story.

Though a work of fiction, this book is based on what archaeologists and pre-historians have told us about Minoa and those events, though with a good dose of conjecture on my part and with what some would call artistic license. For readers who have been to those islands or will go there in the future, my hope is that this book will help put their experiences into a broader, more meaningful context and help them visualize what could happen when—not if—that still-active volcano decides to erupt again.

Lastly, I hope my readers will come to empathize with, perhaps even love, my protagonist, as some have accused me of doing.

Jesse Sisken
April, 2014

PART I

HARBINGER

But it creaked and groaned, heaved and rocked from side to side, as if the whole might collapse.

Sir Arthur Evans, The Palace of Minos, 1928

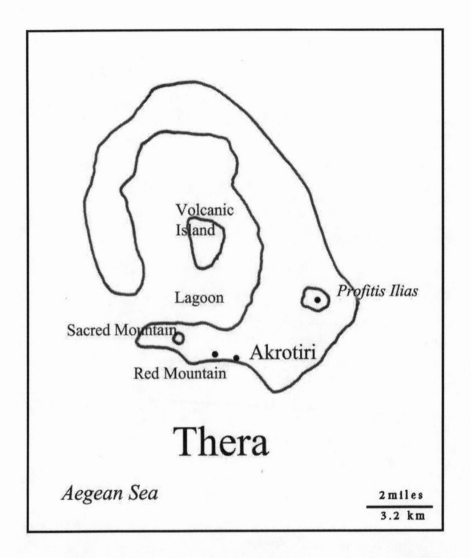

Drawing based upon a U. S. Army Map Service map but modified
to conform with the findings that Thera was a continuous,
C-shaped island prior to the Late Bronze Age eruption.

CHAPTER 1

AKROTIRI, A SEASIDE TOWN ON THERA, AN ISLAND IN THE AEGEAN SEA

Early spring, ~ 1625 B. C. E.

Cavanila was barely on the edge of wakefulness when the dogs started howling. She rushed to her window to see goats in a distant field kicking and bucking and sheep swarming first in one direction and then another. She felt the tremor through her bare feet on the stone floor and heard the low rumble. As the din grew and the shaking intensified, she realized this one would be different.

She snatched up her robe and ran down the stairs.

"Get out! Everyone, get out!" she screamed.

By the time she got clear of her house, the rumble had grown to a roar. Dust rose from the ground and caught in her nose and throat. Her body shook in concert with the trembling earth. She stood with her feet apart to maintain her balance as she struggled to get her arms into the sleeves of her robe.

The outer wall of her bedroom crumbled, and the roof it supported collapsed onto the bed she had just left. Over the noise she heard her father, Rhadamantis, calling for her. She found him lying just beyond a jumble of building stones, holding his knee.

"That wall almost killed me," he yelled. "Help me up."

He had escaped from the other side of their house but Mikami, his favorite concubine who had followed him, was not so fortunate. She lay closer to the house, face down. Cavanila turned to go to her.

"She's probably dead. Help me!"

Cavanila saw he wasn't badly hurt and ignored his command. Stones lay across the woman's legs, others near her bloodied head.

Cavanila knelt, took Mikami's hand into her own and brushed the woman's hair from her face, searching for signs of life. Despite continued shouts from her father, Cavanila lingered with Mikami until she finally closed the woman's unblinking eyes. She caressed her cheek, stroked her dust-covered shoulder and slowly rose to return to Rhadamantis. She took his demanding hand and pulled him to his feet. With an arm around his waist, she helped him limp to where three servants huddled beneath a tree away from the house.

Though the violence in the earth began to subside, nearby walls continued to crash, one after another, in eerie cadence. Fires burned where brush and timber roofs had collapsed onto lighted oil lamps or the coals of burning braziers. Shrieks of pain and terror came from every direction.

Cavanila, a priestess trained to minister to people, left her father with their servants and hurried down the hill toward the center of Akrotiri, fearful of what had happened elsewhere in her beloved town. She was about to enter a narrow, rubble-strewn street when the wall of a house collapsed a few paces in front of her. She froze, looked to be sure other walls weren't about to fall, and started forward again.

Two dust-covered men, clad only in their phallus sheaths, caught up with her, grabbed her arms and held her back.

"Let me go!" she demanded as she tried to pull free.

"It's too dangerous," one of them said. "You can't go in there."

"People need help. Let me go!"

"It really is too dangerous, Cavanila," she heard a deeper voice say. The elderly priest Hekton, limped over to her. He pointed up the street to a wall that resembled a stack of misaligned blocks.

"Look," he said, "that one could fall too."

Her eyes followed his pointing finger, then shifted to a cluster of people trapped in a small, more distant square, staring at the walls above them. They'd be crushed if those walls fell on them, yet they couldn't escape. The bodies of some who tried now lay in the street, partly buried by fallen stones.

Then it happened. One of those walls buckled outward and collapsed.

When the crashing subsided, several young priests dashed toward the square to help the injured and recover the dead. Cavanila tried to follow despite her still-shaking legs but was again held back.

Hekton signaled the men to release her.

"We will tend to them, Cavanila," he said, his somber voice shaking. "Go tell your father what has happened here. He will know what to do."

But she couldn't turn away. With dust and smoke irritating her eyes and throat, and the noise and visions of the devastation flooding her senses, she realized that what she had seen must have occurred throughout Akrotiri. People she loved and served had been injured or killed, and the town she cherished for most of her twenty years had been destroyed during only a few beats of her pounding heart.

She stared at the bodies amid the ruins, one hand over her mouth, the other across her stomach as if to suppress a terrible ache, until an old woman, bent, wrinkled, and with unruly white hair, took her by the hand. With a sympathetic, nearly toothless smile, she silently coaxed Cavanila back up the hill to the house that served as her father's palace. Several times Cavanila stopped to look back, only to have the black-clad woman tug at her sleeve again.

As they neared her house, Cavanila broke away from the kindly woman.

"Mother," she shouted as she raced through the still-standing doorway and up her debris-covered stairway. Her concern was for two pictures painted on the plaster walls outside her sleeping room. Unlike pictures from nature that decorated many houses in this affluent trading town, these were life-sized images of her long-dead mother.

One had been painted shortly after Rhadamantis's brother, King Minos, appointed him regent and high priest of Thera. It showed her mother as a young woman, dressed and made up like most elite Minoan women would be for special occasions; black hair hanging loosely, some in front of her ears, almond-shaped eyes outlined in black, her lips and cheeks reddened. Large, gold rings dangled from her ears and a string of purple stones hung around her neck. She wore a multicolored, flounced skirt and above it a brown, short-sleeved blouse that conformed to the Minoan fashion—laced tightly at her waist and cut so as to leave her breasts exposed. She looked delicate and graceful, as though poised for the first step of an elegant dance.

On the opposite wall, her mother appeared as a more mature woman, her long hair tied in a knot behind her head, the way Cavanila remembered her. An elderly maid, whose bent-over posture accentuated her copious breasts, was shown helping her dress. Her mother looked beautiful, loving, and serene, an image Cavanila revered as though she were a real mother to whom she could talk...and sometimes did.

The paintings were undamaged except for a large crack between her mother's image and that of the maid. Cavanila stood for a long moment, looking into her mother's eyes, wishing she could tell her of the horrors she had seen and the helplessness she felt. With fists clenched at her sides and her body shaking, she began to cry.

Soon, however, she remembered Hekton's instructions but found it difficult to leave. Talking to her father was something she rarely did since a servant told her about how her mother had died.

"She was too sickly to be bearing a child," the maid explained. "She should have used a sponge or even the powder of the sacred crocus once she knew she was with child. But your father wanted a son and refused to let her do it. In the end, your mother and her baby both went to the gods."

When she could delay no longer, she wiped the tears from her cheeks and went to find her father. A servant pointed to a ground-level room where he sat against the far wall, among clay storage jars and amphoras, the food, wine and oil supply of the house. Cavanila picked her way over fallen stones and stepped inside. Light from oil lamps highlighted Rhadamantis's cheekbones and made his eyes look deeper than she had ever seen them. He sat upright, hands gripping his armrests, facing straight ahead.

"Father," she said.

She walked closer, touched the back of his hand and again said, "Father," more softly, as though she were trying to wake a sleeping child.

"Why did you leave me?" he demanded, his eyes still on the doorway behind her.

"I heard people screaming, Father. I had to go to them."

"What did you see?"

She told him about the many people who had been killed or maimed by collapsing walls and roofs, and about the fires, the smoke, and the rubble everywhere.

"You must see for yourself," she added. "And your presence among the people would be a comfort for them."

Rhadamantis remained silent and unmoving before he finally turned to face her.

"You told me what I need to know, and my knee hurts. Tell the high priestess I want her here, and summon the priests and merchants of my council. There is much to be done."

"Father, you need to see what has happened. You can go in your cart."

His body stiffened and the look on his face hardened.

"Do as I say!"

She stared into the shadows beneath his brows.

"As you wish, Father," she said as she whirled around and strode from the room.

The quake that so damaged Akrotiri also roiled the seas. Sloshing waves rocked the two broad-beamed merchant ships in Akrotiri's harbor and displaced their loading planks. Men and the goods they carried spilled into the water. Servants dropped their heavy loads. Clay amphoras already aboard but not yet secured toppled over. A few broke open and spilled olive oil and wine into the ships' holds.

Rhitori, a scribe assigned to record boat loadings, managed to remain standing when the beach beneath his feet shook. He heard walls collapsing and turned to see the ornate front wall of the high priestess's house, Akrotiri's most beautiful building, crumple to the ground.

He dropped the clay tablet that held his records and raced through winding streets toward the house he shared with his widowed mother. It was in a section of the town where the outer walls of most houses, like his own, were composed of stones with inner walls of loose rocks held together by dried clay. Their roofs were of brush laid over wood poles and covered with plaster. Nearly all had collapsed.

He barely recognized what was left of his house. None of its remaining walls stood higher than his shoulders.

"Mama," he cried as he tore at the rubble, pulling brush and stones from the largest piles.

He had yet to reach the floor when he heard her say, "Rhitori," from somewhere behind him. He turned to see her outside a broken wall, sitting sideways atop a heap of fodder on the back of her donkey. Her she-goat was tethered to the donkey. The nanny's kid stood beside its mother.

He rushed to help her down and threw his arms around her frail body. "Mama, are you all right?"

"I fell when the ground shook," she said, "but thanks to the gods I wasn't hurt. I came as fast as I could. But our house...and all the others..."

She laid her head against his chest. "What are we going to do?"

"I don't know, Mama, but at least we are not hurt."

He held her for a moment. They turned and faced the street, where injured people and a few dead now lay.

"Our neighbors need help," he said.

"Go," she replied. "I will follow."

Rhitori joined others who were going from one house to another, seeing to their occupants and providing what help they could.

Rhitori's mother tied her nanny to a still-standing post and took a water bag on her donkey to fill at the nearby spring. She then helped other women tend to injured neighbors and wash and shroud those who were killed.

Later, Rhitori and his mother returned to their house to salvage what they could of their food and belongings.

Rhadamantis's councilors, reeking with sweat, some in dirty, blood-stained robes, filled his makeshift throne room.

"What took you so long?" Rhadamantis demanded. "Where is the high priestess?"

"Sire," a priest with bowed head and drooping shoulders replied, "We had much to do. And I am sorry to tell you that Serivida was killed when the outer wall of her house fell on her while she was trying to help others."

"I am also sorry," Rhadamantis said.

His eyes shifted from person to person. Realizing they expected him to be more mournful for the loss of his high priestess he added, "For her, too."

But he really wasn't. He never forgot how she rebuffed him when he made advances toward her a few days after he arrived to assume his position as Thera's new regent. And he resented that she occupied Akrotiri's most beautiful and ornate house, which he felt should have been his. He had asked Minos to remove her from her position so he could appoint his own high priestess. But Minos refused. Rhadamantis believed it was because she had been Minos's bed partner in their younger years.

"Poseidon shook the earth because we failed to honor him properly," he proclaimed. "See to the injured and dead as you must, but your first duty is to soothe his anger. You will pray and make sacrifices to him every day at dawn and sunset. Tell him of your love and beg his forgiveness. And see to it that all Minoans and Islanders do the same, or he will shake the earth again."

"Sire," Hekton replied while leaning on Cavanila's arm, "of course we need to soothe Poseidon, but our people need help."

Before Rhadamantis could reply, Toran, the former commander of Minos's navy, now a powerful merchant stepped forward.

"Sire, the two ships in the harbor when the earth shook departed as soon as their captains could get their crews aboard. Word will spread that our city has been destroyed and ships will stop coming here. We must rebuild our waterfront shops and storehouses. We need to show we are still the great trading center that we have always been. My son, Bardok, should arrive here in a few days with merchant ships he is escorting. Those captains must see that they can still trade here."

Rhadamantis glared at him.

"There is one more thing, Sire," another priest offered. "Vapors are rising from the little island in the lagoon. We never saw that before. What does it mean?"

Before Rhadamantis could answer, the earth shook again, briefly, yet strong enough to cause everyone to rush for the door. Unlike Rhadamantis's faithful concubine, his council didn't wait for him to exit first.

"You see?" Rhadamantis yelled after he pushed his way outside, "Poseidon reminds us again of our sins. He still shakes the earth and vents his breath. That's what it means. We must appease him. Do you understand?"

His councilors glanced at each other but only Hekton replied, "Yes, Sire, we do."

Without waiting to be dismissed, they all turned and walked away. They had gone only a few steps when Toran spoke in a whisper that only the merchants nearest him could hear.

"That man is so taken by his gods that he cannot see our real problems. Let the priests do as he commands. We must rebuild Akrotiri despite him."

Hekton, still holding Cavanila's arm, spoke to the priests who walked close to him. "Rhadamantis is right. We must do as he commands. But we must also see to people's needs. Somehow, we must do both."

Cavanila walked, her head down, her eyes unfocused, her mind filled with anger. *All he ever thinks about is himself and his gods. How could he neglect his people at a time like this? He didn't even offer water to those tired old men.*

By sunset, thousands of exhausted, dispirited people, surrounded by their salvaged goods, settled down to spend the night on whatever open ground they could find. It was like new villages had sprung up, devoid of walls and with only a few small trees for overhead protection.

Exhausted by their labors and the stresses they suffered, some quickly descended into sleep. Others, still too agitated to sleep, talked in muted tones or lay staring at the stars and the nearly full moon.

"Why?" Rhitori's mother asked him as they lay awake on goat skins recovered from their house. "First Poseidon took your father, and now he's destroyed our house and killed so many people. We have nothing left, yet he still punishes us. What have we done? When will it stop?"

Rhitori reached over and put his arms around her.

"I don't know, Mama. I don't know."

CHAPTER 2

BUT THIS WAS NO FESTIVE OCCASION

As Rhadamantis had ordered, priests sacrificed lambs each morning and evening while praying to Poseidon for forgiveness. Yet the tremors continued.

"Poseidon still is not appeased," Rhadamantis told his council on the third day after the destructions. "We must do more. In two days, we will go to the sacred hill to sacrifice our best animals. Everyone, Minoans and Islanders, must participate and bring offerings. This procession must be the largest we ever had."

"It will take all morning to get there," a priest replied. "We do not often go there when the days are hot."

"I have spoken," Rhadamantis replied.

"Don't go, Mama," Rhitori told her when they heard about Rhadamantis's decree. "You are too old to walk that far and climb that hill in the hot sun."

"The priests have ordered it."

"You are too weak. You cannot go, no matter what Minoan priests say."

"Rhitori, I will ride my donkey, but I will go. I remember the great shaking that destroyed so many houses before you were born. People prayed as the priests ordered, and we never had another like it until now. We must do as they say."

Two days later, Rhitori and his mother joined the crowd that had been waiting in the streets since dawn for the procession to begin. As the sun grew hotter, protesting voices replaced the morning stillness, and the din grew as the delay continued. The march couldn't start until Rhadamantis took his place at its head, but he wouldn't leave his house until he considered himself properly groomed and attired.

Processions to honor the gods were usually festive occasions. People would don their finest clothes and look forward to a happy time. Children would romp and watch sacrifices, and everyone would enjoy the fresh, roasted meat they provided.

But this was no festive occasion. Participants wore what they could salvage. Their faces, even those of their children, seemed lifeless. Like sleepwalkers, they stared straight ahead but saw little. And the hill they were to climb frightened them. Its summit was shaped like the top of a gigantic head emerging from the depths. Though high above the waters, it was strangely strewn with shells of exotic sea creatures, proof, some said, that the emerging head was truly a manifestation of Poseidon.

The procession, when it finally began, was led by two spear-carrying guards and their commander, Gantaros, who wore a bronze sword at his waist. All three wore blue-striped, wrap-around aprons over their blue phallus sheaths. Behind them came two musicians who maintained the pace of the march with the rattle of bronze and clay sistrums. Cavanila followed in the position normally occupied by the now dead high priestess. She carried a small, clay brazier containing live coals into which she sprinkled incense, consecrating the procession and perfuming the air in front of her father.

He had managed to dress well because most of his clothing had been stored in an undamaged part of his house. Strips of red cloth sewn in a diagonal pattern on his purple robe signified his position as the high priest and regent of Thera. His necklace of gold beads, along with his gold armbands, anklets, and bracelets, came from a hiding place in the floor of his sleeping room and attested to his wealth.

He rode his horse-driven chariot until midmorning, when he arrived at the base of the hill. From there, despite his sore knee, he was forced to continue on foot up the steep and narrow path to the summit.

A line of priests and priestesses followed. They chanted in unison, glorifying the charity and greatness of the gods while pleading for pity and forgiveness. Three sacrificial bulls, calmed by the juice of poppy flowers and controlled by nets thrown over them, came next. Hekton had suggested the sacrifice of a horse would be in order but Rhadamantis refused, saying that the few he had were too precious to part with.

Behind the bulls, four kilt-clad servants carried clay rhytons, pouring vessels, for the collection of their blood. One was in the shape of a large nautilus shell, a symbol of Poseidon's role as god of the sea. The second, another representation of Poseidon, was a bull's head that could be filled through an opening in its top and tilted so its contents would pour through a hole in its snout. The third was a giant conch shell, a symbol of Triton, Poseidon's son and messenger. The last, a specialty of Theran craftsmen, was a clay ewer that resembled a large-breasted pigeon with nipple-like decorations on its chest. Its spout looked like a bird's head bent grotesquely backward.

Rich merchants and their families followed with offerings of silver or gold. Some of their women managed to appear in flounced skirts and open-bodiced jackets. Next came craftsmen, common laborers, and others in dull-colored tunics or robes, some of which were in tatters. Among them was Rhitori's mother who sat sideways on her donkey, a brown woolen mantle protecting her from the sun. Rhitori walked beside her.

Not everyone who lived in or near Akrotiri attended. Many, especially those from the poorer Islander neighborhoods, cared little for the Minoan gods and refused to participate. But most who did come brought offerings as Rhadamantis decreed; sheep and goats for sacrifice, grain, cheeses, honey, olive oil, and wine. Some brought skins and cloth goods. Others carried clay figurines, likenesses of animals, humans, or human limbs. From a distance, the procession resembled a serpent with a multicolored head slithering up the winding path.

But it was a somber serpent. No chattering people or shouting children, and no music except for the chanting of the priests and the slow, rhythmic, dreary beat of the sistrums. The only other sounds came from bleating sheep and goats protesting against the herdsmen who dragged them along. The pathway smelled like an animal pen from sun-heated droppings that forced those who followed to step carefully.

Cavanila, hot and sweaty, enjoyed a quiet moment once she arrived at the summit. She faced westward and opened her robe to let the breezes cool her body while enjoying a panoramic view of the lagoon below, the mountains on Kephtor a day's sail to the south, and the sheer multilayered cliffs to the north. Black stones, ranging from pebbles to huge boulders, lay embedded in some of the lighter-colored layers. The sun, already high in the sky, deepened the blue of the waters below. Later, she knew, as the sun approached the horizon, those waters would turn to a shimmering gold, coating the cliffs with a soft, ethereal glow. But now, wispy white clouds rose from the dark little island in the lagoon and drifted eastward in the prevailing winds.

Rhadamantis and his council refreshed themselves with wine and cheese in the shade of the sanctuary at the summit while Cavanila remained outside watching over her people as they crowded as close to the top of the hill as they could manage.

When he considered the time appropriate, Rhadamantis walked out to the altar to stand beside the largest of the tethered bulls. He looked over the crowd and faced the vaporous lagoon. People hushed as he raised his arms to the sky. His voice, loud and high-pitched, almost like a woman's, rose above the sound of the wind:

O Great Goddess,
Our protector from all things,
We have suffered Poseidon's wrath.
Though we offer him prayers and sacrifices,
He shakes the earth and breathes vapors at us.
We beg him to stop,
But our pleas go unanswered.
O Great Goddess,
We have suffered enough,
Ask him to cool his anger before he destroys us all.

Please, Great Goddess,
Help us.

People close enough to hear him joined in as he repeated,

Please, Great Goddess,
Help us.

With his arms still stretched to the sky and his head thrown back, he paused to emphasize the solemnity of the moment and then continued.

O Poseidon,
Great Earth Shaker and God of the Seas,
We have seen your powers.
We come to honor and pay tribute to you.

The crowd repeated his last words, and he began again:

O Poseidon,
You destroyed our great city and killed many people.
You punished us for our sins
And we have suffered.
We now offer you more sacrifices and beg you,
O Poseidon,
Forgive us and still the earth.

Once more, the crowd repeated his final words.

He had just signaled a priest to stun the animal with a large stone hammer when the earth rumbled again. Softly at first but soon much louder until an earsplitting blast, like a nearby lightning strike, shocked everyone. The priest dropped his hammer. Fissures opened in the hill. Rocks rolled down its sides. Goats scattered about the hillsides and sheep bunched closer together. The bulls bellowed, broke loose, and stampeded through the crowd.

Rhadamantis and his priests, even Cavanila, stood mute while the panic-stricken crowds jostled their way down the narrow path or scrambled over low brush down the steep, rocky hillside.

The donkey carrying Rhitori's mother brayed and kicked up its hind legs. She fell to the ground and tumbled down the hill. Rhitori chased after her, slipping on loose stones, yelling for her to stop. But she could not. She slammed against the trunk of a large, woody shrub and lay still. Blood oozed from her head.

He knelt and put his arms around her. "Wake up, Mama, don't die," he pleaded though he knew she was already on her way to the gods.

Cavanila saw what happened to the old woman. She picked her way down the hill to help, but could do nothing for her. She put a gentle, consoling hand on Rhitori's shoulder. He looked up and was surprised to see the beautiful priestess expressing her concern. He mumbled his thanks and turned back to his mother. He cradled her in his arms and climbed back to the path where her donkey still stood. He straddled the animal and, with his mother in his lap, took her down the hill to their broken house.

Cavanila watched his slow progress until she smelled smoke and a foul odor. She climbed back to the summit where a sight, never mentioned in any legends she had heard of, left her stunned. The little island in the lagoon that had been discharging white vapors for days was now belching brown smoke...and fire.

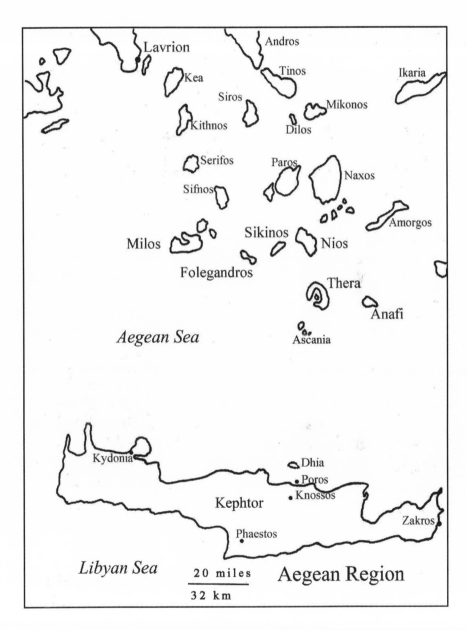

Drawing based upon a public domain map made available
through the University of Texas Libraries.

CHAPTER 3

WE NEED YOUR HELP

With a cloudless sky and brisk, westerly winds filling his sail, Bardok ordered the crew of his longboat, fifteen men to a side, to bring their oars aboard and rest. The captains of the other two longboats under his command did the same. They had spent the last five days escorting two merchant ships loaded with silver ore and copper ingots from the mines at Lavrion on the mainland along a chain of islands that for generations had been infested by raiders. But now, well past the countless sea caves and hidden inlets of Milos and other nearby islands, only the open sea remained between his small armada and Akrotiri. Though the need for constant vigilance had largely dissipated, they maintained their arrowhead formation with Bardok's boat at the point, his other longboats behind and to his flanks, and the merchantmen in between.

Bardok, seated on his boat's afterdeck, let his muscular, sun-darkened body relax and enjoy the sea. He knew his crew was eager to arrive at Akrotiri, a city that offered rest and enjoyment for itinerant sailors, and so was he. He'd see his father again, enjoy the food that only his father's housekeeper, Reda, could prepare, and shave off his itchy, black beard with an obsidian razor he hadn't used since his mission began many days earlier.

As commander of the Minoan navy, he could have assigned other captains to such a mission, but he chafed at the duties that kept him at Minos's palace at Knossos. Like many who spend much of their lives at sea, he could remain land-bound for only so long before the urge to sail again became too overpowering.

"I want to be sure those ships are well protected," he told King Minos after he decided to make the journey. "Their cargos are too valuable to lose."

Those cargos were, indeed, precious; the copper for bronze tools and weapons, and the silver for drinking vessels, jewelry, and ornaments. The silver could also be profitably traded with Egypt, where mines produced abundant quantities of gold but little silver. Bardok's real desire, however, which Minos well knew, was to again feel the seas under his boat, sniff the wind-blown spray, and enjoy the brilliant sunsets so typical of those waters.

But his reverie soon ended. He had just spotted his landmark on Thera, the peculiar red mountain at the western edge of Akrotiri off his port quarter, when Zardik, his second-in-command, pointed to starboard and shouted, "Bardok! Look out there."

He turned to see a pair of overloaded fishing boats bound toward Ascania, a small group of barren islands less than a half-day's row to the south. Despite their steersmen's attempts to keep the winds and waves on their starboard quarter, the way those boats pitched and rolled in the rough seas told Bardok they risked disaster. Even as he watched, one of them turned broadside to the waves as it slid down from the crest of a high one. Its crew worked frantically to turn its bow back into the next wave, but before they could get it around, the wave broke over the boat's rails, nearly filling it with water. The wave after that rolled it over. The other fishing boat, barely navigable in the rough seas and unable to help, continued on to Ascania.

Madness, Bardok thought.

He signaled the merchant ships under his care to continue on to Akrotiri and ordered his crews to unship their oars, lower their sail, and turn southeasterly to position themselves downwind of the foundered boat. Once there, he turned his boat back into the wind and waves to approach the overturned boat in as controlled a manner as possible. His other longboats did the same, spreading out to his right and left.

One of his boats rescued a man who had managed to remain afloat by clinging to a wooden oar. Bardok and his crew found two men clinging to the hull of their overturned boat and managed to get a line to them to haul them aboard. When questioned about their foolhardy behavior, the soaked, shivering survivors only pointed to smoke rising over Thera. Finding no other survivors, Bardok ordered his longboats to give up the search and proceed to Akrotiri's harbor.

As they passed south of the strait that opened into Thera's lagoon, Bardok saw the smoke's source, the small island in its center. But it wasn't until he arrived at the harbor and saw the massive destruction, the ash, and the mobs crowding around the few small boats still there that he began to understand the desperate behavior of those two fishing vessels. He also saw that the merchant ships he had been escorting had turned back out to sea and gone off by themselves.

"Stand offshore after you land those survivors and don't let anyone climb aboard," Bardok ordered as he jumped into knee-deep water and waded ashore.

He found no harbormaster or guards maintaining control. He pushed his way through crowds trying to offer him jewelry in exchange for places in his boats and hurried toward his father's house on the north side of the city. Nearly all the buildings he passed had broken walls and fallen roofs. The second and third stories of some were now masses of stones lying on street-level floors. People sat amid the ruins, staring with unfocused eyes. Women in black mantles rocked back and forth, wailing about their losses. One man sat amid a collection of broken vases in what had once been a pottery shop, shaking his fist at the sky and cursing the gods.

He found his father's house undamaged but unoccupied. He walked around to the cooking area behind it where he found Reda, squatting in the shade, her back against a wall, her head resting on her arms. She looked up as soon as she heard his steps.

Instead of the robust, good-humored woman he had known since childhood, he saw red and swollen eyes and tracks on her cheeks where tears had rolled down her dusty face. She wore a filthy robe, her gray hair a mass of tangles. She looked like she hadn't slept for days.

"Reda! Are you all right?" he asked.

"I am," she replied though her labored rising suggested otherwise. "I can get you something to eat if you like."

"I have already eaten, Reda. Thank you. Where is my father?"

"He left days ago. He said he was going to the north shore and to Anafi to see if the earth shakings had ruined those places too. He said I should care for you when you arrived, but I'm worried about him. I don't know when he'll return. The shakings are so much worse since he left."

Bardok patted her shoulder. "He will be fine, Reda, but are you really all right? Do you have enough food and water? Is your family looking after you?"

"My son's house was destroyed, but no one in his family was hurt. Don't worry about me. I will be fine."

"Have your family stay here in my father's house if you like," Bardok replied. "I am sure he would want you to. But for now, I have to go. I must find Rhadamantis. Take care of yourself, Reda."

"Yes, go," she replied with a gentle smile. "It was good to see you."

He walked away but turned after a few steps to see her sitting against the wall again with her head back on her arms. He hesitated for a moment but continued on.

He was part way to Rhadamantis's house when he saw him approaching. With him were Gantaros, the captain of his guard, an elderly priest in a soiled, saffron-colored robe, and a similarly dressed young priestess.

"Bardok, I heard you arrived," Rhadamantis shouted while still many steps away. "We need your help."

Before Bardok could reply, Rhadamantis waved his arms and said, "Look what Poseidon has done! We offered sacrifices and prayed to him, yet the shaking continues. At night the sky over the lagoon is red from spurting fire. The air is foul. Ash is everywhere. Thera is doomed, Bardok. We have to leave or we will all die. Go to Kephtor. Tell my brother we need help and many ships. And take my daughter, Cavanila, with you. She can tell him what happened here."

"Yes, Bardok, please take me with you," Cavanila said as she stepped forward, her voice self-assured and unusually low-pitched for a young woman.

The short, chubby girl Bardok had seen little of in recent years had blossomed into a tall, graceful woman with a face dominated by high cheekbones and full lips, her eyes soft and expressive.

"I have seen everything," she said, "more than my father. It is as he says. We must leave this island."

Bardok turned to Rhadamantis. "I understand, but to act in panic is foolhardy. One of your fishing boats full of people capsized trying to get to Ascania. We found only three survivors."

"Bardok, don't you see what happened here? We have to get off this island!"

"But does all Thera have to be abandoned? With the winds as they are, northern and western Thera must be clear. Why not move people there?"

"Your father said the same thing. He went to look at those places days ago but has not returned."

"Then why not wait until he returns? He could tell you how safe it is up there."

"No! People could not survive very long there either, even if they could make that trek. And if the winds shift, they'll get the ash there too. We have no choice, Bardok. Don't you understand? We have no time. We must get everyone off this island as soon as we can."

Bardok hesitated because his father had told him things about Rhadamantis that made him suspicious of the man and his judgment. Toran told him Minos had removed Rhadamantis from his previous post as regent of Phaestos and sent him to Thera because of his scandalous behavior. He said Minos might have banished him from Minoa as he did his brother, Sarpedon, had he not appreciated the rules of commerce Rhadamantis was supposed to have developed. But, actually, it was Rhadamantis's wife, Elfida, who developed those rules. Without her wisdom, Akrotiri would never have become the trading center it was. Rhadamantis cared little for his wife and had become impotent so far as she was concerned. He filled his life with wine, other women, and his gods.

Toran never told him how he knew so much about Elfida, and Bardok never asked.

"Very well," Bardok finally said, "I will take Cavanila to the king and leave my other boats here under Vactor's command. He can begin taking your people to Manganari on the south coast of Nios. It's less than a day's sail from here and upwind, so it'll be free of the smoke. They can camp on the grassy plain behind its beach."

"Why not to the great harbor at the other end of Nios? There was once a town there. I could make that place even more prosperous than Akrotiri."

"It's nearly a day's sail farther than Manganari. Not a good choice if you are in a hurry to move people off this island. Besides, I think we should concentrate on getting your people away from here rather than on rebuilding another town."

"Thank you for your thoughts," Rhadamantis answered. "Just tell my brother what I said."

Bardok considered a retort but only said, "My men have had a long day, but we can leave as soon as they are fed and get a little rest. We will depart around sunset."

Cavanila saw the anger on Bardok's face and heard it in his voice.

"That is good of you, Bardok," she said, trying to ease the tension between the two men. "I will be with you by then. I only need to collect a few things from our house."

Cavanila's first act when she stepped aboard Bardok's boat was to draw Poseidon's trident on its forward deck with a piece of charcoal. She then dripped wine onto it from a small flask while she prayed to that god for a safe and rapid journey. As a priestess, she had thus consecrated many fishing boats and ships preparing to leave Akrotiri's harbor. This time, however, she struggled through the words, and her voice lacked its usual conviction. The devastation of Akrotiri had shaken her devotion to him.

Bardok showed her to the small shelter his crew had erected for her on the afterdeck of his boat and offered her some food and water.

"Thank you," she said. "I just need some rest. I have had so little these last few days."

The waters outside the harbor were choppy because of still significant, westerly winds. She tried to sleep but could not. Behind her closed lids she continued to relive the horrors she had witnessed—the shaking earth and crashing walls, the smoke, dust and fetid vapors, the bellowing of the bulls, the cries of terrified children, the wailing of mourners. And she began to ask herself questions.

What made Poseidon so angry, and why didn't the prayers and sacrifices we offered satisfy him? And why didn't the Great Goddess protect us? Has she lost her powers, or has she, too, turned against us? Could we be wrong about those gods?

She realized she was questioning the teachings her father and mentors had drummed into her all her life and it frightened her. But she couldn't stop.

Who is Poseidon, she continued, and, for that matter, who are the Great Goddess and the other gods? Do they really exist? How do we know? We are told they bring the rains, grant us our harvests, and make our flocks fertile; that without them there would be no life. But what if those teachings are wrong? What if they don't control everything, or even exist? What then? How could we explain the sea currents and the winds, the beautiful sunsets and the storms, even the trembling of the earth or its belching of fire? Who or what else could offer comfort and purpose to our lives, or provide a place where people go when their lives end? How could we live without them?

Soon, however, while only a faint glow remained on the western horizon, her weariness caught up with her. She felt herself drifting into sleep, grateful for the respite, yet afraid of what awaited her in the strange world of dreams.

From early in life, Cavanila seemed destined for great things. A pretty child with dark eyes to match her thick, black hair, her innate curiosity made her a favorite of adults. She often spent hours watching stonecutters at work or architects directing the construction of buildings. Though shorter and rounder than her playmates, she was athletic, tough minded, and strong. Boys learned she was not someone to trifle with. As she matured, her parents agonized over her future. It would have been easy for them to arrange a suitable marriage for her, but she refused to consider it.

"I will not be dominated by a husband and his family," she told her parents.

Eventually, her father saw her in a different light. "With her talents," he told her mother, "she should become a priestess. She could be useful to me and might even succeed me as regent of Thera after I die."

As a result, when she was thirteen, he arranged for her to enter the priesthood, the institution that controlled Minoan society and commerce. She easily acquired the necessary disciplines. But her independence of thought often led to confrontations with her father and tutors until she learned it was sometimes better to keep her thoughts and feelings to herself.

She hadn't slept very long before she awoke with unmistakable feelings of nausea. She tried to stop them with sheer willpower but could not, and soon found herself retching over the side. Bardok brought her water, but even that wouldn't stay down. She tried to retreat back into sleep, but was soon heaving over the side again. Even when there was nothing left in her stomach, she continued to retch.

She felt embarrassed to have displayed her inability to control her body in front of Bardok and his crew. She saw the smiles on their faces in the light of the bright moon. They are enjoying my suffering, she thought.

Yet, as miserable as she felt, she rejected the temptation to call on Poseidon to calm the seas. I only need to survive until morning, she told herself.

CHAPTER 4

THE EXODUS BEGINS

After Bardok and Cavanila departed Akrotiri, crowds gathered around Vactor's boats, begging to be taken away from Thera. Vactor and Lendor, the captain of the other longboat, had their armed crews form a picket line to keep people away. Bardok's orders were to wait until Rhadamantis decided whom he would take to Manganari. But Rhadamantis had yet to appear.

"Getting late," Lendor told Vactor.

Vactor looked up at the sun. "I know."

They knew that small islets and subsurface rocks obstructed access to the beach at Manganari, and attempting to take heavily laden ships through them in the dark could end in disaster. And the later their departure, the more likely that possibility became.

Vactor was on the brink of postponing departure until the next day when he saw Rhadamantis approaching at the head of a line of priests, merchants with their families, and numerous servants carrying their goods. Vactor hurried to Rhadamantis.

"Sire, we cannot take all those people and their belongings. We only have two longboats."

"Do not worry," Rhadamantis replied. "You will only take the women and children with you this time. The men are here only to see their families leave."

"Even so, we can't carry them and all their goods, too. Look at our boats. There isn't room."

Rhadamantis looked at Vactor and then at his boats. He turned to those who were to go and told them they could only take their jewelry, some food wrapped in skins, a small bundle of clothing, and a few utensils. The women stood in disbelief that they would have to leave most of their wardrobes and possessions behind.

Their men protested, arguing that their belongings were valuable and that their families would need everything they had with them.

Rhadamantis remained firm but deflected their anger. "Vactor is the commander of the boats," he said. "He decides how much he can carry."

The women and their families muttered beneath their breaths as they rummaged through their goods to select the few most important things. This delayed Vactor's departure even more. Once he thought he had reached his maximal load, and without consulting with Rhadamantis again, he stopped further boarding and ordered his crews to depart. Most left behind complained loudly and bitterly as they watched the boats sail away without them. Others just lowered their heads and trudged off to their makeshift camps or whatever homes they still had, expecting a long night on a rumbling earth under falling ash and fire-lit clouds.

Rhadamantis limped back to his temporary throne room where he sat alone, his wine cup in hand, reliving his meeting with Bardok.

"I acted like a child rushing to meet him in the streets and blurting out our need for help; me, the brother of Minos and regent of Thera. And in front of Cavanila and the others. He questioned me like I was a commoner and he the prince. I can imagine what he thinks of me now. But I did get him to go and take Cavanila with him, though maybe he had other reasons. I saw him leering at her.

"He is probably going to tell my brother how I dishonored him. I can see him smirking when Bardok tells him what happened. Minos never thought I was very smart. But I am not a lout. I am the eldest. I could have been king if I wished, as good a king as my brother, even better. Have I not done well to manage our markets? We have our problems now but I know what needs to be done. And I know how to command people. I will show them. Minos will see how well I have acted and be proud of me.

It was nearly dark by the time Vactor's boats arrived at Manganari. But with light from the moon and torch-bearing lookouts on their bows, Vactor and Lendor managed to thread their way to the beach with only minor bumps and scrapes against submerged rocks. After beaching the boats, crews escorted theie passengers to higher ground where they could camp for the night.

It won't be easy for them, Vactor thought as he watched. They are going to have to settle down and try to sleep in this strange place with no shelter, worrying about their loved ones on Thera and not knowing what the next day would be like for themselves. They probably won't even appreciate that the ground under them is still, and the air they are breathing is free of ash.

"I will remain here tomorrow," he told Lendor after everyone had disembarked. "At first light, you will take both boats back to Akrotiri for more passengers—but with only half your crews."

"Why only half crews?"

"Because I need men to start organizing some kind of village here. The women we brought won't be much help. They have always had servants to care for them. You won't need those rowers to get there because you'll have the winds at your back. You can fill out your crews with Akrotirians for your return here. That way, you can bring back fifteen more men in each boat."

"I don't know if I can find many men there who can pull an oar against heavy afternoon winds," Lendor replied. "We might not be able to get back here by dark."

"Then spend the night there and return here the next morning."

Vactor didn't tell Lendor his real reason for keeping half his crewmen on Nios. He knew the women and children he brought to Nios constituted a rich bounty for any raiders that might be lurking in the area. The crewmen he planned to keep behind were his best fighters.

CHAPTER 5

MINOS'S THRONE ROOM

I defy anyone to enter the throne room without a strange thrill.
J. D. S. Pendlebury, Archaeology of Crete, 1939

Bardok's early morning approach to Poros brought crowds to the beach and the sandy bluffs above it. Located at the mouth of the river that runs past Knossos, Poros was one of the harbors serving Knossos and one of the busiest ports on the north coast of Kephtor. The town that grew up around it was a bustling place for commerce and the arts.

The people watching knew the boat must have been sailing all night, a rarity in those waters. And they wondered why the crew was still at its oars despite its full sail.

"They must be exhausted," a merchant said to the harbormaster next to him, "Why is he driving them so hard?"

"I don't know," the harbormaster replied, "but we will soon find out."

It appeared at first that the boat would run straight up onto the beach at full speed. But when almost there, its sail came down, its crew dragged the oars and rowed in reverse to stop its forward motion, then spun the boat around to ease it onto the beach stern first.

Bardok didn't wait for a ramp. He jumped into knee-deep water and waded up onto the dry sand. He ordered the harbormaster to provide food and water for his men and Cavanila, then sent a messenger to the palace.

"Inform King Minos that Bardok and Cavanila, the daughter of the king's brother, Rhadamantis, have arrived and wish an immediate audience."

Bardok ordered the captains of two longboats beached nearby to make ready to join him for a run to Thera later that day.

"An overnight, upwind run?" one of them asked. "Why the hurry, Bardok?"

"I'll tell you later. Just be ready to go."

He next called together the captains of three merchant ships that sat further down the shore.

"Replace whatever you are carrying with foods of all kinds and with skins and cloth that can be used for shelters. Be prepared to make your way to Nios and Thera as soon as the winds and seas allow."

The largest of the captains, a surly man with a long scraggly beard, glared at Bardok. "We are bound for Egypt with timber, wine, and woolens," he said. "Why should we unload valuable cargoes to go to Nios or Thera? What profit will there be for us?"

Bardok glared back. "I am on my way to the king. He will give you the same orders and provide your new cargos. You will obey him if you wish to continue trading in Minoa."

All three grumbled but argued no more.

Bardok returned to his boat to find his crew enjoying some cold but tasty roasted lamb, thick slices of cheese, and large cups of beer. But not Cavanila, who sat apart from the others.

When he looked at her with raised eyebrows, she shook her head.

"The smell of food makes me sick. I'll try to eat something later. For now, I need to get used to being on land again."

Bardok smiled to himself as he watched her rise and step toward the chariot the harbormaster provided. She walked with her feet spread apart as though her body thought it was still aboard a rolling boat.

The Royal Road paralleled the river southward into the low hills toward Minos's palace at Knossos, but the jarring ride of the chariot proved too much for Cavanila's still unsettled stomach. Bardok had to stop his chariot twice to let her hurry into nearby bushes.

After Bardok left the harbor, Zardik reprovisioned his ship and replaced most of its crew with fresh oarsmen from the harbor's town. Those at the shore soon learned the reason for the boat's hurried arrival.

"Poseidon destroyed Akrotiri and killed many people with a great shaking," one of the relieved oarsmen said. "And the island in the lagoon is spouting fire and smoke and stinking vapors. Therans are fighting to get off that island. We came to get them help from the king."

As he spoke his last words, the earth beneath them began to shake. Like Thera and other nearby lands, mild tremors occurred frequently on Kephtor and seldom caused any damage. But this one was stronger. Everyone knew that Poseidon could become so angry that he would destroy many cities at the same time. He had devastated Akrotiri and Knossos together generations earlier. As news of the disaster on Thera spread and the ground beneath them shook, people feared the same thing might be happening again. Terror spread though the village like a wind-driven fire in a field of dry grass.

Dawn that morning brought little relief to the people at Akrotiri. They congregated in the streets or crowded around storehouses clamoring for provisions. Others stood outside Rhadamantis's house, venting their frustrations. Members of his council were forced to shoulder their way through a noisy, unyielding crowd to reach his temporary throne room.

"You failed to soothe the gods," Rhadamantis told his priests, "and now people have become unruly. I won't tolerate that."

He looked to Gantaros. "Be sure this house and all our storage buildings are protected. Use your weapons if necessary to stop any looting."

He turned to Gridawi, his harbormaster. "Go down to the harbor and select those who will leave on the next boats. Give preference to women and small children and to craftsmen whose skills will be needed on Nios. If necessary, have people draw lots. If the winds are favorable, Vactor's boats should get here before midday. Be certain those you select are ready to board as soon as they arrive. Take guards with you to maintain order."

"Yes, Sire," Gridawi replied with a broad smile and exaggerated bow, "I will be happy to do that, Sire."

Rhadamantis ignored Gridawi's strangely deferential response and continued with orders to the others about food and water conservation.

After he dismissed them, Rhadamantis found his mood had improved.

"Look," he said aloud to the spirits of his father and his brother, who always seemed to be standing behind him, "I can deal with difficult situations. I know how to get things done. I know how to rule."

After Lendor's boats departed with more Therans, Rhadamantis went to examine the dead high priestess's house. He lingered there, admiring the paintings on its walls. He was about to leave when another blast shook the house. He ran into the street and saw an even denser brown cloud shooting up into the sky. Hot, glassy hail stung his skin and began to coat the ground. The air smelled like rotting animals. A rock the size of his head crashed to the ground a few paces in front of him.

People took whatever shelter they could find, huddling under makeshift tents or crowding into the few buildings that still had roofs. A few adventurous young men climbed the western hill to watch the rising cloud and returned with even scarier news.

"The island in the lagoon has cracked open," one of them said, "and fire oozes from it like blood from a wound. And when it reaches the sea it gives off great vapors and turns to black stone."

At Knossos, a kilt-clad servant escorted Cavanila and Bardok up a broad staircase at the north entrance to the palace. They walked through a colonnade, turned right, and climbed more stairs to the central courtyard. Cavanila released Bardok's arm and did her best to walk through the crowd that had gathered to learn why Bardok's messenger had entered the palace in such haste.

Though everyone was watching, Cavanila, like someone who had imbibed too much wine, kept her eyes on her next steps. Another servant ushered them to a stone bench in the king's throne room, where they sat to wait for him.

A brazier in one corner provided heat against the morning coolness. In another corner, several stairs led down into a dry rectangular basin. Flanked by stone benches against the red-painted wall, the throne, carved from soft stone, sat on a low, platform.

A few moments later, the king entered through a door to the right of the throne. The few steps this broad-shouldered monarch took to reach his seat showed that, despite his forty years, his well-coordinated body looked like it could still compete in the games that honor the gods. His sleeveless purple jacket protected his back but left much of his muscled torso exposed. His short, gold-threaded skirt barely reached his knees. He wore a gold-handled bronze dagger at his waist, gold bracelets on his wrists, and gold armbands with lion heads at their ends around his considerable biceps. A gold ring, the seal of his authority, hung from a chain around his neck. His flowing black hair was unadorned. As he sat waiting for his entourage to be seated, he stared at his visitors with quizzical eyes, a slight tilt to his head but no smile, like a father expecting bad news from an errant child.

Jenora, Minos's high priestess, entered behind him. In contrast to the king, she seemed to float on air, her feet barely visible beneath her long, multicolored, flounced skirt. From an early age, she was trained to walk by putting her toes down before her heels and to keep her body upright and still, her arms bent at the elbow and her shoulders back. The posture enhanced the up-thrust of her breasts, which her blue jacket, cinched tightly at her waist, left exposed. Her body and graceful movements exuded sensuality, but her unfocused eyes and erect head signaled that she lived in the world of the gods, not of mortal man.

With slender, graceful fingers, their nails painted red, she pushed back her dark hair as she took her seat. Gold rings dangling from her ears accented her blackened eyebrows, reddened lips, and rouged cheeks. For special occasions lesser priestesses and wives of the elite copied her dress as a symbol of their privi-leged station—and because they believed the jacket with its tight fit beneath their breasts gave them a more youthful look.

For the high priestess, however, this mode of dress symbolized fertility and the nurturing role of females, emphasizing her role as the embodiment of a goddess. As such, she communicated with the gods and passed their will on to the people. She served Minos in other ways as well. He found her well informed and sought her counsel on many issues, including matters such as trade, which Handoro, his chamberlain, considered prerogatives of his own.

Handoro entered next, his deep-set eyes focused on the visi-tors. He wore no jewelry. A simple white cloth held together by a gold pin at his shoulder covered his boney frame. He resembled a wizened old rodent with bald head, hollow cheeks, and an out-sized, beaked nose.

Once all were seated, a male servant wearing just a flap of blue cloth over his codpiece entered. He carried a tall, cone-shaped rhyton, holding his finger over the hole in its bottom from where the wine could be poured. Three young, female servants dressed only short blue skirts came last. They placed vessels of goat's milk, olives, fresh figs, and some cheese on a low table in front of Minos and then departed. Other servants remained at the entrances to the rooms, but no guards were present.

Minos beckoned his visitors to approach.

"Welcome, Cavanila, daughter of my brother. And Bardok, my esteemed naval commander. Let us first pour a libation to the gods and have some refreshment. Your weariness shows, especially yours, Cavanila."

The servant with the rhyton filled gold cups for the king, the high priestess, the chamberlain; he filled silver cups for the visi-tors. They each poured some of their watered wine into hollowed receptacles in an offering table before drinking. Cavanila drank little wine but celebrated newly arrived hunger pains by nibbling on a slice of cheese.

Finally, the king sat up straight in his chair, demanding every-one's attention. He looked first at Cavanila and then at Bardok.

"Why have you requested this audience in such haste?" he asked.

Cavanila spoke first. "My father sent me to ask for your help. Two strong earth shakings destroyed most of Akrotiri, They killed or injured many people. The sky over the lagoon glows red at night, and Akrotiri suffers from bad vapors and ash that falls from a dark cloud. We know how the shaking in the days of our grandfathers caused so many deaths, but this is worse. My father says our island is doomed and we must leave it.

"Sire," she continued, speaking more rapidly, her hands forward in supplication. "Our people have lost their homes and fear for their lives. They mill around the harbor trying to find passage off the island, but there are few boats. A few made it to that barren island to our south on small fishing boats, but they can't survive there very long. Some drowned on the way. We need to move our people to safety. You must send boats to help us."

Minos pointed his finger at her. "Cavanila, don't tell me what I must do. What made Poseidon so violent? Have you not worshipped him properly? What have your father and his high priestess been doing there?"

"Sire, the high priestess was killed in the first earth shaking and—"

Minos sat up straight, his posture rigid. "Serivida was killed?"

"Yes, Sire."

A wave of sadness passed over his face. He remained silent for several moments, then said. "Go on."

"Sire, we prayed to the gods as we always have. We sacrificed our best animals. But the spewing and earth shaking got worse. What else could we do?"

Bardok jumped in. "What Cavanila says is true. The people of Thera are frightened. Those who drowned did so because they took overcrowded boats into rough seas. So far, there has been no violence among the people, but it could happen soon. As Cavanila said, many ships are needed to remove people from Thera. Since Nios is closer to Thera and upwind of it, I think we should take them there first. I ordered Vactor to begin doing that. We can bring them here once everyone is off Thera."

They heard what they thought was thunder from a distant storm, though such storms were rare there at this time of year. The room fell silent until Minos spoke again.

"We know Poseidon is angry and not just with Thera. The earth shook here this morning too. I am concerned for the people of Thera, but I do not know how much we can help. Please leave us so I can discuss the matter with my advisors. I will inform you of my decision."

With the merest smile and a slight twinkle in his eye, he turned to Cavanila. "I see you are still suffering from your journey. Go to our family quarters across the courtyard. Servants will offer you more refreshment and help you bathe and rest in comfort. We will talk again later."

Bardok and Cavanila were about to leave when a scribe rushed into the room and whispered into the chamberlain's ear.

"Sire," Handoro said loudly enough for everyone to hear, "We must see what is happening in the northern sky."

Minos rose and led the others up four flights of stairs to a rooftop from where they saw the dark cloud on the northern horizon. They knew it had to be over Thera. It grew even as they watched, spreading southeasterly in the prevailing winds, toward the eastern end of Kephtor. They stared at it for a while until Minos led them back to his throne room.

"I understand now," he said to Cavanila more sympathetically. "I will do what I can to help."

He turned to Bardok. "Return to Thera and take any longboats here in the harbor with you to begin moving people to Nios, as you suggested. I will order the merchantmen in port to load up with food and water and proceed there as well. It could take many days for them to arrive. But once they unload their cargos, they can proceed to Thera, take on passengers, and bring them back here. I will also send runners to all our harbors with orders for other boats to do the same. Cavanila, you will remain here as an attendant to the high priestess."

"But Sire," she objected, "My people need me. I must return to them."

"You are in no condition to help anyone. You will remain here. Go to our family quarters. Bardok, I wish to speak to you in private before you return to your ship. Please follow me to my rooms."

He turned to his high priestess and the chamberlain as he rose. "I will speak to you both after I send Bardok on his way."

CHAPTER 6

THEY ARE ALL OUR PEOPLE

"You look exhausted, old friend," Minos said to Bardok once they were alone. "I hate to send you off so soon. Have you had any sleep?"

"Very little, Devterex." Bardok spoke to the king using his birth name. "We were only at Akrotiri a short time. The merchant ships we were escorting turned around and headed back to sea as soon as they saw the chaos and damage there. Did they come here?"

"I have had no word of them. They might have gone directly to Egypt. We needed those cargoes."

"I'm sorry."

"What about Cavanila?"

"She had a difficult night at sea, but she's a brave girl. You can be proud of her."

"She does seem bright, but she needs to learn some respect. I will have the high priestess find a place for her."

"If it is all right with you, I'll send a message to my captains that I'll be back at the harbor in time to depart just before sundown. Then I'd like to get a little sleep here before I go."

"I will send the orders myself. You stay here and rest. May the gods grant you a safe and speedy journey."

Shortly after the king left him, two serving girls arrived to help Bardok disrobe and bathe. They anointed his body with refreshing oils and saw to it that he would have a restful sleep.

The two men had been friends since Devterex's father, the previous Minos, decided his son, then fourteen years old, needed to learn about maritime trading and experience the toughening that going to sea would offer. He knew that Toran's son, Bardok, though the same age, was stronger and more mature

than Devterex and would be a fit companion, even a protector
for him. So the king arranged with Toran, then commander of
his fleet, to have the two boys work on merchant ships together.
They grew to be friends and shared many adventures aboard ship
and in many ports. They also shared a few misadventures they
preferred to forget, such as the time they found an open amphora of wine and drank themselves sick.

Their pathways diverged during their middle teens. Devterex
continued his training at court while Bardok joined his father in
Minos's navy. By his early twenties, Bardok commanded a longboat that patrolled trade routes throughout the northern seas
and was a veteran of several fights with pirates. It didn't take
him long to acquire the confidence of his crews and other ship
captains, and promotions came with his successes. He became
a squadron commander and later commander of the navy after
Toran retired.

While still a ship captain he took for a wife a young woman
named Lovanna, the daughter of one of his father's squadron leaders. She was tall, graceful, and had a smile that radiated an innate
intelligence and gentle serenity he had never seen in anyone else.
Their marriage was one of deepening love made even more joyous
by the impending arrival of their first child. But it ended for him
the day he returned from a long mission and was met at his house
by his father, not his wife.

The sadness he saw in his father's face frightened him.

"What happened? Where's Lovanna?" he asked, as he placed
the bundle he carried on a low table.

Toran reached out, put his hand on Bardok's shoulder, and
said, "I'm sorry, Son. Your baby, a boy, came too early and was born
dead. The priests couldn't stop Lovanna's bleeding and she too
went to the world of the gods. I am so sorry."

Bardok stood still as a statue, trying to grasp the enormity of
his father's words. He pulled a chair from the table and sat. He
leaned forward, his forearms on his thighs, his hands folded together, his head bent down. He shut his eyes, took several deep
breaths, and looked up at Toran. "Where are they?"

"We put the baby in Lovanna's arms in a sarcophagus that we have not yet placed into the ground. It's on the northern hill. I'll show you where when you wish to go."

After a long silence, Bardok said, "Thank you, Father, but I need to be alone for now."

"I understand. Send for me when you wish to talk or go to where Lovanna lies."

Bardok filled a cup with wine his elderly servant had left for him and drank it down. He sat, eyes unfocused, picturing Lovanna, trying to accept the fact that the woman he so loved and the child she bore were both gone. And it was his seed that led to her death.

He filled his cup a second time, opened his bundle, and placed the two things he had brought for her on the table: a sheet of filmy blue cloth he had hoped she'd wear that evening, and a gold pin with a sacred knot twisted into its design to hold the sheet together at her shoulder. They sat untouched, the pin atop the cloth, while he drank more wine and slept when he could no longer stay awake.

Early in the morning three days later, he appeared at his father's house, a bundle in one hand and a small clay brazier containing live coals in the other. The two men looked at each other for a moment and, without speaking, walked to where Lovanna and her baby lay. Bardok set the brazier down next to the sarcophagus and stood staring at it while his thoughts dwelled on her beauty and gaiety, their times of greatest joy, and how lovely she looked when he last saw her. But he choked up when he envisioned her on her deathbed and how she now lay with their son in her arms.

When he could stand there no longer, he took the blue cloth from his bundle, and placed it directly over the still burning coals. He waited until smoke began to rise from it, and then turned to walk back to his house.

Moons passed before he left his house again. He ate little but drank a lot of wine. His hardened body weakened, his sun-browned skin paled. He saw no one except the servant who cared for him and, sometimes, his father, who tried to offer solace and ease him from his sorrow. Priests came to talk to him, but he refused to let them into his house. On one occasion, his friend Devterex, the new Minos, came to try to help him through his mourning and encourage him to look to his future. But it did little good.

Eventually, his father convinced him to return to the sea. Not long afterward he found himself and his crew in mortal combat against a pirate ship. It was then that he vented his anger, becoming a reckless, unrestrainable fury, hacking and killing, until all of the pirates, some of whom could have been taken as valuable servants, were dead. Only in the calm after that fight did he finally grieve for his lost wife and son—and for his loss of self-control. As time passed, his pain receded, but he never took another wife.

After seeing to Bardok's comfort, Minos returned to the throne room to find his high priestess and chamberlain in the midst of an argument.

Jenora, on the edge of her seat, turned to face him and spoke first. "Sire, it's folly to bring all Therans here. We don't have enough houses, and Handoro thinks we could have problems feeding everyone. We can bring our Minoans here if necessary, but Islanders should go back to their northern islands.

"It's true," Handoro added. "If the falling ash comes this way and gets worse, our crops and grazing lands will be hurt. I agree that bringing Therans here will be costly. And losing our marketplace at Akrotiri makes things even worse, but..."

"Then why bring them all here?" Jenora demanded.

"They are all our people," Handoro replied. "Those Islanders have lived on Thera for generations. We can't let them starve. Besides, we will need their help to increase our food production and work on our roads."

"Why on our roads?" Minos asked.

. "Because we are going to need larger tributes from other places. Zakros and Malia will likely suffer more than we will and won't be much help. Kydonia might help some, but Phaestos has a fertile plain, the Mesara, on the other side of the mountains. It will probably be less affected. That will make it our best source of food. With our ships occupied elsewhere, we will have to transport food and everything else over those mountains. That means improving our roads before before the rain and snow of the cold season make them impassible."

"Suppose the regents in those places say they can't help?" Minos asked. "Remember the problems we had with Phaestos when Rhadamantis was regent there?"

"I do remember the troubles he caused, and Jawana hasn't been overly generous with his tributes since then. But if he refuses to help, you'll have to remove him from his position and take what we need."

"I would need an army to do that and I don't have one. We have never had one."

"Then you'll have to build one."

"I will think about it. Is that all?"

"One more thing," Handoro replied, his face looking as serious as ever. "If you believe Poseidon is responsible for our problems, now is the time to ask him for rain to wash away the falling ash. Unfortunately, our dry season will continue for several more moons."

He then broke into a smile like Minos had seldom seen. "But if you do manage to get us some rain, even I might become a believer."

Jenora jumped up from her seat. "Outrageous!"

Minos raised his hand, motioning for her to remain calm.

"Your views about the powers of the gods are dangerous," Minos said to Handoro, "but I trust your judgment about our needs. Begin your work. The high priestess and I will deal with the gods."

Jenora glared at the chamberlain.

"Sire," Handoro continued, "I am not a young man any more. I have considerable wealth and could have retired to my villa years ago. I continue in my position because of my love for Minoa and my respect for you. Whether you agreed with me or not, I could speak my mind, even be critical of you without fear of your anger. That's the mark of a great ruler. In this you are like your father. Whatever may befall us, we will deal with our problems as well as any mortals could."

"Thank you for speaking your mind, Handoro. Meet with me again tomorrow."

"I know you are upset by Handoro's attitudes about the gods," Minos told Jenora after Handoro departed. "But he is a wise man. He understands the needs of Minoa. You and I must deal with Poseidon's anger."

"Sire, I too have labored for Minoa all of my life, and I have tried my best to satisfy the gods—and you. Despite what your chamberlain says, our problems are the work of Poseidon. We must appease him."

"And what can we do that we haven't already done?"

"I don't know, but I will think of something."

"Then do so. We will discuss it in my chambers tonight."

CHAPTER 7

IF THE GODS ARE WILLING

"The king ordered us to begin removing people from Thera, like I said he would," Bardok told the merchant ship captains he had spoken to that morning. "He will provide the food and other provisions you will take to Nios. From there, you will go to Thera, take on as many people as you can carry, and bring them back here. Start out by sailing eastward around the cape to Zakros, westward along our south coast to Kythera and then to the mainland. The king is sending messengers overland to ports along your route with orders for all merchant ships to do the same. Longboats in those ports will escort you for the rest of your journey."

"You don't have to tell us about routes, Bardok," one of them replied. "We've been sailing these seas since before you were old enough to grow a beard."

"Or grow hair anywhere else," another added.

Bardok smiled. "Have a safe journey."

"The winds will be against us," he then told the captains of his longboats, "but they might decrease enough after sunset so we can make it to Akrotiri by dawn. Strip all unnecessary gear and offload as much ballast as you think prudent."

"Bardok," one of the longboat captains said, "the seas can be rough this time of year. We need that ballast to stabilize the boats."

"I know. We'll replace some of it with more men so we can rotate oarsmen for maximum speed. By twilight, we should be to the west of Dhia. If the winds are light enough, we will continue on to Thera. If not, we'll spend the night on Dhia and try again tomorrow night."

He was about to climb his boat's boarding ramp when he saw Cavanila approaching in a donkey-drawn wagon.

"What are you doing here?" he asked her.

"My people need me. I'm going with you," she answered as she brushed past him and climbed the ramp onto his boat.

Bardok shrugged his shoulders and shook his head in disbelief as he followed her aboard. Let's depart," he ordered Zardik, "and stop grinning."

About halfway to Dhia, Bardok made his way to the bow.

"What are the winds telling you?" he asked Zardik.

Zardik, a short, broad-shouldered, deep-chested man, had fought many battles beside Bardok and his father. He was not a Minoan, but like others who came from the northern islands, he had spent most of his life at sea. His sense of the winds and currents had been ingrained in him through generations of seagoing ancestors. If not for his loyalty to Bardok and Toran, he would have been captain of his own ship.

"We won't know about the winds further north until we're out of the lee of Dhia. If they're too strong, we'll have to return there. But by then, it'll be dark. I say better go directly to Dhia and rest there tomorrow, like you said. The men will enjoy a free night and be in good spirits for the shorter row tomorrow night."

Bardok suppressed a smile. He knew Zardik had a favorite drinking place on Dhia and was not unfamiliar with the women there. Yet he respected Zardik's analysis and told him to head directly to Dhia.

Zardik passed Bardok's order to the steersman and explained the plan to the crew. He saw the grins on their faces and knew they were thinking about the enjoyments Dhia had to offer and the time they would have to sleep off any ill effects.

"But be careful," he added, "you need to be fresh for the long row tomorrow night. I will personally dump overboard anyone who can't pull an oar."

It was twilight by the time Bardok's three ships beached at Dhia, a small, mountainous island that, as seen from Kephtor, resembles a huge crocodile floating on the sea. Several protective bays on its lee side, the side facing Kephtor, provide convenient harbors for ships traveling between Kephtor and the islands to its north, or to ships traveling southward and eastward on their way to Egypt or the Levant. The villages in those bays depend upon visiting ships for their livelihoods and are hospitable places where sailors with valuables to trade could satisfy their wants.

Cavanila waited until most of Bardok's crew had gone ashore and then told Bardok she preferred to spend the night in her stern shelter rather than seek lodging with a local priest.

"It will be more peaceful here," she said, "and after the last several days I'll enjoy the quiet."

"As you wish. You can sup here and retire when you are ready. I'll dismiss my lookouts and sleep on the foredeck."

"I think I would only like a little cheese and bread with something to drink. We can sup together, if you wish."

Bardok set an oil lamp and food and drink on the afterdeck. They ate in silence, listening to the waves while barely looking at each other. Cavanila's thoughts were about the destructions she had witnessed and what she might find upon her return to Akrotiri. And she couldn't shake the feelings of guilt that tormented her since the previous night, when she began to question the gods.

Bardok's mind was on his mission to get the people of Thera to safety and organize things on Nios so they could survive there until they could resettle. He wondered how long it would take for the supply ships to arrive and whether they could bring enough necessities to support the many displaced Therans.

Cavanila broke the silence first.

"I must thank you for taking me to my uncle and for being so kind last night when I was sick. I know I might be causing you trouble for taking me against my uncle's wishes, but I must get to Thera."

"I hope he won't be too angry with either of us," Bardok replied. "What will you do when you get there? Will you stay there to help your father or will you go to Nios with us?"

"I won't know until I talk to him. If his priests remain on Thera, I might be more useful on Nios."

"Whatever you do, I will do my best to help. We will be faced with many difficulties, but if the gods are willing, everything will turn out all right."

51

Cavanila became more alert and attentive. "That is something I wanted to ask you about. You talk about the gods being willing, but you have no shrines on your boats, like other ship captains, and I haven't seen you make any offerings. Don't you think you have to appease the gods? Aren't you afraid to go to sea without honoring them?"

"Cavanila, I have been to sea for many years. I have fought many battles and seen many people die, some by my own hand. I lost my wife and a son at childbirth. I have sailed on calm seas and on seas so rough they nearly destroyed our boats and drowned us all. I have seen the lushness of Kephtor and how destructive an earth shaking can be. I have seen them all, good and bad. Were gods responsible for those things? Did they happen because I did or didn't make appropriate sacrifices and offerings? If all of those things were in the hands of the gods, is there any way I could have influenced what they did?

"Maybe some gods are greedy or demanding and easily upset, like Poseidon is supposed to be. Maybe some are truly benevolent, like the Great Goddess. I don't know. What I know is if I use my wits properly when I'm at sea or in a battle, things go well. If I do something stupid or reckless, I put myself and my men at risk. It is my doing. I cannot seriously ascribe my misfortunes or successes to the gods, even though I might say 'the gods were with us' when something good happens. You are a priestess who deals with the gods and teaches people to worship them. I am only a simple sailor."

As a priestess, Cavanila knew she should try to strengthen his faith in the gods. But, she asked herself, how can I tell this man what he should believe if I am beginning to have doubts of my own?

"I understand," she finally said. "You have seen much in your life and seem comfortable with your disbelief in the gods. I can only wish you well and ask the gods to look after you."

The conversation discomforted Bardok as well. I don't know why I made such a long speech, he thought, or why I said things to her I have never said to anyone, not even to Lovanna. And her response was not what I'd have expected from a priestess.

But he only said, "Thank you. I think I had better get some sleep. Sleep well."

"Good night," she answered as she pulled sheep skins over herself.

But neither slept immediately.

Bardok could not get Cavanila out of his mind. She's spirited, beautiful, and committed to helping her people, he thought, even if she knows she will suffer for it. She reminds me of Lovanna. But she is the daughter of a prince and a priestess besides. How can I even be thinking about her?

He's loyal to his king and willing to risk his life when necessary, Cavanila thought, but he can also be warm and sensitive, like when he tried to comfort me when I was sick. Even tonight. He thinks about things and has an unusual inner strength. I wish my father was more like him.

CHAPTER 8

SOMETHING ABOUT THE BOY CAUSED HIM TO WORRY ABOUT HIS SON'S VIRILITY

Minos sat in near darkness, his shoulders sagging, his wine cup in his hand. He had never been faced with so many serious problems in a single day. His thoughts turned to his father.

I wish he was here. He'd know what to do. He could deal with anything. What must he think of me as he watches from the world of the gods? He always worried about me, that I might not be a fit ruler for Minoa. He worried about many things. But if he didn't, I would never have known Serivida.

His mind turned back to his early life. His mother, Moxila, died in childbirth when he was only six, leaving him and his brothers, Rhadamantis and Sarpedon, under the care of the priests and priestesses of the palace. They taught the boys about the powers of the gods, and the consequences of disobedience. As they grew older, his father also tried to teach them about Minoa and the duties of a king, but neither of his brothers had any interest in such matters.

Unhappy with his other sons, the king decided Devterex would be his successor. He let Rhadamantis and Sarpedon wander about the palace and town, but he ordered Devterex to sit in his throne room whenever he held court. Devterex saw how his father dealt with people and governed Minoa and how he could be wise and gentle, or harsh, even ruthless, when he thought it necessary. And he came to understand how his father, as high priest, controlled Minoa through his grip on religious beliefs and taboos.

From early in life, Devterex's father urged him to participate in foot races, wrestling matches, and other games, and to become expert in the use of weapons. While not yet into his teens, his father had him escorted into the countryside to see the food production that supported Minoa. In the spring he watched the planting of grain and the collection of young grape leaves that would eventually be wrapped around bits of meat and other tasty things. He learned about beehives, watched farm animals breeding, and witnessed the birthing of their offspring. He saw how milk was made into cheese and watched as sheep were sheared and their wool washed, spun into yarn, and woven into cloth of the highest quality.

He visited verdant fields during the summer, though in one year of drought, he saw little but ruin, and he witnessed how his people suffered from it. When the weather turned cooler he helped harvest and thresh grain and pick grapes. It was the time when villagers celebrated their harvests and thanked the gods, often dancing within circles of fire.

He learned the lore of the olive, Minoa's most valuable crop. He saw young trees that would not bear fruit for many years after being planted, and others, hundreds of years old, with their twisted and separated trunks, still bearing enormous quantities of olives. He watched people knock the fruit from the branches with long sticks and saw how they pressed the olives for their oil.

Priests walked him through storerooms and showed him how food, cloth, and skins were distributed in exchange for other goods or services. His father and teachers saw to it that his head was constantly crammed with the knowledge of what it took to feed and clothe the people of Minoa.

Even in sexual matters his father left nothing to chance. He knew his son would have many available servant girls and would find other compliant women. Yet something about the boy caused him to worry about his son's virility. After his wife died, he saw to it that the priestesses and maids who cared for Devterex included the young Serivida, who was three years older. He selected her from among many offered by their parents because of her apparent intelligence, endearing personality, and potential beauty. She participated in bathing and dressing the young prince and was instructed by the priestesses to be young Devterex's playmate, servant, and confidant. She was given a room to herself next to his, and was trained so that when the time came, she would be capable of initiating him into the pleasures of the bed.

The youngsters were well matched and became good friends. Their intimacies began well before the priestesses had anticipated and continued until Devterex went to sea with Bardok. At that time, his father's high priestess, who had monitored the young couple's activities, inducted her into the priesthood and sent her to serve in a community near her family's home. When Devterex became king and assumed the name Minos, he appointed Serivida the high priestess of Thera.

The thought of her death turned Minos's mind back to his present world. He sighed, rose from his seat, and, still holding a cup, went to his sleeping room, where his servants bathed and perfumed him in preparation for Jenora's visit.

Jenora arrived through a long hallway that connected their sleeping quarters on the floor over their throne rooms. She too had bathed and perfumed. She wore only a light, filmy gown held together by a tie around her waist. Her long black hair flowed smoothly down her back.

"I know what we should do to please Poseidon," she said when she arrived.

"Not now," Minos replied as he took her hand and led her to his bed.

CHAPTER 9

A GOLDEN BULL

"Our people need to worship Poseidon with much greater passion than they now do," Jenora told Minos the next morning while they still lay in his bed. "They need a new image, a symbol of that god, something to make them feel his presence and see his power. Something so beautiful that Poseidon himself will be pleased with it. I think a bull would be fitting. The stone bull's head with golden horns that stands in our great hall is magnificent, but we need something smaller, something we could lead processions with. And it should be made of gold."

"A rhyton for pouring special libations," Minos said. "We will do it. Have your priests determine an auspicious time for its dedication."

"I already have. Last night before I arrived I spoke to Negorti, my eldest priest. He is our watcher of the heavens and keeper of the days. He said the night of the next full moon would be the most propitious time for a dedication. As you know, at this time of year, the sun rises a little farther to the north each day. At its most northerly position, it will rise in the same place for two successive days, as though it had stood still before it begins its southward journey again. Moonrises move in the opposite direction.

"Negorti has a place on the west roof where he uses a bronze rod to follow the sunrises as they move across the row of double horns on the east roof. He says the morning when the sun rises exactly in the middle of the northernmost horn will also be a night of a full moon —a rare event and the best time for a ceremony. The next most propitious time will occur three moons later when both orbs will rise from the same position in the middle of the row of horns."

"Then we will dedicate the rhyton on the sacred mountain the night of the next full moon," Minos replied. "Let us summon the goldsmiths."

Alkabar and his son Alpada had just melted gold for a bracelet they had been commissioned to make when two of Minos's guards entered their workshop. The older of the two ordered both goldsmiths to accompany them to the king. But Alkabar protested.

"We can't go now. We are about to pour gold. Wait until we finish."

Anger flashed across the guard's face.

"The king wants to see you now, so you will go now."

The threat in the guard's voice frightened them. Alkabar removed the clay crucible from their oven, called to his wife to watch their fire and, along with Alpada, went with the guards.

They entered the palace through a narrow corridor on its south side and climbed the stairway to the courtyard that they crossed to get to the king's throne room. They fell to their knees in front of Minos and Jenora who sat beside him.

Minos ordered them to rise.

"Poseidon is angry again," he said. "He destroyed Thera and shakes the earth here too. We must soothe his fury and do it soon before he destroys Knossos like he once did. I command you to make a symbol of that god, a golden rhyton in the shape of a bull, an image that will excite people and make them more passionate in their worship. It must show the power of that god and please him with its beauty so he will stop shaking the earth. It must be ready for dedication by the next full moon."

"But Sire," Alkabar pleaded, "Work like that will take at least two moons and a lot of gold."

"You will have the gold, but I will tolerate no delay. Complete it by the next full moon or you will be severely punished. Early tomorrow you will be brought before the high priestess to show her your design. Go and begin your work."

Alkabar and Alpada bowed, said "Yes, Sire," in unison and backed out of the room.

The earth had been silent since a mild shaking earlier that day, but most of the people at Knossos still avoided their homes, choosing to eat and sleep in the open. The goldsmiths, however, were more fortunate than most. Their house, a short walk along the Royal Road to the south of the palace, had a little courtyard for their furnaces and workbenches, and an awning under which they could sit, away from dangerous walls.

Immersed in a discussion of the king's demands, Alkabar and Alpada were oblivious to all else—the light ash that had begun to settle, their wives, and even the meal their wives had set on the table for them.

"Eat!" Alkabar's wife said. "I didn't put all this food in front of you to see it go to waste."

"Leave us alone!" Alkabar replied. "We've had enough orders for one day."

Absorption in their work was nothing new. Their wives left their house to commiserate and trade gossip with the other women of the town. Alpada's younger brother, Rengori, went out to join his contemporaries who were happy to be away from their houses. The trees around the fields provided them with cover and, once the sun sank below the horizon, a degree of darkness they were eager to exploit.

Alkabar's roots as a craftsman went back hundreds of years to ancient Babylon, where the great masters perfected gold-working techniques. His ancestors migrated through Anatolia and eventually to Thera and Kephtor, plying their craft and training their sons to do likewise. While at Zakros on the eastern end of Kephtor, Alkabar's work caught the attention of Minos's father, who brought him to Knossos to make jewelry for the royal family and the elites of the palace.

From the time Alpada was able to walk, he watched his father work the beautiful metal that could be melted, poured, hammered, twisted, drawn, or pressed into almost any form without breaking. When he was about three years old, he could form clay into recognizable animal shapes. He progressed to human heads and, by the time he was six, fashioned surprisingly good portraits of his parents and newborn baby brother. As his dexterity improved, his father taught him how to use sculpting tools to enhance the details of his pieces.

Among his works was a series of small heads, realistic, even grotesque in some cases, yet full of personality and feeling. Other craftsmen of the town considered them ugly and an affront to the gods, but his father saw those pieces as the work of a creative talent. When he was about eight years old, his father took him into the shop to clean, carry wood, and maintain fires for the ovens.

His moments of greatest delight came when his father broke a clay mold from around a gleaming object. He also learned that things didn't always work out perfectly. Occasionally, a piece came out with a flaw so minor only his father could detect it. Yet he never hesitated to melt it down and redo it. The lesson, he once told Alpada, is that one could judge the skill of an artisan by the quality of the work he refuses to accept.

Unfortunately, like potters whose work exposed them to hot kilns, Alkabar began to lose his eyesight despite the clay mask he should have worn more often when at the furnaces. As the years passed and Alpada mastered the requisite skills, his father assigned him an increasingly larger share of the work.

By the time of Minos's summons, Alpada was nineteen and had mastered all that his father could teach him. He enjoyed the challenge of tedious filigree and granulation work, but his real joy was sculpting. He had the genius to endow his pieces with dynamic and emotional qualities, whether a predatory animal on the hunt or a pregnant woman like his wife who was then aglow with health and pride.

Alkabar and Alpada decided the piece would consist of a bull's body that could be filled with wine or other liquids through an opening in its back. It could stand on a table without spilling its contents and be easily tilted for pouring through a hole in its snout.

Alpada's younger brother, Rengori, who had returned home still excited by his nocturnal activities, sat quietly and listened to his father and older brother argue about the possible designs for the bull.

When he could no longer contain himself, he blurted out, "If you really want something different, give the bull a big cock to pour the wine through. I'm sure there will be serving girls and maybe even some men and women who wouldn't mind holding their fingers over that spout. Some might even enjoy drinking directly from it."

That brought a sound cuffing from the older men who forcibly removed him from their shop while biting their tongues to avoid laughing. But Alkabar didn't completely dismiss the notion. A rich noble might pay handsomely for such a piece to spice up one of his parties.

The goldsmiths decided to model their bull after a fierce, aggressive species that had been bred to be fighters. These huge animals, their shoulders well above the height of a man, held their heads erect on gracefully curved necks despite the weight of their huge horns.

The pose they chose was of a bull in the act of goring an antagonist. Its left front leg would be planted to give force to his head as he lifts and swings it to his right, impaling his prey on the point of his left horn. Such a piece, they agreed, would have the power worthy of Poseidon.

But Alkabar was still worried. "What if she doesn't like it?"

"We could design more than one bull, Father, and some other things too. We could even make a likeness of the Great Goddess."

Alpada's suggestion about a statue of that goddess came from feelings he couldn't express, even to his father. He was smitten by Jenora's graceful posture and movements, especially her narrow waist and still youthful breasts. But it was her face with its high cheekbones and full lips that he dreamed about. He had only seen her mouth drawn and intense as she exercised her authority over them, but he imagined how soft and warm her lips might be during times of joy.

In his mind she was the perfect model for his golden goddess. He hoped his father would like the idea and bring it to Jenora's attention. Then, if the gods favored him, he might be *ordered* to sculpt the statue he yearned to create.

"Son, I like your ideas, but they want a bull, so let's work on that."

CHAPTER 10

CONDEMNATION AND DREAMS

"This whole island is shaking," Toran told Rhadamantis when he returned to Akrotiri, "even the far northern and western coasts. Anafi is quiet and the people hospitable, but it's just outside the path of the smoke. No one could live there very long if the fires continue and winds shift to the west."

"We can't live here either," Rhadamantis said. "The sky glows red at night, and fire runs down the sides of that island in the lagoon. Bardok arrived two days ago and took Cavanila to Knossos to ask Minos for more boats to move people away from here. The longboats he left behind under Vactor's command have begun taking women and children to Nios. What else can we do?"

"We could begin moving some people to the north coast. It's free of smoke and ash and closer to Nios. Boats could easily make it from Nios to there and back in a single day."

"But it's a long walk through ash to get there. What about food and water?"

"A day's walk will get people beyond the ash to where animals can have cleaner forage. They can drive their flocks and use donkeys to carry what they need. Even goats can carry packs."

Rhadamantis looked down at the floor. "I'll think about it. Right now I am going to watch the loading of Vactor's boats. Come with me."

Along the way, Rhadamantis stopped in front of an old couple who sat with their backs against the remains of a wall, their arms cradling their heads on their knees. He inquired about their health, but received no reply. The man looked up at Rhadamantis and rose. He shook the ash from his head and shoulders, turned his back to him and Toran, and helped the woman struggle to her feet. They stared at Rhadamantis for a moment, then limped silently down a street of ruined houses.

Rhadamantis, his face flushed, quickened his pace. As they approached the harbor, they saw that guards had restricted most of the crowd to the upper beach. Those selected to depart on the next boats stood waiting closer to the water. Rhadamantis and Toran saw an older man, a rich merchant from his dress, hand something to Gridawi and, with his family, pass through the guards to join those closer to the water.

Rhadamantis's first impression was that Gridawi had instituted the lottery system he had suggested. But once closer, he saw Therans pressed against the guards' spears, holding out items of gold or silver toward his harbormaster. And he saw Gridawi take something from another man, place it in a bag he carried over his shoulder and motion to a guard to admit that man and his family to the lower beach. He soon realized that his harbormaster was taking bribes for places in the boats.

Angered and embarrassed because he knew Toran had seen it as well, Rhadamantis rushed across the beach.

Gridawi noticed people turning their attention toward the town and looked up to see Rhadamantis approaching. He removed the bag from his shoulder and put it down next to an overturned hulk.

"What is in that bag?" Rhadamantis demanded when he reached him.

"Only some of my possessions."

Rhadamantis put out his hand. "Give it to me!"

When Gridawi hesitated, Rhadamantis snatched up the bag and pulled out a handful of gold and silver jewelry. He turned to the frightened group on the beach. "Did you give these to Gridawi?"

Their hesitant nods told him all he wanted to know. He replaced what he had in his hand and threw the bag at the nearest man in the group.

"Take back your jewels," he shouted. "Gridawi no longer needs them."

With his teeth clamped shut and his jaw muscles twitching, Rhadamantis stepped in closer to Gridawi, a much shorter man, who tried to move backward. But Rhadamantis grabbed the front of his robe and held him fast.

"I ordered you to select women, children, and craftsmen for places on the boats," he shouted, loudly enough for everyone on the beach to hear, "but you defied me. You chose elderly merchants who offered you gold. You used the authority I gave you to enrich yourself."

Gridawi stood in horror as Rhadamantis's words, foul breath, and spittle struck his face. He didn't even try to break Rhadamantis's grip on his robe. His eyes widened, his jaw moved with unformed words. He pleaded with outstretched arms as he began to realize his fate.

Rhadamantis continued, his face crimson, his voice rising in pitch. "Poseidon is destroying our island because of corruption like yours. You dishonored me and the House of Minos. Therans have died because of you and your greed. We could all die here. You are a thief and a murderer, and you don't deserve to live. And I, Rhadamantis, Regent and High Priest of Thera, Prince of Minoa, condemn you to death."

Without pausing even to take a breath, he drew a gold-handled dagger from the jeweled sheath on his belt and plunged it upward into Gridawi's belly. He withdrew it, took a deep breath, and stabbed him again. Only then did he release his hold on the man's robe and step back.

Gridawi's eyes opened even wider as he stared into Rhadamantis's face. His hands pressed against his gushing wounds, his jaw went slack. He coughed up bloody vomit and slumped to the ground, his knees drawn up to his chest, choking and gasping for air. Blood ran from his mouth. He lived for a few more weakening heartbeats before blackness overtook him.

Rhadamantis stood silent and still, his right hand and the dagger bathed in blood. A whirlwind of thoughts coursed through his mind. *He disobeyed me to fill his own coffers. He was a thief who had to be punished. What else could I do? What would any ruler have done? I had to take his life, and I did it with my own hand. I showed Toran that I am a man. Minos will know it too.*

The crowd on the beach stood mute in amazement.

"Do not move his body," Rhadamantis told his guards. "Let the ash cover it—a lesson for all who disobey and dishonor me."

He shouted to the crowd. "Our situation here is dire. You saw what happened to Gridawi. I will tolerate no disobedience. You older men waiting to go will be replaced by stronger men. Your families can go but you will wait for later boats."

He turned to Toran, who stood nearby. "Please take command of this harbor. See that order is maintained and that people and goods are ready to load as soon as the boats arrive."

Rhadamantis turned back to the crowd. "Toran will command this beach until Gantaros arrives. He will punish anyone who disobeys me. He will tell you of our plan to move people to the north side of this island."

He then whirled about and strode off to his palace.

That same morning at Dhia, Bardok's men, singly and in small groups, wandered down to the beach. Some, still relishing their activities of the night before, smiled as they walked. Others held their heads very still as they slowly navigated the rocky path. Zardik, with little sympathy, drove them to tidy up their boats and refill water jars for the coming night's journey. With those tasks completed, most spent the remainder of the day making up for lost sleep in whatever shade they could find. Later on, they ate a quick meal and, at Bardok's command, launched their boats. They pointed their prows into the setting sun until well past the rocks of Dhia and then turned northward toward Thera.

Cavanila sat in her stern shelter, relieved that the seas remained calm, her eyes on Bardok, his broad shoulders and tapered back silhouetted against the orange horizon. She thought about her conversation with him the night before and felt comforted by his presence. But she worried about what the smoke over Thera could mean for her father and the people of Akrotiri. And her problems of the previous days, and her feelings of guilt continued to plague her.

It was well into the night by the time sleep overtook her. As her body relaxed and her breathing slowed, curious images streamed through her mind. She saw her boat rocking on the open seas until an island, venting smoke and fire, suddenly grew beneath it, lifting it high into the mountains. She saw herself alone in a downpour, running naked through a forest, her rain-soaked hair, long and strangely golden, trailing behind, tangeling in the wind-driven branches. Covered with scratches and shivering in the cold air, she ran until she found herself in a steamy bower surrounded by a wall of rich greenery. The air was heavy with the pungency of wet moss. Butterflies of every color flitted among fragrant, nectar-rich flowers. She eased herself into a warm, mountain pool, closed her eyes, and let herself doze, thankful for the respite, until the sounds of cooing doves and rushing water caused her to look up. A rainbow had formed in the sky above her, and swallow-tailed blue birds swooped in to feast on flying insects.

She rose from the warm waters to take the hand of her lover who walked her to the entrance of a cave that she entered alone. Surrounded by oil lamps, her skin glowed like polished amber. She stood before a pillar of stone, a symbol of the gods. Offerings of food and gold lay at its base. She knelt and embraced the column, her cheek finding comfort in its unexpected softness and warmth. From deep in the darkness she heard the howling of dogs, and her body began to tremble. She couldn't tell if the trembling came from the shaft in her arms or from within her. But it filled her with joy until the entire cave began to shake. She tried to run, but her leaden legs turned each step into an agonizing chore. She fell to her hands and knees and dragged herself to the cave entrance, to blue skies and a blinding light, until a protective shadow fell over her.

She awoke to see Bardok, shading her from the newly risen sun. She thanked him for the water and cheese he offered and consumed them without the nausea of her previous trip. She looked past him over the port bow and saw the remains of her beloved city, ash-covered and broken, and could eat no more. Looking forward, she saw good-natured smiles on the faces of the tired crew, not the snickers of two nights earlier. Instead of humiliation, she felt acceptance, more like a budding crewmember who had proven herself to be a sailor.

The boats drew up on the same beach from which they had departed two days earlier, but the landscape had changed. Pumice and gray ash covered the rubble and had piled up into drifts.

Gray-powdered citizens were clearing pathways through the rubble and ash, and were moving clay jars of foodstuffs to the beach for loading onto boats. Tethered sheep and goats stood waiting to be transported.

Rhadamantis now stood straight, strutting with his usual arrogant air, shouting orders at everyone.

"What did my brother say?" he demanded from Bardok without a greeting or acknowledging Cavanila's presence. "Is he sending more boats?"

Bardok described the conversation he and Cavanila had with Minos and the orders the king gave for ships to help Thera.

Rhadamantis nodded. "I hope they get here soon. It is now ten days since the first destructions. We survive, but I don't know for how long. Your father is leading a group to the north coast where they can be out of the ash and closer to Nios."

"Your people seem more active today than when we left," Bardok said.

"I showed everyone I will tolerate no disobedience. Anyone who wants to get off this island will have to work for it. Unfortunately, I was forced to execute my harbormaster who was taking bribes in exchange for places in Vactor's boats. He deserved to die." He pointed to a mound on the beach. "His body is under that pile of ash. People learned I am serious."

Bardok tried to hide his dismay.

"I suppose you did what you had to. We'll be off to Nios as soon as my crews have some rest and refreshment. We can take some passengers with us."

"Take Cavanila with you," he said. Then turning to her, "You will be the high priestess of Nios. A council of priests will help you and see to it that the gods are properly served."

Cavanila too was shocked to learn that her father had killed a man, and more so that he left his body to rot on the beach.

"I will gladly go, but first I need to select priests and priestesses to serve on my council. We will go on the next boats."

"I have already chosen the priests who will go with you."

She looked straight into his eyes. "If I am to be the high priestess there, I will select my own council."

"But I chose my most senior priests for you. They know how to serve the gods."

"Father, I will select my own council."

"But my priests know how I want Nios governed."

"Then choose someone else to be your high priestess."

Rhadamantis' face turned red. His eyes narrowed, his voice became louder

"What happened to you, Cavanila? You dare to disobey me?"

She stared back at him, defiance in her eyes and posture, but remained silent.

Rhadamantis glared at Bardok, as though blaming him for Cavanila's attitude.

"Choose your council if you must. Just be sure you serve the gods well."

"I will do my best..." she started to say, but he was already walking away.

Cavanila took a deep breath to regain her composure and then looked to Bardok.

"Please save a place for me and my priests on your boats tomorrow. And thank you again for bringing me here."

Bardok's ships had just rounded the southwest corner of Thera on their way to Nios when they pulled alongside Vactor's two boats inbound to Thera.

"We might have problems with raiders," said Lendor, who commanded those boats. "An old shepherd who lives on Nios came down from the mountains yesterday. He told Vactor that pirate boats had landed at Manganari in the past. Sometimes three or four boats would come and stay for a few days. He said he thought at first we might be them. Vactor sent lookouts to both ends of the bay and up the mountain, but so far they haven't seen any pirates. He ordered me to ask Rhadamantis for fighters and weapons. He's afraid we might not be able to fight off a sizable band with what we've got."

"I understand," Bardok said. "The men I have with me should help with Manganari's defenses. But make your request as Vactor ordered. We could use whatever he sends. We will meet again when you return to Nios. Have a good journey."

"Good journey yourself, Bardok. I will see you there."

CHAPTER 11

JENORA

Alpada and Alkabar had barely swallowed their morning meal of olive oil-soaked barley bread and soft sheep's cheese when Jenora's guards came for them. They marveled at her throne room until she appeared. Everything was in blue, an attribution, they understood, of the sea, where Poseidon reigned. The huge fresco of dolphins and fish on her wall, the tiles on her floor, and even the spirals and rosettes that framed her doorways and windows were done in some shade of that nautical color.

Jenora, made up and dressed as though attending a formal ceremony, seemed to float into the room. She didn't look at them until she sat on her throne. Alpada's eyes followed her in amazement, captivated by her beauty. But a chill passed through him when she spoke.

"Show me your design," she demanded.

Alpada let his father reply while he absorbed every detail of her face, her body, and her dress.

"High Priestess," Alkabar answered, "we have two suggestions for the bull rhyton and drawings of other things you may like."

"Show me!"

The goldsmiths laid their drawings at her feet, the two bulls, a double axe, and a goddess with snakes wound around her arms.

"King Minos ordered you to make a gold bull. What is so good about your designs?"

Alpada felt he had to speak.

"We think the poses of the charging bull show the most important qualities of Poseidon." He held up a drawing for her to see. "In this one, his head is down, he is about to gore an enemy with a powerful, sideways movement of his head."

He picked up his other sketch.

"In this one his legs are firmly planted, but his head is up as though he has just thrown his enemy. It shows what he can do to those who anger him. He looks victorious. As my father said, we think either of these bulls will please Poseidon."

Her eyes went from one drawing to the other. "It is fitting to show what Poseidon can do when he is angered," she said, "but he seem lifeless as you have drawn him. I want him to look more alive."

"High Priestess, these are only rough drawings," Alkabar answered. "Please tell us how you would like them to look."

She sat up straight in her throne, imperious yet beautiful.

"You are supposed to be artists. You decide. Return to your shop and bring me something better by the time the sun is overhead. Leave your sketches of the other things. I will show them to King Minos."

The goldsmiths hurried their work and rushed back to Jenora's throne room by the appointed time.

"Well, do you have a better design?" she demanded.

"We have, High Priestess," Alkabar replied as he handed her a drawing. "This is the one we like best. The bull is throwing his head up as though he has just gored his enemy. His front legs are off the ground but his back feet are firmly planted. He has shown his prowess and punished the one who angered him. He is all powerful and pleased with himself. It's the most heroic of the poses we have drawn. We hope you like it."

She looked at the drawing and then at the goldsmiths with raised eyebrows.

"It is the best you have done so far. Proceed with it. And one more thing. King Minos considered the double axe a fitting symbol of the Great Goddess. He wants it made of gold along with golden dove, the Goddess's messenger, that will sit on the axe. We will carry the axe and the bull atop bronze staffs when we hold a procession so people can see and pray to them. Return before dark with your final designs. If I approve, I will have gold brought to your workshop. Be ready to form those pieces in two days. Nine days from now, the sun will rise at its northernmost point and the moon will be full. That night we will dedicate these pieces at the sanctuary atop the sacred Mount Juktas. You will be severely punished if your pieces are not finished in time."

Despite the Jenora's commanding tone and her warnings about failure, the goldsmiths sensed a softening in her voice.

"She likes our work," Alpada said to his father as they walked back to their shop. "But how can we have it all done by that time?"

"We have no choice," Alkabar replied.

Jenora did like the goldsmith's work, but she wouldn't tell them so. She ruled by fear, a tactic she acquired early in life.

Her father, a tough, aggressive merchant who was now dead, left her, while still a baby, in the care of servants after her mother died of the coughing disease. They taught her to beware of vindictive gods who could punish people, even other gods, for any disobedience or misbehavior. She learned before she reached her teens that she could rule her household in the same way. Her servants obeyed her or suffered her father's wrath. Sometimes, out of spite, she told her father untrue stories about their servants just to see them suffer. Her haughty attitude caused her to have few friends among girls, but as her body developed, she learned to use it to attract boys. And like a queen bee, she found ways to punish the few whom she allowed to enjoy her favors.

Her father's wealth grew from his ability to trade fine woolen cloth, wine, and oil of the olive for gold, silver, ivory, and anything else of value. He bought ships, hired tough captains to command them, and paid them well so they would not cheat him. He instructed his captains to fill their crews with fighters who could defend his ships and cargos against pirates. His were the first ships to sail in open waters when warmer weather brought milder winds and calmer seas, and they were the last to operate late in the year when the high winds and rough seas of the approaching cold season made sea travel almost impossible. Any captain who refused to sail under those conditions soon found himself without a command.

Her father once explained to Jenora: "I can make better trades by sailing when timid shippers are afraid to. Sometimes I lose a ship and a crew, but that's the price I pay for greater profits. I don't like to lose good boats, but my captains and crews know the risks when they sail for me. They take them because I pay them well. It is their choice."

He used his influence with Devterex's father to gain Jenora's acceptance into the priesthood, where she found comfort, even delight, in its dogmas. She learned that the gods controlled the world and needed frequent appeasement to remain sympathetic. What fascinated her most was that the high priestess could, on special occasions, become the embodiment of the Great Goddess on earth, even rise into the world of the gods. She vowed she would play that role one day.

Though her father's contributions to Minos's storehouses gained her acceptance into the priesthood, she advanced because of her intelligence and cold aggressiveness. She ingratiated herself with her mentors and superiors and made no friends among her peers. Eventually, she became one of the major priestesses in the hierarchy. When Minos had to choose a high priestess to replace the one who had served his father, she made sure he was aware of her talents and willingness to serve him in whatever way he wished. Minos selected her when the most beautiful and accomplished of her competitors suddenly became ill and died of a strange stomach ailment.

Under Minos's direction, Jenora controlled nearly every aspect of Minoan life through the priesthood she commanded. She governed the towns and villages, determined the levies farmers contributed to central stores, and meted out punishment to those who failed to obey the taboos she handed down. She was both feared and revered as an agent of the gods.

But her power came with a cost. She found herself nearly always on display. She had no private life and no family of her own. Her only lover was Minos.

Alkabar and Alpada arrived at Jenora's throne room long before their deadline.

"Your designs are adequate," she told them. "You will have your gold. Just be certain the bull looks alive and powerful."

Jenora and her guards appeared at the goldsmith's workshop two days later with the gold she had promised. But when she demanded to see their work, they could only show her wax carvings of their figures.

"You were supposed to be ready to pour by now."

"Two more days, High Priestess," Alkabar replied. "We still need to coat the wax with clay and then burn off the wax. Only two more days, High Priestess, please."

"You had better be ready by then."

CHAPTER 12

MANGANARI

Five longboats filled with Therans arrived in the afternoon two days later.

"Welcome to Manganari," Bardok said as he reached out to help Cavanila off the ramp of Zardik's boat. "I hope you had smooth waters."

"We had no problems," she replied. "I'm beginning to understand why you love the sea. I wish I had more time to enjoy it."

He looked into her eyes and smiled.

"Maybe you will someday. If you wish, I can take you to your new home. Zardik and Vactor will care for the others who came with you."

"Yes, please."

Bardok escorted her across the broad beach to the grasslands beyond it where he had set up a lean-to for her close to his own.

"We have much to talk about. But I suggest you rest while I speak to Vactor and Zardik. I'll have refreshments brought to you. We can talk afterward."

But she was too excited and apprehensive to rest. She had some food and drink and walked through the encampment, greeting people, mostly women and children who stared back at her with expressionless faces. She stopped to talk to a few but elicited only one-word answers from most of them. Once past the last of the shelters she walked westward along the hard sand and climbed a rocky outcropping that extended from the hills down into the sea. She saw two more bays, each with a sandy beach, and climbed down to the nearest one. She sat on the warm sand, hugging her knees, enjoying the quiet and solitude. She looked out across the sea toward Thera, visible through a light haze, wondering how the people she had left behind might be coping with the smoke and ash that still spewed from that island in the lagoon.

After a while, she removed her short robe and loincloth and waded out for a shallow dive into the cool sea. She arched up to the surface after a few underwater strokes, pushed her hair back, and wiped the water from her eyes while she gulped for air. She swam a few more strokes on the surface and dived again to search for fish and to examine the bottom. She tried a handstand on the bottom but couldn't keep her feet out of the water without falling over.

For the first time in many days, she felt invigorated, like a young girl again. She allowed herself one more dive and then returned to the beach, thinking she could stretch out on the sand and let the heat of the sun dry her body. But her worries about Thera and her impending responsibilities wouldn't let her relax. Still wet, she dressed again and retraced her steps to the encampment.

After he left Cavanila, Bardok went to find Zardik and Vactor.

"I reminded Rhadamantis about the pirates and our needs for fighting men, weapons, and more food," Zardik told him. "I also asked for some fishermen to come to Nios. I offered to tow their boats here if necessary. As you saw, he gave us a few guards and weapons, and we brought more goats. Fishermen will come some morning when the seas are calm and the winds not so brisk."

"What do you think about our defenses now?" Bardok asked Vactor.

"Aside from Rhadamantis's guards, and I am not sure about them, our own crews are the only fighters we can depend on. It will be a long time before the few scribes and tradesmen here could match battle-hardened pirates. They'd be slaughtered if a fight were to occur today."

"We will have to do what we can," Bardok replied. "We will at least have an advantage in numbers once more Therans arrive here. We need to develop tactics to make the best use of everyone."

As sunset approached, Bardok brought some strips of roasted goat meat and watered wine to Cavanila in her lean-to. She thanked him for his thoughtfulness and invited him to join her.

"I walked around our beach and settlement," she said. "It's beautiful here but we have so many problems. How will we accommodate everyone?"

"I saw you up on the rocks," he replied smiling. "It won't be easy but we'll survive. I can see to our defenses and transporting people here from Thera. My men can set up camps and help provide food and water. But you are the high priestess now. You are the one to organize people and get them to work together until everyone is transported to Kephtor."

"I know how my father distributed food, but I won't use it to control people like he did."

Bardok was impressed that she had already turned her mind to the task of finding a way to govern Nios. He also felt it best that she continue to develop her ideas without too much contribution from him.

"Then you'll have to think of another way."

"What other way?"

"I don't know, but let's consider the possibilities."

Their discussion continued until well after the sun had set. It was only when one of Cavanila's priests brought them a small, lighted oil lamp that they realized daylight had turned to near darkness.

Bardok jumped to his feet.

"I'm sorry. I didn't realize it was so late. You must be tired. And we both have much to do in the morning. Let us meet again tomorrow."

Cavanila looked up at him, amused by his sudden awkwardness. She knew he didn't want to end their discussion, and she didn't either.

"Yes," she said, "let us sup together tomorrow before sunset. By then, I'm sure I will have many more questions for you. Good night, Bardok, and thank you."

Cavanila doused her lamp and lay back on her bed of sheep-skins. She watched the moon and listened to the waves breaking on the shore. Were it not for a child's cry and a goat's bell somewhere in the distance, she could have been alone in the world.

As she drifted into sleep, her last thought was to thank the gods for Bardok.

The next day, Vactor reported to Bardok and Zardik. "Our scouts found some old campsites in a bay to the north, but no sign pirates were there. I'm still worried about the supply ships from Kephtor. They should begin arriving soon."

"What do you think, Zardik?" Bardok asked.

"If I were a pirate captain hunting for rich prizes this time of year, I would want a temporary base somewhere closer to the shipping routes. I think the big bay at the other end of this island would be more to their liking."

"We need to send escorts out to help protect our supply ships. What routes do you think they'll take? When should they arrive?"

Zardik drew a map in the sand that showed the mainland, Kephtor, Nios, Thera, and a few of the islands in between. He drew arrows to indicate wind directions as they had been since they left Kephtor.

"I think they'll go from the south coast of Kephtor past Kythera to the mainland, then take an easterly course to the strait between Sifnos and the islands north of Melos, past Folegandros and Sikinos to here. They could overnight on Milos, where they would be welcomed. They might also pick up some obsidian while there. But they could beach for the night on any of the islands. I figure it would take seven to ten days for them to get here. If we want to go out to escort them in, we should do that about two days from now."

"That gives us two more days to continue bringing people from Thera," Bardok replied.

While Bardok conferred with Vactor and Zardik, Cavanila spoke to the priests who came to Manganari with her.

"Our settlement here will soon include almost everyone from Akrotiri. Bardok and I have decided that those who are already here will form a small, temporary village. It will include my lean-to and a shrine they could set up. The next groups to arrive will form separate villages, but those with family already here can join them if they wish. Each village will select a chief to look after its affairs according to my orders and keep me advised of our progress and any problems that arise. Those chiefs will form my council. You will remain as priests to help me maintain this organization and to pray to the gods as you wish."

"Some of those supply ships must be getting close by now," Zardik told Bardok two days later. "Let me go look for them."

Bardok knew that Zardik could help ensure the safe arrival of those ships if he actually met them, but he worried that the ships might have taken a route different from one Zardik expected. To divert longboats from the evacuation of Thera would slow that process and prolong Theran's suffering and risks. But he decided to trust Zardik's judgment.

"Five days but no more," he told him. "We need those boats."

Zardik wasted no time. By sunset that same day, his boats made it around the south side of Sikinos and across the gap to a tiny beach on the northeast coast of Folegandros, where they camped for the night. The next day, they made it to the northern end of Kimolos, a chalky island near Melos that wore a silvery sheen in the afternoon sun, where they again camped.

"Look sharply," he told his crews. "This island has always been a haven for pirates."

But the night was uneventful. The next morning, after rounding a point on the northern coast of Kimolos, Zardik's lookout pointed deep into a large bay and shouted.

"There!"

Zardik made his way up to the prow where he could see what appeared to be two boats on the distant beach. He ordered his steersman to turn toward them and signaled Lendor, who commanded his second boat, to follow his lead. But once closer, they realized those boats were only the derelict hulls of a cargo ship and a longboat. Both had been stripped of everything useful, even their masts. As they approached the beach, the crews spotted several bodies that had washed up on the sand. Scouts Zardik sent up and down the beach found several more bodies displaying stab wounds and slashes. They found no survivors.

"This happened only two or three days ago," Lendor told Zardik after they buried the dead in deep sand high up on the beach. "Those raiders can't be far away. We should go after them."

"They could be almost anywhere on the far side of this island by now," Zardik replied, "or in any of the sea caves on the south coast of Melos. I'd like to go after them too, but we can't. Our other supply ships need our protection. Besides, seeing what they did to those two boats, there might more of them than we can handle."

The next day, on their way northward toward Sifnos, Zardik's lookout reported sails near the horizon to their west. He steered his boats toward them and ordered his crews to be ready for a fight if they turned out to be raiders. To his relief and that of his nervous crews, they turned out to be two of Minos's merchantmen with a pair of escorting longboats. After greetings and celebration among all the crews, Zardik led the group back toward Nios. They made it to Folegandros that night, bypassed the big bay at the north end of Nios, and sailed into Manganari late the next morning.

The sight of Zardik's approaching flotilla had everyone at Manganari racing to the beach to greet the arriving sailors and help unload the boats. Zardik was the first ashore.

"They're out there somewhere," he told Bardok and Vactor, who came to meet him.

Cavanila was as happy as anyone to see the arriving boats. Soon after the lookouts reported their approach, she called together her four priests and the head men of her villages. She told them each of the villages would get a share of the cargoes, but the rest would be stored and doled out as needed. When she learned the ships carried some wine, she ordered a ceremony to thank the Great Goddess that night after all had supped.

The next morning the supply ships and four longboats proceeded to Thera and boarded as many Therans as they could hold. Three of the longboats returned to Nios with their passengers. The merchantmen, filled with Therans and with one escorting longboat, set out for Kephtor.

That day more than two hundred people were taken off Thera. With Bardok's fleet now up to six longboats, and more people trekking to the north shore of Thera, he began to think that the relocation could be completed before the onset of the cold season.

CHAPTER 13

YOU WILL HAVE YOUR JEWELS

That same morning, Handoro sat next to Minos, whose wine cup was already filled. Handoro drank only goat's milk.

"A shepherd from the east said ash is still settling on this side of the mountains," Handoro said, "but none on the south side. So I ordered our flocks to be driven through the passes to our southern feeding grounds. I sent messengers with your royal seal to order the farmers there to make whatever accommodations are necessary."

"And in other places?" Minos asked.

"The ash fall gets heavier as one goes farther east. Trading at Zakros has stopped. And if you don't already know, two houses here in Knossos collapsed during the last shaking, but there has been no damage to the palace."

"Is that all?"

"No, Sire, we have two other problems."

Minos reached for his cup. "Is there no good news?"

"Some merchants complained to me yesterday that our use of their ships has reduced their profits. I reminded them there is little we can do about destructions caused by the gods and that they had little to complain about. I told them they had all managed to build great villas when times were good, so they should expect to contribute their share when help is needed. I warned them they would suffer consequences if they refused to comply with your orders."

Minos smiled for the first time that morning.

"So you, who does not believe in the gods, told them their problems were the fault of the gods?"

"Sometimes the gods are useful." Handoro replied with a smile of his own.

"What else?"

"I ordered my engineers to improve our roads over the mountains, like we discussed two days ago. They are worried about getting the workers they will need."

"Where will you get them?"

"The ships we sent to Nios and Thera will soon return with many Therans. They should be willing to work for their food and shelter. I assume the high priestess will agree."

"Did you ask her?"

"No, Sire, I didn't. She refuses everything I request, even though she doesn't mind asking for large quantities of gold and jewels. It would be better if you asked her."

Minos sat back in his seat and bit into a fresh fig.

"When did she ask for those?"

"A few days ago, for the gold. This morning for the jewels."

"I'll talk to her about your workers. You look tired. Are you well? As you said two days ago, you're no longer young."

"Do not worry about me, Sire. I am fine."

"Then continue with your work, and return to me when you have more news. And try to get some rest."

"Good morning, Jenora," Minos said later when she entered his throne room.

"Good morning, Sire," she replied, and with a knowing smile added, "I trust you slept well last night."

"Yes, I did. I didn't hear you rise this morning. Handoro told me he provided you with gold and jewels. Have the goldsmiths finished our pieces yet?"

Jenora's smile disappeared. She had only moments earlier provided the jewels to the goldsmiths.

"They have, Sire. They are beautiful. Wait until you see them."

But Minos saw uncertainty on her face and hesitated for a moment. "Don't forget. The moon will be full in four days."

"They will do as I say. Is there anything else you would like me to do?"

"Two things. Handoro needs workers to improve our roads over the mountains. See that he gets them. Use whatever

Minoans and Therans are available." And with a suggestive look he added, "The second thing can wait until tonight. In the meantime, be certain that everything will be ready for the dedication."

"I will, Sire."

But the fabrication process was far more complex and time-consuming than either Jenora or Minos had expected, and not all of the pieces were completed when she left the goldsmith's workshop earlier that morning.

Once Jenora approved their design, the goldsmiths worked long hours to meet the deadline she and Minos set for them. They sculpted wax models of their pieces, encased them in clay, and then burned off the wax in their ovens, leaving behind molds into which the gold could be poured.

Jenora had gone to the workshop the day after they received the gold Handoro provided. She watched them pour the gleaming metal into molds for the double axe and the two halves of the gold bull. Alkabar explained that they would pour the gold for the dove the next morning. He told her the double axe and several parts of the bull rhyton would be cool enough by then to break away the clay molds. Then all that remained would be to glue the two halves of the bull's torso together and attach the head and legs. The innards would remain hollow.

By the time she arrived late the next morning, the gold had been poured for the bird, and the pieces poured the day before sat cooling in their molds.

"When will you break those molds?" she asked. "I can't stay here all day."

"It's a little early, High Priestess," Alkabar replied, "but soon."

"I want to see them now."

The goldsmiths looked at each other. Alkabar felt the mold for the double axe to see if it had cooled enough. He shrugged his shoulders again and tapped the clay with a small bronze hammer, gently at first and then harder until it broke away from the double axe. The striking beauty of the piece seemed assured until the final bits of clay came away from the thin edges. Delight turned to horror. The axe lacked one of its edges.

"The gold didn't penetrate to that side," Alkabar explained after a moment of silence. "We have to do it again."

Jenora shook her finger at Alkabar and spoke through clenched teeth.

"Only four more days," she said. "I will see to it that you and your family are banished from Minoa if your work isn't done by then."

She stalked out of the shop without waiting to see how the parts of the bull turned out. When she returned three days later, all of the pieces were completed. The bull was now completely assembled. But again she shook her head in anger.

"The axe and dove look good, but the bull is just a statue with no character. You said it would look alive. You failed me and the king."

"We did our best," Alkabar replied.

"It's unacceptable!"

Alpada had not spoken directly to Jenora during any of her visits, but this time he spoke up.

"I know what we could try."

"Speak!"

"High Priestess, we could set jewels into his eyes, like we do with golden daggers. That would make him look more lifelike, especially if they were red. And they would sparkle at night in the light from a fire."

Jenora looked at him as though seeing him for the first time. That young man is clever, she thought. He is also comely and well formed. But her face remained scornful.

"You will have your jewels."

While Jenora was assuring Minos that the pieces were already completed, the goldmsiths were just beginning the work of setting two ruby red stones, faceted and polished by the palace's lapidary workshop, into the bull. Their first task was to hollow out the bull's eye sockets with their bow lathe, an implement with a sharply- pointed bronze cutting tool attached to a shaft that could be rotated at high speed with the use of a bow. They then cemented the jewels in place with fish glue.

"Now your bull seems alive," she said when she returned to them after seeing Minos. She even smiled a little. "My guards will soon come for the pieces."

"Thank you, High Priestess," Alpada replied. "We are most happy you like it. Would you grant me a wish?"

Her smile vanished. "What do you want?"

"Please, High Priestess, we are proud of our work. I would like to see how people respond to our pieces. And I would like to be present when you dedicate them."

"You may attend the ceremonies as one of our servants, if you wish, but you will have to do the work of a servant as well."

"Thank you, High Priestess," Alpada replied with a deep bow.

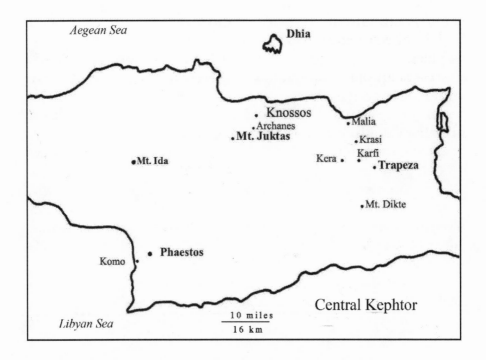

Drawing derived from a map made available from
the Wikimedia Foundation under CC BY-SA 3.0.

Chapter 14

THE DEDICATION

"Where is your chamberlain?" Jenora asked. "It is the day of our dedication. He insults the gods even as the earth rumbles."

"He is an old man with many problems," Minos replied. "He would probably not come even if he did believe in the gods. Let us begin."

Jenora signaled two flute players outside his throne room to begin the procession. After a few heraldic notes, sistrum and timbrel players joined them with a lively beat as they led the way to the altar at the center of the courtyard. Behind two guards parading their spears at arm's length, the king carried the gold bull atop a bronze staff. He wore no jacket. Tassels hung from the bottom edges of his white skirt which had gold threads woven into it. His belt held a gold-handled, jeweled dagger.

Jenora walked behind him. She held the bronze staff that supported the double axe with the gold dove perched on it. She wore a ceremonial gown composed of a multicolored flounced skirt and a purple, short-sleeved, open-bodice jacket edged with strips of red cloth. Miniature representations of birds and the moon, further symbols of the Great Goddess, sat atop her hat. Bracelets on her wrists, snakes on her upper arms, and rings that dangled from her ears, all of gold, sparkled in the bright morning sun.

Wives and children of the elites of Knossos who sat in the stepped courtside gallery ceased their chatter and fell silent, captivated by the gleaming gold pieces.

Jenora watched their eyes as she walked. Just the effect we wanted, she thought smiling to herself.

Alpada, waiting in the northeast corner of the courtyard since shortly after dawn, felt his heart race as he watched Jenora and

Minos parading the pieces he and his father had fabricated. His charcoal flew over his clay tablets, but the only images he drew were those of the high priestess.

As the marchers approached the altar, the crowd parted to clear a path, then closed in behind them, like water around a passing ship. A large, poppy-fed bull, his head down, stood tethered on one side of the altar. A fire burned in a pit on the other. Jenora raised the double axe as high as she could, stared up at it, and in a voice that reached the rooftops of the palace began:

> O Great Goddess,
> See the beauty of this golden axe,
> And the dove, your messenger.
> They glow in your honor,
> Symbols of our love and loyalty.
> We dedicate them to you,
> And ask your help to soothe Poseidon.
> Please, O Great Goddess, help us.

She maintained her pose until the crowd repeated her last words, and lowered her staff. Minos then held up the golden bull and prayed:

> O Poseidon,
> See your symbol I hold before me,
> Gold and shining,
> Powerful and bold,
> Victorious and triumphant.
> We ask your forgiveness.
> We offer you sacrifices and plead for your understanding.
> Let the earth be still again.
> Hear us, O Great Poseidon.
> Let the earth be still.

Again, the crowd repeated, "Let the earth be still."

Minos lowered his staff to the ground and nodded to a priest who slammed a great stone hammer onto the bull's head, just behind its horns. Stunned, the animal crumpled to the ground.

Six priests struggled to haul it up onto the altar but let its head hang down over the side. Another priest cut into its throat and two elderly priestesses collected its spurting blood into bronze rhyta. They handed the vessels to the king and high priestess, who appealed to the gods as they circled the altar three times, each time dripping blood into the fire. Other priests cut pieces of meat and skin from the bull and dropped them into the fire while murmuring more chants to the gods. The smoke, the stench of burning hair, and the smell of roasting meat permeated the courtyard.

Musicians and guards led the king and high priestess out the north end of the courtyard, down a stairway, past a colonnade, and down a second flight of wide, sloping stairs to the Royal Road, where horse-drawn chariots waited to carry them through the town. People lined the streets to watch the procession and gaze at the gold pieces. Many stood in doorways so the chariots and marchers could pass. Priests and priestesses offered olive branches, symbols of goodwill and connection to the gods, to the bystanders. Adults and children followed behind, and the procession grew as it advanced. The marchers then turned south and reentered the palace through the same portal by which they had left.

Commoners who had followed remained outside. The palace grounds were not for them. But they were not unhappy. Priests left roasted meat and jugs of wine on stone benches built onto the outside of the palace walls.

After feasting, Minos, Jenora, six young priests, and six priestesses changed into tunics for traveling and left the palace through its south portal. Waiting chariots carried them south along the river that poured from a cavern high in the mountains.

The dusty road into Archanes took them past a dome-covered reservoir fed by a perpetual spring, then through a street lined with two- and three-story buildings, many with window boxes containing flowers. The local governor and his wife greeted them in their courtyard. Their palace was smaller than the one at Knossos but nearly as grand. Like Minos's palace, its thick walls were composed of large, polished stone blocks. Red-painted pillars on marble bases supported upper-story walkways and provided entrance ways into the interior.

The governor's servants showed them to luxurious rooms on the second floor where they retired for a brief rest. They ate an evening meal with the governor and his wife beside a torch-lit, outdoor, paved area. They were entertained afterward by wrestling and boxing matches between teenage boys, and by young girls who danced to the music of a lyrist. Minos and Jenora watched politely but excused themselves as soon as the dancers were finished.

The next morning, they continued their journey up the east side of the Juktas mountain, the crest of which, when seen from the northeast, resembled the face of a reclining bearded man. They left the chariots and continued on foot when the path became too steep and narrow. The priests and priestesses took turns carrying the gold pieces.

Their path took them near an abandoned, stone building that sat on a bluff on the north side of the mountain. Weeds and shrubs obstructed its doorway.

"It must be an old sanctuary," one of the young priests said. "Let's look inside."

But when several of them began to walk toward it, Jenora stopped them.

"Do not go there," she said. "It's an old shrine where ancient peoples are said to have held strange rites. Some say their gods still occupy it. I forbid you to enter. We must continue on."

She didn't tell them what an elderly priest had once told her, that it contained a large stone altar that had been used for sacrifices many generations earlier.

Once past the shrine, their route took them around to the west side of the mountain, where a rocky path led to a huge cave that had several entrances. Minos stopped the procession and sent servants inside with torches to light its interior. He sent others ahead with the gold pieces.

"The goddess of the lands and mountains dwells in this cave," he said. "It contains pillars that represent the gods of the earth, and a hidden lake that never dries. The high priestess and I will purify ourselves in its waters and pray to the gods before we continue up the mountain. The rest of you will then do the same."

Minos and Jenora entered the cave and disrobed. Shadows on the walls mimicked their movements. The still water, like a mirror, reflected stalactites, walls, ceilings, and the flames from multiple torches. The ripples that Minos and Jenora caused when they entered the cool water abolished the reflections and made the cave walls shimmer in an undulating light.

After a brief immersion, they dressed in fresh robes, left offerings of wheat and barley in clay cups on a stone altar set against one of the walls, and walked out into the daylight. They continued their steep climb with several servants while the young priests and priestesses who had accompanied them entered the cave to purify themselves as well.

Minos and Jenora arrived at the summit of the mountain by late afternoon. They sat side-by-side on thrones in front of a roofed, multiroom sanctuary while waiting for the others to arrive. A fire burned near an altar on the largest of the terraces. The gold pieces stood in front of them in stone stands carved to resemble the horns of a bull. After the priests and priestesses joined them, Minos ordered most of the servants to leave the mountain and to return two mornings later to help with the trek back to Knossos. Several serving girls, a pair of servants to tend to the fires, and a few musicians remained. So did Alpada.

The worshippers ate an evening meal, their last food until the next night, sitting in sunshine watching the valleys below sink into darkness. They spent the next day in quiet contemplation, enjoying the expansive views from the mountaintop: Archanes below to the east, Knossos on a low hill to the north, and the seas beyond. They could see the mountain to their east, where many believed

Zeus was born, and the snow-covered one to the west, where legends said Zeus grew to manhood.

The sun had just disappeared behind the western mountains when the priests and priestesses gathered before Minos and Jenora on the upper terrace. Minos now wore a long purple robe with diagonal stripes that signified his authority as the high priest. Jenora wore an ankle-length, red robe over the skin of a black panther, its forepaws tied around her neck. The others wore leopard skins under their robes.

Two priests sacrificed a lamb, dripped some of its blood onto the now roaring fire, and set its meat to roasting. Then Jenora stepped forward with a brightly painted ewer of wine, held it up for the gold bull to see, and poured its contents into a mixing bowl that already contained water. By then, the full moon, as red as it had been every night since the cloud rose over Thera, appeared above the eastern mountains. The fire, its heat reflected by a wall of gigantic stones that surrounded the terrace, warmed the entire area, while the smell of lamb roasting on a spit over another fire tormented the fasting participants. A musician strummed his lyre and sang of their trek up the mountain.

The ceremonies began after serving girls filled clay cups for all participants with the watered wine. Minos rose and held his cup in front of him.

"May the Great Goddess protect Minoa, and may Poseidon still the earth," he said as he poured a few drops into a depression carved into the center of his table. He drank the rest and threw his cup into a deep crevice not far from the altar.

Jenora stood, repeated Minos's words and added, "May the Great Goddess watch over our people and protect them."

She drank the wine and, like Minos, threw the cup into the rift before returning to her seat next to him.

One by one, the others repeated the actions of Minos and Jenora and went to sit around the fire, where fresh cups of wine and numerous plates of food awaited them. With the rising full moon, their cravings for food satisfied, and a mellowness induced by wine consumed on empty stomachs, they relaxed in their seats and began to enjoy the night. They picked at cheeses, roasted almonds, olives, and fresh figs as they listened to the lyrist, who continued to sing of their journey and their mission to dedicate the gold pieces.

But it was the soulful tunes of the flute player that touched them more deeply. So when the musicians and a sistrum player joined in a harmonious rhythm, one of the priestesses rose to stand before the golden bull and began to sway with the music. The other priestesses soon joined her, forming a half-circle with their hands on each other's shoulders. The priests then rose to form another half-circle behind the priestesses. As the music continued, the dancers closed the circles. They reeled first in one direction and then the other, slowly at first and then more rapidly as the musicians increased their tempo. The wine, and the fervor of their dancing in the heat of the fire brought sweat to their bodies and brows. Along with Minos, Jenora watched the dancers until she could no longer remain seated. She rose to stand in front of the gold pieces. She poured another libation onto the ground and, gazing up toward the now whiter moon, raised her arms and began:

> O Great Goddess,
> Who protects us and our homes,
> Who makes our vines grow,
> And provides us with life-giving waters,
> Who sees to our crops and the fertility of all things,
> O Great Goddess, who provides our sustenance,
> We need your help.
> The earth trembles and fire comes from the sea.
> Poseidon is angry but we know not why.
> We honor him with sacrifices and offerings,
> But the earth still trembles.
> O Great Goddess,
> We beseech you,
> Tell Poseidon to forgive us and let the earth rest.
> O Great Goddess,

Who always protected us,
Give us a sign you hear our prayers,
Let us feel your presence.

She then moved to the center of the circle of dancers, where she joined in the dancing, chanting over and over:

O Great Goddess,
Protect us.
O Great Goddess

The others took up the chant as they danced. She led them to the golden bull. Its eyes, reflecting the fire, were flickering and alive. Poseidon was near, summoned by the dancing. She addressed her prayer to him:

O Great Poseidon,
We dedicate this bull to you,
This bull that gleams with your power and strength.
We give you our love,
Our sacrifices and offerings,
We give you our trust and loyalty.
We beg you,
Listen to our voices.
Quell the fires in the sea and stop the shaking of the earth.
We give you all,
And ask only for the safety of Minoa and our people."

She again began to dance, her arms outstretched, her head back, her body lost in the music and euphoria of the night. The other dancers formed concentric circles around her. She whirled around in one direction and then the other, until she suddenly stopped and raised her hands to halt the music.

She ordered servants to fill the gold bull with undiluted wine. In the silence of the night, she poured some into everyone's cup and dripped a few drops directly into the fire, causing a hiss and the pungent odor of burnt wine. She stood in front of the bull again, raised her arms and, with her open hands facing up in supplication, she looked to the moonlit sky, closed her eyes, and again called on Poseidon:

We beg you, O Poseidon, listen to our voices.
Quell the fires and quiet the earth.

She drank her wine and signaled the musicians to begin again. She repeated the incantation while her hands and arms fashioned graceful figures in the air. Her body swayed and her feet moved to the music. Her motions no longer came from her consciousness but from her soul. A strange lightness settled on her. She felt she had left the earth and was looking down on herself from above. She had become the Great Goddess, and it was she who had to protect her people and cool Poseidon's anger.

Already sweating, she felt the heat of the magnificent bull. She gazed into its eyes and slowly removed her robe, leaving the panther skin and her loincloth as her only covers. The others shed everything but their leopard skins.

But Jenora paid them no attention. She saw only two piercing, red eyes. Her devotion to that god was all that mattered. She stood swaying before him, her hips moving in new ways, slowly at first, then more rapidly. The others again mimicked her movements. They became a group of swaying, thrusting, heated bodies moving to the incessant, penetrating beat of the music. She called out to the god, but her words were only deep-throated grunts in rhythm with her movements. She was with him, begging, offering. Her eyes fluttered, her breathing became rapid and shallow until, in exhaustion, she slumped to the ground.

The music stopped. The dancers, filled with their own passions, saw the transformation of their high priestess. They too ceased dancing and moved off in pairs to the far corners of the terraces.

Alpada, who had been sketching furiously from his place in a corner, put his charcoal and clay tablets down but continued to watch.

Minos left his throne to kneel beside Jenora. He slipped his arms beneath her nearly unconscious body and carried her into the sanctuary, where he placed her on the sheepskin-covered altar. He arranged her long hair to frame her face and removed her panther skin. The rays of the moon beaming down through the light well gave her body a soft glow, like a figure carved in translucent marble. He removed her loincloth and his own robe, his only garment. Adoringly and with the lightest of touches, he spoke to her with his fingertips, moving them slowly and tenderly over her body.

Jenora remained somewhere in her dream, where only the radiant eyes of her god pierced the blackness. But sensations from her skin soon roused her to awareness. With tears in her still-closed eyes, she took her god, her king, her lover, into her, feeling him in her very soul. For a while, neither moved, only reveled in each other's essence. She opened her eyes and looked into his, knowing then that she had returned from the gods. She gripped him with tightening muscles as they fell into a slow rhythm, only contracting their deepest sinews until, losing control, they entered still another realm.

CHAPTER 15

I AM NOT JUST ANOTHER WOMAN

"Last night was glorious," Jenora said as she and Minos ate a morning meal in the privacy of their sanctuary. "I saw the Great Goddess. She was dressed in my sacred gown and looked like me. Then I was her. I pleaded with Poseidon. I offered him everything if he would still the earth. I saw his red eyes in the darkness and heard a distant laugh that echoed over the earth. I awoke to find myself staring into your eyes and feeling unbounded pleasure before I drifted back into a peaceful sleep."

"I slept well too," Minos replied as he finished a cup of wine and rose to leave the room. "I think we should join the others."

She followed him, seething with anger. What's wrong with him, she thought. We had a wonderful night, yet he walked away from me like I was only a servant girl for his pleasure. Is that what he really thinks of me?

Out on the terrace, the priests and priestesses sat around the rebuilt fire, absorbing its heat while eating their morning meal. The scarlet sun had just risen and seemed, for a moment, to perch on an eastern mountain.

"You performed well last night," Minos said to them. "Surely, our dedication of the gold pieces and your supplications must have pleased the gods. Let us pour another libation to ensure that Poseidon will listen to our pleas."

When it was her turn to speak, Jenora said, "You participated in a most important ceremony. The gods will surely favor us. The king and I thank you."

But in her mind, she added, I shudder to think what we might have to do if the gods refuse us now. She then led another appeal to the gods with more libations.

They used a shorter, more direct route down the mountain this time, one that avoided both the cave where they had sanctified themselves and the mysterious shrine they passed on the way up. They refreshed themselves with the governor of Archanes again and changed back into the garments they had left there two days earlier. Waiting chariots returned them to Knossos, where people lined the streets to greet them.

Two days later, the thick cloud that had been rising over Thera was gone and the earth no longer rumbled. A man in a crowded street proclaimed, "It's over! Poseidon has listened to our priests!"

More earthquake- and ash-free days followed. People moved back into their houses, cleaned out the ash, and swept the streets clean with straw brooms. Their world would now be safe and happy, they thought, so long as they continued to supplicate the gods. A brief cleansing, rain shower, a rare event during the warm season, drenched Knossos three days later. People raced naked into the streets to enjoy the refreshment provided by the gods.

"Libations, Jenora," Minos said when Jenora entered his room. He handed her a cup of wine. "Our ceremonies on the sacred mountain were beautiful and fitting. Your dancing was marvelous. We were with the gods. Our joy was their joy, and now happiness has come to Kephtor."

Jenora wondered if she had misunderstood his coolness that morning on the mountain. "O Minos," she said as she threw her arms around him. "I agree. It's a time to rejoice."

The embrace caused her to spill some of her wine before she finally put her cup down on a table. For them, it was another libation before they again communed with their gods.

"You look unhappy," Minos said to the chamberlain, who came to him the next morning. "Were not the rains wonderful? Now do you believe in the powers of the gods?"

"No, Sire. I am pleased the earth has stopped shaking and our people got to enjoy a little shower. But it didn't wash all our problems away."

"What bothers you now, old friend?"

"Many things. Despite our little rain, the ash in eastern Kephtor is going to hurt our animals and crops. We may not have enough food to see us through the winter, especially now that Therans are increasing the drain on our supplies."

"You said you were going to order our flocks to be moved south."

"I did, but as I predicted, it caused some serious fights. And to add to our problems, some of the animals in the east are dying from a strange illness, and people have begun to steal from each other's flocks."

"Then see to it that they are caught and punished."

"I will, but those aren't our only problems."

The king shifted in his seat. "What else?"

"As I also predicted, the loss of our markets on Thera and the use of our boats to move Therans has ruined our capacity to trade with other lands. We are almost isolated, except for foreign ships sailing westward along our south coast. But that benefits Phaestos, not us."

"What about food from the south and west?"

"They have paid some levies, but not enough."

"What do you want me to do? Reduce distributions? Let Therans starve? Do I have to use force to take food from other regions? Am I going to need an army?"

Handoro sensed he was again a tutor who had to lecture his pupil. "That time may come, but we also need men to work on our farms and roads. I sent a message to Nios to tell Cavanila to send us her strongest workers. I think you should also order Bardok to return here to help with these problems and start building an army."

"I will do that, but don't worry. Minoa is rich and strong. We will survive. In the meantime, I am on my way to confer with the high priestess."

"There is more."

"You have given me enough problems for now. Just do what you think necessary. I must go."

Handoro crossed the courtyard to his quarters, anger in his stride. His lips moved as he muttered to himself. I tell him about the great threats to Minoa, and he gets angry and dismisses me because he has to go to his whore. I don't know what she has done to him, but he acts like a young boy who has just had his first woman. I fear for Minoa.

Jenora induced Minos to sit on her bed and offered him some wine.

"You look unhappy," she said. "What's bothering you?"

"If what Handoro says is true, we are going to face difficult times. He thinks we won't have enough food to see us through the cold season and, worse, that we are too feeble to do anything about it. What am I supposed to do?"

She sat next to him. "He always frets too much," she replied. "The gods favor us now. We will be fine."

"I hope you are right," Minos said as he reached for her hand.

"I know I am. Look how successful our ceremonies on the sacred mountain were. I think we should have the goldsmiths make a new piece to celebrate our successes, perhaps a seal ring. And don't forget, they need to be rewarded for their work. Why don't you summon them now?"

The walk to Jenora's throne room was slow and difficult for Alkabar; the left side of his body suddenly lost most of its function while Alpada was on Mount Juktas. His left hand and fingers had little life, and he carried that arm in a contracted position. His face was pulled to his right causing his speech to be slurred. His right leg was still strong, but he could only shuffle along. Alpada walked on his left side to shoulder some of his weight.

Minos motioned them forward when they appeared, saw it would be difficult for Alkabar to bow and indicated with his open hand that they should remain standing.

"You have done well," he told them. "The gods were pleased. You will be rewarded, but now we want you to make another piece to celebrate our ceremony on the sacred mountain."

"Sire," responded Alpada, "we are happy you and the gods are pleased. We will gladly craft anything you wish."

"The high priestess and I have decided it will be a seal ring to commemorate her encounter with the gods. Bring her a design. You can then tell her what reward you wish to have."

After the goldsmiths departed, Minos and Jenora dismissed their servants, enjoyed some refreshments, and walked arm in arm through the passage to Minos's quarters.

The next day, Alpada appeared alone for his audience with Jenora.

"High Priestess," he said as soon as she motioned for him to speak, "I have an idea for the seal ring to commemorate your ceremonies. I think it should be an image of you dancing before the gods."

Her smile relieved his fears of being rebuffed. But her only words were, "That seems appropriate."

"Then please tell me how you would like to be shown."

"I thought you made sketches of our ceremonies when you were there?"

"I did, High Priestess," he replied as he removed two tablets from his bag. "I made many. Here are the ones I like best."

The first drawing he showed her pictured Jenora encircled by the dancers, her head back and both arms held high. She and the dancers were still dressed in their robes. In the second, she and the dancers wore only their animal skins, their arms to their sides, their hands palms up as though pleading to the gods.

"I like them both. What about the other sketches?"

"High Priestess, I like these best because they show your graceful movements as you danced."

He didn't tell her of the one he drew of the king carrying her limp, nearly naked body into the sanctuary.

"I like these, but I want something better. I want to be shown as a goddess. The others should be my supplicants. And I should be wearing my sacred gown, as I am now dressed, not my animal skin. I should look something like this..."

To his surprise, she stood and performed several graceful steps, ending in a pose with one arm held up, as to a god in the skies, while her other arm was lower, like she was reaching out to her earthly subjects.

He was both flustered and elated by her unexpected attention. He sketched as rapidly as he could, profusely thanked her, and said he would return with more sketches the following day.

After he left, the high priestess sat surprised that she had enjoyed displaying her movements to that young man. "He is just a craftsman," she said aloud with a shrug of her shoulders.

With his hands clasped behind his head. Alpada lay awake that night beside his sleeping wife. Over and over, he saw Jenora undulating to the rhythmn of the music on Mt. Juktas. He saw the dancers sweat and shed their garments and Jenora, in her panther skin, lost in a trance-like state. He saw her collapse and the king gently carrying her into the shrine. Unable to shed his visions or contain his excitement, Alpada turned to his wife, took her into his arms and woke her.

The next morning he was up and sketching at first light. He had his basic design. He had drawn Jenora in her sacred gown, her womanly torso erect and tapered to the narrowest of waists, one hand reaching to the skies, the other to dancers who were shown paying homage to her. He represented her ascension to the gods with a miniature figure, a suggestion of a sacred gown, above her. He brought his sketch to her at midmorning.

"I am pleased by the way you have shown me and the other dancers, but your design contains no sign that the ceremonies were performed under the eyes of Poseidon."

Alpada thought for a moment and took back the sketch. He drew an eye into the design to represent that god watching over the ceremony, and added snakes as protectors and flowering plants to represent the goddess of fertility.

"Yes, that will do. I am pleased with your design. But can you put all this detail into a ring?"

"I can try, High Priestess. Our bow lathe should make it possible."

Fourteen days later, Jenora brought the ring to Minos.

"It is a good likeness of you," he said examining the reverse image stamped in soft clay. "Reward the goldsmiths well."

"I will. I like it too." Then a coy smile appeared on her face. "But I won't look like that much longer."

Minos' eyebrows went up. "I don't understand."

She enjoyed his confusion for a moment. "My blood didn't flow with the moon this time. I think I am with child."

Minos jumped up and embraced her. "The gods gave us this child on the sacred mountain. This is their child. We will call him Staphylos, to commemorate the sacred wine we drank. He will be my successor."

"Yes, dear Minos. This will be a child favored by the gods. I pray for a boy who will grow into a man like you. I will be watching for the signs."

"We must thank the gods for this great gift."

He filled two cups with wine and began an incantation.

O Great Goddess
Who is kind, and protective,
And brings fertility to all beings,
I thank you for the seed you nurture in the High Priestess,
And ask that it grow into a fine man.
O great Goddess,
I thank you.

He then poured some wine onto the coals and Jenora began:

O Great Goddess,
Thank you for taking me into your world,
After many years a seed grows within me.
Give it life,
O Great Goddess.
Let it be a boy with strength and wisdom,
A successor to our great Minos.
We thank you for your goodness and bounty."

She drank down her wine and put her arms around him for another tight hug. "I am so happy. I know it will be a fine son for you."

But when she tried to give him a soulful kiss, she found him stiff and unresponsive. He took her arms from around his neck and held her away from him.

"Jenora, we can no longer make love. It could end my son's life and anger the gods. Sup with me when you wish, but we must not do anything to hurt Staphylos."

She forced her arms down and stared into his eyes. Instead of loving warmth, she felt only a sudden coolness from him.

"Shall we sup together tomorrow night?" she asked.

"Perhaps, if you wish."

"Then let us see what tomorrow brings." She wheeled around and left the room. Once outside, her serving maid had to run to keep up with her.

Minos was bewildered. First she said she was happy because she carries a son for me, then she turned angry. She knows that if we get too close we could be tempted to do what everyone knows is not good for a baby. She must understand that.

Jenora's fury kept her awake that night. I understand his worry about the baby, but why did he push me away? I'm still the same person. I have been his lover for years and finally have his seed growing in me. Yet he again treats me like I'm a concubine, or a cow that carries his bull calf. Suppose it's a girl and not the son he wants? Will he accuse me of failure? Will he tire of me? Would he appoint another high priestess like he once threatened?

She rose from her bed and paced the room in the semidarkness of a solitary oil lamp. But I am not just another woman. I am the high priestess. I speak to the gods. And what about me? Will the people and my priests still revere me when my belly grows big? Will they rejoice that my baby is a gift from the gods, a sign they still favor us? Or will they see me as just another woman Minos bedded. I will not allow this baby to turn me into a useless old woman. If I lost it, I could tell Minos I was mistaken, that my blood finally came.

She summoned Alpada the next morning.

"The king and I are pleased with your work, but you haven't asked for your reward. Tell me what you would like."

Alpada went down on his knees. "High Priestess, there is something I have long wished for, but am afraid to ask."

"What is it?"

He looked up at her. "I wish to make a statue of the Great Goddess. I would like to model it after you."

"Rise."

He stood with his head down, afraid to look at her while she studied him in ways she hadn't done before. He is strong, she thought, and would be obedient.

"Bring me a drawing of what you propose. If I like it, I will let you proceed."

He tried to restrain his excitement, knowing that he could finally show her a picture he had already drawn.

"I will, High Priestess."

She smiled when she saw his sketch the next morning, a full-length image of her in her sacred gown, with snakes around her arms, and wearing a tall hat with animals representing other gods on its top.

"I like it. It signifies good fortune. Bring your clay to my rooms in the morning and you can begin."

Early the next morning, he carried a simple tall table, a heavy bag that contained his sculpting tools, and a large lump of clay. When he was finally shown into her living quarters, he found her dressed in her sacred gown sitting under a light well. She directed him to set up his table in front of her and ordered a servant to bring a bowl of water and leave.

He worked quickly to form a crude, upright figure around a wood support. He asked her to stand for a short time so he could get her proportions right, and she complied. He roughed in her flounced skirt and her narrow waist.

"I must confer with my priests," she said after a while. "I will sit for you again tomorrow morning."

His nascent piece took on greater definition as she sat for him the next morning. But as he worked to model her torso in the clay, his hands began to shake, and he seemed unable to progress further. She watched him struggle and understood why. She smiled to herself but put on a harsh face.

"Return to your shop if you can't do anything."

"I can work, High Priestess."

He swallowed hard, took a deep breath, and turned his attention to her waist, making it even narrower than he had left it the day before. From there, he progressed to her neck, causing her to look taller and more elegant. He formed knots in her hair that resembled snakes.

When he could delay it no longer, he began to mold her breasts. His body felt hot, and his heart pounded as he worked to perfect their shape. He feared she'd see what had happened to him and turned away to adjust his phallus sheath. But she already saw the flush in his face and the source of his discomfort. She knew she had chosen the right man. She enjoyed his distress and decided to let him suffer a while longer.

"Stop your work," she ordered when she thought the time was right. "Wash the clay from your hands."

When he had done so, she rose from her throne to stand close to him. With her eyes on his and a smile on her face, she ran her hand down the front of his skirt and let it linger there for a long moment. She then turned her back to him and began to lift her own skirt.

"Help me," she said, "and don't be meek. Show me how strong you can be."

Later, as she readjusted her dress, she said, "Perhaps your hands will be steadier when we begin again tomorrow. And if you speak to anyone about this, I will banish you and your family from Minoa."

She sat for him two more days, each time taking advantage of his lust, yet with no signs of any change in her pregnancy. The next time he arrived, she refused to sit for him and made him destroy the statue.

CHAPTER 16

"WAIT," SHE WHISPERED.

The first supply ships that made it to Nios established the circular route Bardok envisioned. They brought supplies from Kephtor to Nios, proceeded to Akrotiri to take on Therans, and returned to Kephtor to offload passengers and load up with more supplies for Nios. Many of the escorting longboats remained at Nios, adding to Bardok's defenses and speeding up the evacuation. Those whom Toran convinced to make the trek to northwestern Thera also helped speed the transfer.

As people continued to arrive at Nios, more villages were established and the number of potential fighters increased. Men and older boys practiced armed combat every morning, and Bardok soon had the beginnings of a small, though still unskilled, army. Nevertheless, his crewmen, despite their involvement in various chores, remained close to their weapons.

Younger boys served as lookouts on the hills at each end of Manganari beach to warn of approaching boats. Children were put to work: the older ones tended goats and sheep and saw to their milking. Others collected firewood from the few small trees and large shrubs that grew in the foothills. Women had to fend for themselves and their children, performing routine chores like preparing food and maintaining cooking fires until servants began to arrive from Thera. Delicate hands soon became dirtied, even blistered.

Gatherers pried mussels from partly submerged rocks and dug for clams in shallow waters with their hands or sticks. Some learned to locate clams in chest-high water by digging into bottom sands with their toes and then diving to retrieve them. They built a dam to collect water from the little stream that trickled down from the hills, hoping the reservoir could supply water if the stream dried up in the coming hot weather.

The sea also provided the settlers with one of their few enjoyments. Around sunset, their chores completed for the day, people bathed in the refreshing water or dug for more clams. The beach resembled a communal bath that many, especially the elite women, would never have attended back on Thera. By dark, most had returned to their simple shelters. Others remained on the beach to enjoy their freedom under moonlit skies.

Bardok and Cavanila met daily to discuss food supplies and distribution, problems with new arrivals, and the successes and failures of the governing system they adopted. Afterward, they often strolled into the foothills or along the beach. During one such walk, he took her hand to help her up a rocky hill at the east end of Manganari. He didn't let it go when they reached the top, and he could tell she didn't want him to while they explored a cave that overlooked the sea. They then climbed down to a tiny beach encircled by tall outcroppings of rocks.

For a while, they sat in silence on the still sun-warmed sand, an arm's length apart, looking out toward Thera, listening to the lap of waves against the shore. Neither spoke until Cavanila turned to Bardok and said, "Do you remember our conversation on Dhia that night?"

Bardok looked at her. "Of course."

She leaned back on her elbows but kept her gaze on him. "Seems like a long time ago. I remember what you said about how things happen because of what we do and not because of what the gods determine. I feel like it was our plans and our people's hard work that helped us survive despite our problems. I sometimes say to myself, 'I thank the gods for Bardok and what he has done,' though I know you are the one responsible for what we accomplished here, not the gods."

Bardok's face flushed. He reached out to pat her on her shoulder.

"I've only done what any ship captain would do. The way you organized the villages and the goodwill the people perceive in you are really what made Manganari successful. In the short time we have been here, your Therans came to appreciate and love you, and so do I. You should feel proud of yourself."

Cavanila stared into his eyes, stroked his arm for a moment and jumped to her feet. "It's time to bathe," she yelled as she stripped off her robe and raced to the water.

Bardok waited until she resurfaced from her shallow dive, removed his tunic, and called out, "I'm coming too."

She watched him enter the water and thought of her dream about the pool in the forest and how her lover led her to a cave. She remembered its sacred pillar and its softness before it began to shake.

They swam and surface-dived, playing in the waves like they were children again, free of problems and responsibilities. After one such dive, they stood in water up to Cavanila's shoulders, laughing and talking about how wonderful and refreshing it felt. But they soon stopped talking and, with eyes fixed on each other, moved closer. Bardok reached out to support her with his hands at her waist. Her arms went around his neck. They fell into a gentle kiss that soon became more urgent. Their bodies enjoyed the warmth each provided the other against the cool sea. Bardok lifted her into his arms and carried her back to the beach where he gently set her down on her robe. Their passion grew until Cavanila pulled her head back. Holding Bardok's face between her hands, she whispered, "Wait, let's go up to that cave."

Days later, Zardik returned to Nios with six longboats filled with Therans.

"We have another problem," he told Bardok as soon as he arrived at the beach.

"I saw your approach," Bardok replied. "Only some of your oars were in the water."

"Because by the time we were halfway here, the rowers we took on at Thera couldn't pull an oar anymore. Some got real sick. They complained about their stomachs or were throwing up their food. One shit all over the boat."

"What happened?"

"I don't know. Some passengers were sick too."

"I hope it doesn't spread. On your next trip, find out how many others on Thera are affected the same way. And watch for it among your crews."

Bardok told Cavanila about the problem later that evening.

"Maybe that explains one of my priest's complaints. He said the newcomers were weak and unable to do their share of the work. It sounds bad. I will discuss it with the village heads."

"How are the people in your villages faring?" she asked her headmen the next morning. "Do you have enough food?"

A farmer, one of the first arrivals on Nios, answered first. "Our share of what the ships bring is too small. We need more food."

"What about water?"

"Only a little is collecting behind the dam. Most of the trickle from the mountain just soaks into the ground. We dug wells below the dam, but the water we collect from them is barely enough to keep us and our animals alive. Some of the sheep and goats have stopped giving milk."

"What else?"

A potter spoke up. "High Priestess, we could do better if the new-comers did their share of the work." Others nodded in agreement.

A woman, a weaver of fine cloth who headed the newest village, rose to her feet. "What are we supposed to do? Many in my village can't even walk. Some have died. How can you expect people to dig wells or try to fish when they are barely alive?"

"High Priestess," the farmer replied, "my people refuse to go near the newcomers, and they don't want their flocks mingling with theirs."

"My people are unhappy too," another said. He was a powerful looking man who was a builder of houses. "There is a large bay at the other end of this island. Some of us think we should go there."

Cavanila was surprised to find herself besieged by such outspoken people, yet pleased that her subjects felt free to express their thoughts. That could never have happened under her father's rule.

But she refused to be intimidated. She gestured to the standing woman that she should sit.

"Be calm. I agree that healthy animals should be kept separate from sick ones, but we can't abandon sick people. We don't know what the sickness is, or if healthy people or animals can get it from those who are not. We will watch for it. But remember, we are all Therans. We have to stay together and look out for each other."

Bardok, until then sitting quietly beside Cavanila, spoke up.

"Cavanila is right. We must stay together. Yes, there is a large bay at the other end of this island with an old, deserted city that might still be habitable. A boat I sent found fresh goat droppings and a small stream that was still running, even this late into the hot weather."

"Then why can't we go there?" the builder asked.

"I will tell you," Bardok replied. "First, to go there across the mountains would be nearly impossible. The only way to get there is by boat, and we can't spare any. We still need to escort incoming merchant ships and finish removing people from Thera and transporting them to Kephtor. And that bay seems to have been a pirate den in the past. Maybe that's why there is no one there now. You know pirates destroyed two of our boats and killed the crews. It would take many fighters to protect those who move there, and we don't have the men for that."

"Then what can we do?" asked a merchant who sold wine he made from the grapes of Theran vines. "If we stay here, with more sick people coming, we are going to get sick too."

Cavanila held up her hand for silence. "Our situation here is difficult, but it will improve. When we are finished moving people from Thera, which should be soon, we can begin taking people from here to Kephtor. I will see to it that our sickest people go first."

The village heads looked at her and at each other but said nothing. Cavanila rose to her feet, signaling that the meeting had ended.

"You will have to trust me."

Two days later, Zardik returned to Nios with four longboats filled with Therans, nearly all of whom were so sick that they had to be helped off the boats. Bardok and Vactor met him and the three men walked along the beach to confer in private,

"Gantaros told me nearly everyone there is sick and a few have died, including the old priest, Hekton," Zardik said. "They are calling it Poseidon's Punishment. Gantaros wasn't feeling too well either."

"I'm glad my father is upwind of that smoke and ash," Bardok said. "Is Rhadamantis well?

"Gantaros said Rhadamantis stays in his house and refuses to see anyone. Gantaros seems to be the real regent there."

"Anything else?" Vactor asked.

"Most of the animals are also sick. It's why we didn't bring many back with us. Gantaros would only let me have a few healthy ones. He said he needed the others for the people still there. What do we do now?"

"We continue what we've been doing until everyone is off that cursed island," Bardok replied.

Two more cargo ships arrived at Nios a few days later with fresh supplies and a message for Cavanila.

"Since the removal of people from Thera is nearly complete," one of the captains told her, "some of the next boats will begin moving Therans from here to Kephtor. The chamberlain orders you to send your best workers first. He said they are needed there."

"I will not do that," Cavanila told Bardok once they were alone again. "We cannot survive here without our strongest people."

"You have little choice," Bardok replied. "The chamberlain speaks for Minos. To defy him would be an act against the King."

"I am surprised at you, Bardok. I don't care what they want. I have to do what's best for my people."

"You acted against the king's wishes when you boarded my boat, and now you want to defy him again. How much disobedience do you think Minos will tolerate?"

"I told my council I would send the weakest people first, and that is what I will do. I will send a message to Handoro that we cannot survive here without our best workers. I'll tell him that as more supply ships arrive and the number of people here gets smaller, we can start sending him stronger workers."

With a rare hardness in her voice, she added, "That should convince him to get supply ships to us more quickly, and more of our people to Kephtor as soon as possible"

Neither Cavanila nor Bardok expected that the next ship to arrive would bring an order from Minos for Bardok's immediate return to Knossos.

CHAPTER 17

MINOS'S COUNTENANCE SUDDENLY CHANGED

"Tell the king I have arrived," Rhadamantis ordered a messenger on his arrival at Poros.

He then left his servants to transport his possessions on donkey carts and proceeded to the palace on a chariot the harbormaster provided. A servant at the king's throne room set a table for him with fruit and a ewer of wine that he had nearly finished by the time Minos entered.

"Greetings, Brother," Minos said as he clasped Rhadamantis's hand. "We did not expect you so soon. I hope your journey was not too difficult. Tell me about Thera."

Rhadamantis drank down the last of the wine. "I had no difficulties getting here, though I did not like leaving any of my people behind. The situation there gets worse all the time. I will tell you about it, but first I need to bathe and have a short rest. I am not feeling well. My head hurts, and I nearly fell asleep waiting for you. Are rooms ready for me?"

Minos's smile disappeared. "You do look tired." He signaled to a servant. "I will have you shown to your quarters. We will hear what you have to tell us at our evening meal."

Once in his room, Rhadamantis drank more wine with a little cheese and a few olives, bathed and slept for a short time. As the sun approached the horizon, a servant came to usher him to Minos's dining room.

"Tell the king I will be there soon," he ordered.

He selected his attire from bundles his servant brought; a short-sleeved, purple robe that opened down the front, gold bands for both arms, gold bracelets for his wrists, and large gold rings for three fingers on each hand. He knew Minos was waiting for him, but he took time to have a servant outline his eyes with kohl and perfume him from a tiny ewer. Before leaving his room, he donned a headdress with three peacock feathers attached.

Minos, Jenora, and Handoro waited for him in a large hall near the foot of a fresco-decorated staircase that led down from the central courtyard. Because the palace was built on a hill, the room, though below courtyard level on its west end, had windows that faced east across a river to a high ridge beyond it.

Minos tried to hide his impatience and embarrassment over his brother's tardiness. He spoke to them about how fortunate they were that the earth no longer shook, that the smoke had stopped rising over Thera, and how favorable the weather had been for their ships.

"We have done well to soothe the gods," he said.

All three were dressed informally. Handoro wore only a cloth of fine wool, Jenora a simple robe, no makeup, and no jewelry except for the seal ring of her office on a gold chain around her neck. Even Minos wore only a plain, blue robe and, like Jenora, his only jewel was the gold chain that held his own seal ring.

Rhadamantis's entrance caused Handoro to raise his eyebrows at Jenora, who returned his stare with an unmistakable smirk. Minos failed to conceal his surprise at Rhadamantis's extravagant dress. His brows furrowed for a brief moment.

"Welcome again, Brother," the king said with a smile while motioning his servants to begin putting food on low tables in front of them. "Sit here next to me."

As Rhadamantis sat, Minos's countenance suddenly changed. For a brief moment he looked like a threatened man about to do battle. Handoro and Jenora both noticed the sudden change and knew Minos well enough to understand his subsequent smile was forced and no longer hospitable.

"We have been waiting to hear what you can tell us about Thera," Minos said as they began to eat, "and about how Cavanila is doing on Nios."

"She is still young but she appears to be an able leader," Rhadamantis replied. "I have heard the people there are surviving well."

"I heard that too, but it seems she is doing it without attention to the gods. And the priests there have little authority. Is that what you taught her?"

"I tried to teach her how important the gods are, but she defies me. I wanted to send priests to Nios to help her, and I ordered her to not change the way we rule our people, but she refused to listen. She even thinks commoners should choose their own leaders. So far the gods have not made Nios suffer for her ways. I pray they do not."

"She defies me too," Minos offered. "Now tell us about Thera."

As they ate, Rhadamantis told them about the disasters and how he had remained in control and dealt with them even though he was nearly killed by a collapsing wall. He also told them he had decided it would be most efficient to first move people from Thera to Nios before bringing them to Kephtor and how he shortened the sail between Thera and Nios by convincing people to go to Thera's north coast.

His eyes shifted from one to the other as he spoke. But instead of rapt attention, he perceived little interest, which caused him to speak even more rapidly of his exploits. Eventually he related how he had executed Gridawi and his justification for it. He ended by saying, "And now, with most Therans here or on the way, I am ready to help rule them."

Minos knew his brother was not entirely truthful but only said, "I can see the difficulties you and your people must have suffered. We have our problems here too, and your Therans have added to our burdens, especially those who are sick. But we will do what we can to help them."

"We indeed have difficulties here," Handoro added. "We have done our best to settle your people into nearby homes and farms. But as more arrive, we are forced to place them in settlements more distant from Knossos. It has gone well in most cases, but not all. We need someone the Therans respect to counsel them to be patient while we try to deal with both their problems and our own."

"I don't often agree with the chamberlain," Jenora added, "but there is merit in what he says. I sent some of my priests to talk to Therans. Some are thankful for the help we give them. Others are suspicious of our priests and don't appreciate what we do for them. There have even been some fights. We need your help to control your Therans."

That's unacceptable, Rhadamantis thought to himself. They want me to worry about the behavior of a few Therans because they can't manage their own people.

"I will do what I can," he said, turning to Minos. "I assume you will find proper living quarters for me and for my priests and councilors. My guards, with Gantaros at their head, will be the last to come and will also need accommodation."

"We are crowded here in the palace," Minos replied. "For now, you and your servants can stay in the rooms where you are. We will try to find additional space for the others when they arrive."

Rhadamantis didn't reply and no one else spoke except to comment on the food they were eating.

At the end of the meal, Rhadamantis rose. "I must retire, now."

Handoro and Jenora wished him a good evening, but Minos remained silent.

They were not happy to see me, Rhadamantis thought as he returned to his rooms. They treated me like I was a lowly scribe they could order about. And Minos accepted it and said nothing. But I am of royal blood and deserve to be treated accordingly. When the time comes, they will know who I am.

After Rhadamantis's departure, Minos, Handoro, and Jenora sat in silence until Minos finally spoke. "He didn't seem very happy when he left."

"No, he did not," Jenora said. "He seems to think you should give him half this palace because he proved his manhood by killing a man. I doubt he really had to do that. It only showed his own failings as a leader, something we knew about from the problems he caused when he was regent at Phaestos."

And then laughing, she said, "His attitude when he came into the room reminded me of the birds who donated the feathers for his hat. He even wore it while he ate. He looked like the pouting dove that the potters on his island reproduce on their ewers. If that is an indication of how he governed Thera, he will not be much help here."

But Handoro didn't laugh. He turned to Minos and asked, "Something troubled you when he sat next to you. What was it?"

Minos looked at him but only said, "We'll talk tomorrow." as he left to go to his sleeping room.

What Minos didn't want to explain was that the reek of Rhadamantis's perfume when he sat next to him unleashed a string of painful memories. As he now sat next to the bed where his father had spent his last hours, he once more saw the priests wiping his father's face and bathing his feverish body with herbal extracts. He remembered the pungency of the oil lamps and beeswax candles that burned around the room, and the acrid vapors from herbs steaming in a bronze vessel. But they didn't cover Rhadamantis's scent. He and his brothers, along with Handoro and Suvlana, his father's high priestess, stood close to that bed, waiting to hear the final wishes of his weak but still cogent father. The future king already knew his father's wishes, and he feared the reactions they would provoke from his brothers.

The problem began many years earlier.

"Devterex, my son, you are growing into a fine man," his father told him after he had returned from his years at sea with Bardok. "But you still have much to learn before you are ready to occupy this throne. You frown at my words but I have decided. You will be the next Minos after I go to the gods."

"But Rhadamantis is the eldest, and what about Sarpedon?"

"I said I have decided. You and your brothers will abide by my decision."

"If it is your wish, Father," Devterex replied. "I hope I can be as good a king as you are."

"I hope so as well. Tomorrow, Handoro will begin teaching you what you must know to rule Minoa. He has served me well and will serve you too if you act wisely. He can be a difficult man, but you can trust him."

"I understand."

"Then let us pour a libation to the gods."

The king filled two gold cups with wine, handed one to Devterex, and poured a few drops from his own into hollows on a three-legged offering table. "May the gods favor the next Minos as they have favored me," he said.

"May that be so," Devterex replied as he did the same, "but may you have many more years as the great King Minos."

Minos embraced Devterex, something he rarely did, and then held him at arm's length. "My son," he said looking into his eyes, "Make me proud of you. Go now, but be at Handoro's quarters early in the morning."

Instead of returning to his room, Devterex walked out the north portal of the palace and into the town. He wandered through the noisy marketplace, seeing everything as a king who would control it all—the works of weavers, potters, and metal smiths; the smells of ripe cheeses and fish brought up from the harbor; children struggling to carry bundles of sticks or jars of water that Handoro's engineers had piped down from the mountain.

He turned southward along the Royal Road and ambled past some of the great villas of Minoa before he re-entered the palace and climbed out onto its highest roof. With the sun nearing the horizon, the burdens and challenges of his future crowded his thoughts. Can I really govern Minoa? Can I make my father proud of me? Will I have to fight my brothers?

He awoke the next morning to the prodding of a servant who said that the chamberlain was waiting for him in his quarters. Still sleepy in the predawn darkness, he gnawed on a piece of dry, brown bread while he followed the servant to Handoro's rooms. The chamberlain sat in the light of a single flickering oil lamp that emphasized the hollows of his cheeks.

He growled rather than spoke. "Your father said he chose you to succeed him, even though you are not the eldest of his sons. It is a good thing he doesn't have any daughters, or he might have chosen one of them. He wants me to teach you how to be a Minos, as though I don't have anything else to do while I manage this kingdom. You will have to listen carefully and work hard, even if you are your father's son."

During the next three years, Devterex became steeped in nearly every aspect of the Minoan economy. Engineers taught him about construction, harbor improvements, and roads. He saw how building blocks were quarried and was allowed to try his hand at squaring a large stone. He spent months in the major trading centers on Kephtor—Kydonia in the west, Phaestos in the south, Zakros at the eastern tip of the island, and Malia not far to the northeast of Knossos. He learned how they were ruled and the circumstances that made each of them unique. He spent time at Minoan trading centers at Thera and Rhodos, and visited such places as Egypt, the Anatolian coast to the east, and Sicilia to the west.

On one such trip, the Egyptian Pharaoh offered him one of his daughters as a wife to cement relations with Minoa. Since he could not refuse without insulting the Pharaoh, he returned home with a lovely young wife named Moxila.

In the year he turned twenty, he noticed that his father's gums appeared bloody and that he often bled from the nose, a symptom not uncommon in the hot, dry summers of Kephtor. Later, he realized his father tired more quickly during his exercises and that bruises accumulated beneath his skin.

Confounded by his father's condition, he could only watch the high priestess and her priests make sacrifices and offerings as they appealed to the gods on his behalf. But the king became progressively weaker. What scared Devterex and perplexed the priests were the sore lumps under his arms and in his groin, which made it painful for him to wear his codpiece.

When his father finally accepted that his path led only downhill, he called his sons, the chamberlain, and the high priestess to him. As he lay propped up on silk-covered sheepskin pillows, his voice was strong despite labored breathing, but he spoke slowly.

"I will soon be going to the gods. I want you to hear how I want Minoa governed after I am gone."

His eyes narrowed, almost to slits, as he shifted his focus to each son in turn.

"I and my fathers before me have always acted to keep Minoa strong and prosperous, though it sometimes required difficult and unpleasant action. But it was what we had to do. Now, before I depart, I have one last duty to perform. For the good of Minoa and as the gods watch, I have charges to place on each of you."

He stopped, took a few labored breaths, and spoke again. "You, Rhadamantis, will go to Phaestos to work with the regent there. He is getting old. You will assume his position and carry on his work when he no longer can. Do not fail me."

Rhadamantis glared at his father and clenched his fists, but he said nothing.

"And you, Sarpedon, will do the same at Malia." Sarpedon's eyes widened, but he too remained mute.

The king then turned his attention to his third son, gazing at him for a few moments before speaking. "You, Devterex, will be the next Minos."

Rhadamantis could no longer contain himself. "I am the eldest," he whined. "It should be me."

The king stared at him with one eye half-closed. He took a few more breaths before he could speak again. "So you think you should be Minos. How could you be? You never showed any interest in Minoa. You were too busy enjoying our servant girls. You will do as I command."

Now, years later, what still bothered Minos about that scene at his father's deathbed was the look on his brothers' faces as they stalked from the room. Sarpedon was no longer a problem. Minos had banished him many years earlier. But he worried about the kinds of problems Rhadamantis might cause now that he was back in Knossos.

CHAPTER 18

OUR PROBLEMS HAVE BECOME UNMANAGEABLE

The next morning, Rhadamantis sent a messenger to Minos to say he needed time to rest but would speak to him the following day. He sent similar messages to Handoro and Jenora, inviting them to come to his quarters. He then spent the rest of his day eating, drinking, and contemplating his situation.

Handoro saw through Rhadamantis's attempt to be assertive but went to meet him anyway. Rhadamantis greeted him with cool politeness but offered him a seat next to a low table that contained a ewer of wine and an empty cup.

"How are my Therans being treated?"

Handoro ignored the table and its contents.

"We found work here in Knossos for some according to their skills, but we had to send many to work on our roads and farms."

"I see. You are turning my scribes and craftsmen into farmers and road workers. No wonder you are having problems with them."

Handoro's bony body stiffened but his voice remained calm. "What choices do we have? The destruction of Thera ruined our most important marketplace. We are using all our resources to help Therans survive and to move them to safer places. Our storehouses are being drained because we now have to feed Therans as well as our own people. We have more merchants, craftsmen, and scribes than we can use. Our greatest needs are to produce and acquire more food, and your sick Therans are too weak to help."

"Then what do you expect me to do?" Rhadamantis asked.

"Counsel Therans to be patient. As I said before, our situation is difficult but it will improve."

"And what about your people? They need to remember what Therans have suffered and be hospitable."

"Minoans are a hospitable people, but ugly things sometimes happen. In fact, a serious problem arose this morning that you can help with."

Rhadamantis's eyes narrowed. He reached for his wine cup. "What kind of problem?"

"It came from our attempts to house Theran families with similar families here. It involved a fight between stonecutters, a Theran and a Knossian. Both were injured and one might have been killed had neighbors not separated them. They must be punished to show that such behavior cannot be tolerated."

"Then punish them. What do you need me for?"

"We want you to help pass judgment so Therans will know it is not just our punishment. We will meet after our morning meal tomorrow. The high priestess will also help decide on their punishment."

"I will attend, but after this, my priests will deal with such problems. I assume you will find quarters for them when they arrive."

Handoro rose from his seat. "We will do what we can. Is there anything else you wish to discuss?"

"No. I just want to be sure you don't forget I need appropriate rooms for me and my people and a shrine where we can pray to the gods."

"You can talk to the high priestess about your shrine. As we mentioned last night, we would like your help to see to the welfare of your people. But we will do what we must with or without your help."

"And as I said, my priests and I will do what we can, but the main responsibility for how people behave remains on Minos's shoulders, and on yours."

"If that is all," Handoro replied, "I will return to my quarters."

Rhadamantis received a message from Jenora saying it would be inconvenient for her to go to his quarters. Instead, she invited him to her throne room after midday. He agreed to go but decided to retaliate. He lingered over his meal and didn't arrive at Jenora's quarters until well after the sun had passed its zenith.

Except for a brief visit from Handoro, she had spent her morning being made up and dressed. Because of the way Rhadamantis leered at her the night he arrived, she chose to wear a long, woolen robe instead of her formal gown. Unlike Handoro, she was not amused by his obvious ploy. She didn't offer him a seat and provided no refreshments. He recognized her insult and stood glaring at her.

"I hope you slept well," she said.

"We have much to speak about," he replied.

She cocked her head. "Such as?"

"I need more rooms for myself and places for my priests, who will soon be here. And we will need a shrine where we can pay homage to the gods. The chamberlain said I should speak to you about them."

She turned her eyes to the gold bull that stood on its shaft to the left of her throne. Such a contrast between that beautiful rhyton and this man, she thought.

"I know about your conversation," she said when she turned back to him. "He was here before you came. We don't have rooms to spare. We can house your priests with ours and, if you like, you can honor the gods with us in our shrine."

Rhadamantis's face reddened, his jaw thrust forward. "That is not acceptable. I need my own shrine. I will speak to my brother about it."

"Then what else did you wish to speak to me about?"

"When there are problems between Therans and Kephtorians, punishment for both must be rapid and harsh."

"I agree, but we need to act together, as I hope we will tomorrow. I trust you will be there."

"I will be," he replied and departed without even a polite good-bye.

The next morning, the three sat to judge the stonecutters. One of Jenora's priests first described what had happened. When

Handoro asked the Knossian stonecutter to speak in his defense, Rhadamantis interrupted.

"Wait! It doesn't matter what he says or what the Theran says either. We cannot tolerate such fighting. If one had killed the other, a skilled worker would have been lost. The Theran mason should be banished from Knossos and put to work elsewhere. You can punish your stonecutter as you like."

The chamberlain looked at Rhadamantis in disbelief and had the stonecutters removed from the room.

Rhadamantis didn't wait for Handoro to speak. "Why do we have to discuss this in their absence? We know what happened. They had a fight."

"But you failed to ask why or who was at fault," the chamberlain replied.

"What does it matter?"

"Because it was the Knossian who started the fight," Jenora said.

"How do you know?" Rhadamantis asked.

"I had a priest question both men and their wives and neighbors. The Knossian got too friendly with the Theran's wife, who rebuffed him. When he saw his own wife making eyes at the Theran, he became furious and accused the Theran of trying to seduce her. Their argument then grew into the fight. The Theran was only defending himself."

"In any case," the chamberlain added, "you should have waited to hear the facts before making your pronouncement. Now we either have to punish both of them, or you have to change your mind. Or we could embarrass you by overruling you in public."

"I gave my verdict and will not change it." Rhadamantis stood up to leave the room. "Do what you will. I have nothing more to say."

"It seems he is in the habit of walking out on us," Jenora said after he had gone. "He could be more dangerous that we thought. What shall we do with the stonecutters?"

"We can't change his decree," Handoro replied. "That would destroy any authority he may have over his own people. But perhaps we can temper his decision."

After calling the stonecutters back into the room, the high priestess spoke first to the Theran stonecutter.

"We know you did not start the fight but you should have avoided it. You and your family will be sent to Zakros to work in the quarries near there."

To the Knossian, she said, "You were responsible for the fight. You will work at your job every day from sunrise to sunset with no days of rest for three moons. We give your wife the right to leave you and, if she wishes, to marry someone else."

News of the judgment spread through both communities. Therans learned how Rhadamantis condemned the Theran stonecutter before he even knew the details of what had happened. To them, the man they hoped would be their advocate and protector had left them isolated and unprotected in foreign surroundings. Such incidents were rare at first but became more frequent as more Therans arrived and food supplies dwindled. It also became more difficult to match families on the basis of occupation.

Many Therans who had been city dwellers and craftsmen found themselves assigned to farms though they had never done such work before. They enjoyed friendly welcomes in some cases and gladly participated in the work. In others, where Therans were unwilling or too sick to perform the more demanding or disagreeable chores, or where they were treated like servants or even slaves, they protested or worked with little enthusiasm. Their hosts considered them lazy and punished them by reducing their share of food, leading some Therans to steal to survive.

Similar problems arose among Therans sent to work on the roads. Unaccustomed to such physical labor, their hands blistered, their backs ached, and their legs gave out early in the day. Local workers often jeered them, calling them lazy slackers who refused to do their share of the work. Arguments and sometimes fights broke out until overseers decided to assign them to segregated crews. The Theran crews received smaller rations because their work progressed more slowly.

Rhitori was one of those sent to work with road crews. After his mother's death, Gantaros assigned him to keep count of people and food stuffs transported from Akrotiri to Nios. He was then sent to Nios when Cavanila called for scribes to help her maintain the orderly supply of food for her villages. She recognized him from the time of his mother's death and had one of her priests monitor his performance. Later, as more Therans transferred to Kephtor, she sent him with the message that he was a skilled scribe who should be assigned appropriate work. He was put to work on the roads to keep accounts of materials, food distribution, and the daily progress of the work. He was sometimes used as a messenger between work sites, so he saw the difficulties Therans were having at several places.

As a result of those difficulties, Therans banded together and, as on Nios, chose spokesmen to take their grievances to their overseers. The crew where Rhitori worked chose him. When he approached his overseer and told him that Theran workers were upset with their treatment, the man pushed him away.

"Get back to work," he yelled, "I don't care about your complaints. You will do as I say or you won't eat."

The Therans crowded around him. One of the largest of them stood only at arm's length from the overseer. "We are not servants or animals," he said.

The overseer tried to push him away but the man pushed back. Kephtorian workers rushed to protect the overseer, and the pushing and shoving turned into a massive brawl until cooler heads on both sides separated the two factions. No serious injuries occurred, but no one worked on that section of the road for several days. As a result, all workers received reduced rations.

Some Theran road workers stole goats and sheep from local farms and ran away to the mountains. Others left the roads and made their way to more distant towns, where they hoped to find work. To make matters worse, more of the recent arrivals from Nios suffered from Poseidon's Punishment. Rhadamantis himself became ill.

"Our problems have become unmanageable," Handoro told Minos. "Cavanila has finally stopped sending us her sick people, but those we have are a burden on everyone. I am impressed, though, with how well she appears to have done on Nios and with what her people say about her. I think she could help with our problems."

"I do not know if she can," Minos replied. "She is still very young. But I will order her to come to Knossos."

CHAPTER 19

UNTHINKABLE

The community on Nios had thinned considerably by the time the hot weather reached its peak. Most Therans who wanted to go to Kephtor were gone. A few went northward to larger islands. Some who thought they could survive off their flocks and the sea decided to stay at Manganari, where they constructed houses of the flat stones so readily available on nearby hills. Vactor and most of his longboats had returned to Kephtor leaving Lendor to govern the few Therans still on Nios.

The day before Cavanila was to leave for Kephtor, those still on Nios decided to celebrate their good fortune. That night, under a moonless sky peppered by a myriad of bright stars, they ate newly caught fish, drank what little wine remained, and danced within rings of fires they built on the beach. Some of the women donned their Minoan gowns for the first time since their arrival from Akrotiri. Cavanila had none of her own, but a woman supplied one she insisted Cavanila wear.

At first, Cavanila stood aside watching the revelers. They appreciate what we've accomplished, she thought, and they treat me like a goddess. But goddesses don't cry like I did when they gave me that lovely little stone figurine that has only a nose for a face. It was the most precious thing they could offer, a symbol of their ancient gods, they said, that had been handed down for generations. It will always be with me, as they will always be in my heart.

Zardik, however, gave her little time for sadness. He took her hand and led her into a circle of dancers. That squat, powerful man, a killer of pirates who bore many scars of battle and whose movements were far less graceful as a dancer than as a warrior, became the leader of the festivities that lasted well into the night.

Cavanila learned about the problems on Kephtor almost as soon as she arrived at Poros. Priests directed her fellow passengers to their assigned destinations, but she found a charioteer, a man who had once been a scribe at a mercantile house at Akrotiri, to take her to the palace. A talkative man who now earned food for his family by driving people between the harbor and Knossos, he recognized Cavanila and didn't hesitate to tell her what he thought.

"No one is happy here," he said as they made their way up the Royal Road. "Kephtorians are angry because they have to share their houses and food. Therans are upset because they are treated like servants and, worse, they have no one to stand up for them."

Cavanila paid little attention to him at first. She was remembering the last time she was on that road, when she made Bardok stop the chariot so she could go off into the bushes. But the charioteer's last words caught her attention.

"Why do you say that? Why is there no one to help them?"

He told her about the fight between the stonecutters and how it was resolved. He ended by saying, "The Theran couldn't even get a fair decision from the man who was our regent. Priestess, you must to do something about it."

"What do you think I should do?"

The charioteer suddenly realized it was her father he had criticized. "I don't know," he said, and then remained silent for the rest of the trip.

Cavanila studied his face from the side but asked no further questions.

At the palace, she went first to Bardok's rooms where, after a warm hug and soulful kiss, she stepped back from him. "I wish I could stay longer, but I must go to my father and then to the chamberlain and Minos. I don't know why they summoned me. I will come to you as soon as I can."

"I'll see you at the throne room. Minos wants me there too."

She found her father sitting in his outer room, a frown on his face. "What is it, Father? Aren't you well?"

"No, I am not. But if you care so much for me, why didn't you come to me before going to your lover? I know you arrived here a while ago."

"What's wrong?" she asked, ignoring his criticism. "Why do you seem so sick?" After he described his stomach ailments, she replied, "You have the same sickness as many who came to Nios from Thera. We think it's from the smoke and ash."

But he wasn't listening.

"What did you do on Nios?" he asked. "Your Therans care nothing for the gods and won't listen to the priests. They have become thieves and get into fights. Why are you here?"

"Minos summoned me. I don't know why."

"I don't know why, either, but I will find out."

"I will too. Rest well."

Handoro welcomed her with a friendly handshake and offered her some grapes and cheese.

"I know you need some rest after your journey," he said, "but I need to talk to you before you go to Minos. We have serious problems I hope you can help with."

"I heard something about them. But what can I do?"

"I don't know yet. It depends upon how much Minos is willing to defy Jenora. She isn't happy with Therans who don't worship her gods or respect her priests. And she won't be happy to share any of her authority."

"Then why did Minos summon me?"

"It was my idea. As I said, I think you can help us, but you will have difficulties—and maybe even face some danger."

Cavanila shrank back in her seat. Everyone is piling problems on me, she thought. Why me? What am I supposed to do?

"What difficulties and dangers?" Her voice was soft, almost pleading.

Handoro realized he should have been more careful with his words. He rose from his chair and took her hand. "We can talk about them later. I think we should go to Minos now."

Bardok and Jenora were already in Minos's throne room when Cavanila and Handoro arrived.

"Welcome, Cavanila," Minos said. "You look tired but stronger than when I last saw you. Perhaps this time you can enjoy some refreshments with us while we wait for your father."

Before she could reply, he added, "But I have not forgotten how you defied me the last time you were here. Don't do it again."

Rhadamantis soon arrived, walking as though he felt very weak. Once he was seated, Minos asked Cavanila to explain how she ruled the settlement on Nios and how well she solved the problems there. She had hardly begun to talk when her father interrupted.

"You put people in charge who were not priests. That's not what I ordered you to do."

"And you taught those people to ignore the gods," Jenora added.

"But we had so many other things to worry about," Cavanila replied. "We..."

"Cavanila is right," Bardok interjected. "Despite all the hardships people suffered and the problems she faced, her organization worked well and the settlement survived. People did what they had to and worked hard with few complaints. And when the village headmen did bring complaints to her, she listened and dealt with them."

"Maybe your ways worked on that little island," Minos said, "but Minoa has long prospered according to the ways of my father and his fathers before him. Without the gods and our priests, we would only have chaos."

"That's what I've been saying," Rhadamantis added. "It is folly to let common people determine how they should act."

"I can say little about how Minoa has survived," Cavanila responded, "but our way of doing things on Nios kept people fed, even happy."

"Yes, but you relied on shipments of food and other things from here, didn't you?" Jenora said. "It was our prosperity, brought on by our priesthood, that let you survive."

Handoro sat quietly during this argument, staring into Cavanila's reddening face with an intensity that made her feel even more uncomfortable. He noisily cleared his throat and began to speak, gently at first, and then with more authority in his voice.

"I think the kind of organization Cavanila developed could be useful to help control Therans here. They are mostly skilled craftsmen, not laborers. Their attitudes would improve if they were organized into groups with a voice over their own activities. And," looking at Rhadamantis, he added, "they would be less hostile if their own people helped resolve their disputes."

"What about *our* own people?" Jenora asked. "They will want the same privileges and won't worship the gods. They will be just like Therans and refuse to obey our priests. We can't allow that."

"That is a problem," Handoro replied. "Our people might well want the same privileges. We could lessen that danger by ordering priests to listen more carefully to people's concerns and bring them to us, much like Cavanila's councilors brought them to her. Yet they could still determine how people worship the gods."

Minos hesitated. He respected Handoro's judgment but wasn't willing to endure Jenora's wrath. "I see good and bad in your suggestion, Handoro, but I wish to think about it. We will discuss it again tomorrow."

Handoro took Cavanila by the hand again when they left Minos's throne room.

"I would like to discuss these matters further with you," he said. "Please sup with me tonight."

"Thank you," she replied. "I am so upset. I do need some rest, but I will come to your quarters at dusk."

She started toward her own rooms but changed her mind and went to Bardok's instead. Later, while lying in his arms, with her head pressed against his muscular chest, she tried her best to fight off her tears.

"They were so angry with me," she said when she finally pulled away. "All we did was organize our settlement for the good of our people under those difficult conditions."

"Yes, but don't you understand? You threatened them."

Cavanila sat up, shocked by the accusation. "How did I do that?"

"You showed them you could govern without invoking the gods. Even worse, you showed that commoners, if given the chance, could rule themselves without the need for priests or the gods. Jenora told you exactly what she was afraid of."

"What?"

"She said your way of doing things could not be allowed to develop on Kephtor because it would destroy the power of the priesthood...her priesthood."

"Did Minos feel that way?"

"He is the high priest as well as king, Cavanila. You cast doubt on his beliefs. How do you think he would feel?"

Cavanila said nothing for several moments. His chastisement on top of all the other criticisms she received that day deepened her depression. She had stepped into a world where everyone made demands but criticized her attempts to do what she thought necessary. Maybe she didn't belong in a world where she had so little experience. She looked again at Bardok and brushed her loose hair back with both hands.

"Maybe I should just return to Nios."

Bardok took her into his arms again. "You know you can't return to Nios. You are needed here."

"That's what Handoro said. He asked me to sup with him this evening."

"Listen carefully to him. He is a good man."

While they dined, Handoro explained to Cavanila that he liked her system but that it would have to be altered to work on Kephtor, where Therans were so scattered and mixed in among Kephtorians.

"What is needed," he said, "is another level of leadership, a council that would give the Theran leader better control."

"My father won't agree to anything like that."

"Forgive me for saying so, but your father is not the kind of leader we need. I was thinking about you, not him. Therans were pleased with your rule. Who else would have the confidence of the Theran people?"

Jenora, Cavanila, Rhadamantis, Handoro, and Bardok all arrived at Minos's throne room at about the same time. Even Rhadamantis arrived at the time requested. They sat before small tables that contained a variety of cheeses, fruit, gold and silver cups, and a ewer of wine.

Minos began the discussion by directing his words at Cavanila. "Priests have always governed Minoa. Your way was to let people help govern themselves. Even if it worked on Nios, why do you think it could work here? Why do you think we could allow two separate ways of ruling, one for Therans and another for everyone else?"

"We cannot do that," Jenora said before Cavanila could reply. "It will weaken my priesthood and upset the gods again. Is that what you want to happen?"

Handoro ignored her objection and talked about the system he discussed with Cavanila the night before. "If the people would have them, we could use priests for those positions as well."

Rhadamantis, who had just emptied his second cup of wine, slammed it down on his table. "Unthinkable! What do you mean when you say, 'If the people would have them'? It is not their choice. I will not rule that way."

Handoro bit into a grape from the bunch on his table and spoke in softened tones. "Then perhaps you are not the best person to govern them."

"I am the regent of Thera!" Rhadamantis shouted again. "I rule over Therans!"

Handoro looked first at Minos and then to Rhadamantis with the merest suggestion of a smile, a rarity for that crotchety old man. "But as you once learned, you serve at the pleasure of the king."

Rhadamantis pushed his table away and jumped up, fumbling for words to express his anger. But Minos held up his hand, commanding silence, and motioned for him to return to his seat.

Minos then turned to Jenora. "What do you say, High Priestess?"

"I oppose the whole idea. It goes against the gods."

"And you, Handoro?" Minos asked.

"I say we should try Cavanila's way."

"But if neither the high priestess nor Rhadamantis favor it, what then?"

"Then appoint someone else to help govern the Therans."

"Who?"

Handoro looked directly into Cavanila's eyes.

"Cavanila," he said.

Minos saw rage on Rhadamantis's face and anger on Jenora's. Handoro had the quizzical look of a tutor waiting for his student's reply to a difficult question. Bardok smiled at Cavanila who sat quietly, her hands in her lap, looking from one face to another. Minos looked up at the image of a blue-gray dolphin on the wall above his doorway and then back to the group.

"Except for Cavanila, you may all leave," he said.

"I don't like your ideas about how to organize people," he told her after the others had gone, "but Handoro says they can work here and that your Therans respect you. Do you think you can really control them?"

"I don't know, Sire, but my people need justice and deserve to be treated fairly."

Minos raised his eyebrows. "That's something your father never seemed to worry about. I have my doubts, but I am willing to appoint you to oversee Therans on Kephtor. You are to bring them under control and stop their violence and thievery. But you will have no authority over Kephtorians."

"I accept those responsibilities, but only if you agree to my conditions."

"Which are what?"

"I will no longer act as a priestess and will not answer to the high priestess. I will work hard to improve the living conditions of Therans who are here. I will try to see to it that they behave as you say, but also that they are treated properly. If they are, it will be to the advantage of all Minoa. I must be able to speak to you when there are problems that require your help and, finally, I want to appoint my own assistants, people I already know."

"I'm not sure you can do all that. You will have a difficult time ahead of you, but you may come to me any time you think I can help."

"Thank you, Uncle, I will do my best. What advice would you offer?"

"The first thing I would tell you is that you can trust my chamberlain. He is a difficult man sometimes, but his only desire is to help Minoa. He will do what he can for you."

"What about the high priestess?"

"She too wants what is best for Minoa, and she's not happy you will have power over Therans. Work with her as much as you can. So far as Bardok is concerned, I have heard you know him well, so I need say little about him."

"Yes, Sire, I do know him well." She hoped the sudden heat in her body didn't show on her face.

"You will also need to work with Drondak, the captain of my guard. He may appear unfriendly at times, but I believe you can trust him."

"Thank you, Sire. Anything else?"

"Do what you think you must. I will support you as much as I can. Go to your work, but remember, do not disappoint me."

CHAPTER 20

WHAT WILL HAPPEN TO MINOA NOW?

"The chamberlain is sleeping," Handoro's manservant told Cavanila, "but he asked to be awakened when you arrive. I will inform him of your presence."

He entered the Chamberlain's sleeping room but came out screaming moments later. "I can't wake him! I must call the priests!"

Cavanila rushed in to see the man who had led Minoa's fortunes for so many years lying on his back, eyes closed, cold and lifeless. She too tried to rouse him but could not.

Tears welled up in her eyes. She held his hand and stared at her new but suddenly lost friend until priests raced in and shouldered her aside.

Minos and Bardok arrived soon afterward and watched as priests ministered to Handoro's body.

"He seemed so well just a short time ago," the king said. "How could he die so quickly?"

"He was not a young man," one of the priests replied. "At least he doesn't seem to have felt any pain."

Jenora, one of the last to arrive, only glanced at Handoro.

"He was a nonbeliever who angered the gods," she said to no one in particular and walked from the room.

Minos shook his head as he watched her depart. "He was a good man and a faithful servant of Minoa," he said. "We will miss him."

"Yes we will," the priests replied in unison as they turned Handoro onto his side and folded his arms and legs to his chest. They had to do this before the body grew rigid so it could fit into a sarcophagus.

Bardok took Handoro's manservant by his arm and walked him into an outer room. He sat him down in a chair normally reserved for the chamberlain's guests. The servant looked up at Bardok and said, "I must see that visitors are attended to and provided with food and drink,"

"Later," Bardok said as he stood over him. "I know you grieve. We all grieve for him. But I want to know what the chamberlain did after he returned here from the king's chambers. Did he seem unwell or say anything to suggest he was ill?"

"No, Sire."

"Did he speak to anyone?"

"He spoke to his assistants and then told me he wanted to rest before Cavanila came."

"Did anyone else enter his room?"

"No, Sire."

"Were there any visitors to his rooms today?"

"No, Sire."

"Did you touch his wine container or any of his cups or food plates since you found him lifeless?"

"Sire, the servants took everything out and replaced them with clean vessels and containers of wine for King Minos and the others."

Bardok stared into the man's face for a while, then told him to return to his duties.

Late the next morning, four priests, led by musicians who rattled sistrums in a slow rhythm, carried Handoro's clay sarcophagus to the burial hill north of the palace. Minos, Jenora, Cavanila, and Bardok walked behind. A long line of priests, Handoro's assistants, scribes, and many other people of Knossos followed.

Rhadamantis did not attend. He had sent a message to the king saying his stomach ached too badly for him to leave his rooms.

The priests set the sarcophagus down on a nearly level path, bounded by rock walls, that led into a small cave hollowed out of the hill. With a view of the sacred mountain to the southwest and the sea to the north, Minos led a chant to ask the gods to accept his good and deserving chamberlain into their world. He then turned to the group that stood around the burial site.

"Handoro and his father before him served Minoa for many years. Minoa could not have achieved its greatness without them. He will be missed, especially in this time of great troubles. May the gods look after him, and may he have cause to smile when he looks down upon us."

"May that be so," everyone present responded.

The priests moved Handoro's sarcophagus into the cave and wrestled a large boulder into position against its entrance. Minos then led a somber procession back down the hill to the palace. The high priestess, who had remained silent during the ceremony, walked behind him until they approached the north entrance to the palace, where she stopped and waited for Cavanila and Bardok to catch up to her.

"Come see me later today if you wish to talk," she said to Cavanila.

Cavanila shook her head. "Not until tomorrow. I am still too upset."

"Yes, of course. Come tomorrow."

"What will happen to Minoa now?" Cavanila asked Bardok once back in her rooms.

"I don't know," Bardok replied. "As the king said, Handoro and his father controlled the fortunes of Minoa for many years, but he failed to train a successor. No one was ever good enough for him, and now we are left with no chamberlain and no one to help Minos with his problems except the high priestess. That worries me."

"I'm worried, too..." Cavanila began to say when a messenger arrived at her rooms to tell Bardok that the king wanted him in his throne room.

After Bardok left her, Cavanila went to her father's rooms, found him in a chair, his wine cup in his hand.

"I heard you were ill again, Father. What is wrong?"

"I have many aches but this wine helps," he grumbled. "How do you feel now that you have taken the position that is rightfully mine?"

"That was not my decision, Father," she replied as gently as she could.

"You could have refused it and told Minos that I should have it. My own daughter went against me!"

Cavanila stood in silence, feeling the guilt her father had thrust on her but angered by the injustice with which he treated her.

"I'm sorry father," she said as she turned to leave. "I hope you feel better soon."

"Where is your father?" Minos asked Bardok as soon as he arrived.

"The last I knew, he was at a settlement near the north coast of Thera. He may still be there."

"Find him. I want him to be my next chamberlain. Inform him that Handoro has gone to the gods and that I need him here."

"I'll go down to the harbor and send a message on any ships that might be there. I should return before dark."

"No. Send a messenger and return here immediately. I have more to say to you."

When Bardok returned, Minos waved him to a seat. "Our problems get worse all the time. First it was the earth shakings and the ash. Now our trade suffers and our stores are being drained. Both Kephtorians and Therans are causing trouble, and the man we need to deal with these problems went to the gods. I need help, Bardok, and I can't wait for your father to get here. Until he does, you will act as my chamberlain."

Caught by surprise, Bardok hesitated before replying. "Sire, I will help as much as I can, but I am only a sailor."

"There is much you will need to learn. To relieve some of your burden, have Drondak help you build the army. He may be a little jealous about his authority, but he is a good man."

"I know he is, and I have Vactor to help as well. What about the high priestess? I know Handoro had many disagreements with her."

"Handoro was too sensitive and didn't appreciate all that Jenora did for Minoa. She can be unpleasant at times, but she means well. You needn't worry about her. Just do what needs to be done."

"I will do my best, Sire."

"Be sure you do."

CHAPTER 21

WE CAN'T IGNORE THOSE INJUSTICES

The bull rhyton to the left of the high priestess's throne caught Cavanila's attention as soon as she entered the room. Alone, she stood before it, staring into its jeweled eyes until she heard the high priestess say, "It's beautiful, but be careful. It can have strange effects on a woman."

Cavanila turned to see Jenora dressed in her formal Minoan gown, gold jewelry hanging from her ears and neck and around her wrists, arms, and fingers. Her eyes, cheeks, lips, and even her fingernails were made up as completely as Cavanila had ever seen her. Jenora sat on her throne and waved Cavanila to a seat.

"I assume you had your morning meal?"

"I did. What kind of strange effects?"

"When its eyes sparkle before a fire, it's like Poseidon can see deep into a woman's soul."

"What did he see when he looked into yours?"

"He saw my love for him and took me into a wondrous world where I was a goddess among the gods, ready to serve him in any way he desired. And you see the results. The earth has stilled."

"I see what you mean, but I doubt Poseidon would take me into his world. Or if he did, I doubt he or the other gods would think of me as a goddess. But not everything that happened here has been good. We lost the chamberlain. It is sad and also strange that he died so suddenly."

"He often offended the gods. Perhaps that is why they took him. But Minos did not really need him. Handoro was just passed on to him by his father. With him gone, Minos and I can now deal with Minoa's problems without his interference."

Cavanila smiled to herself. She had spent the previous night with Bardok and knew differently. But all she said was, "I hope we will all do what's best for Minoa."

"I hope so too. We will have few difficulties as long as your Therans honor the gods and appreciate what we do for them."

Cavanila's amusement disappeared. "As long as they are treated with respect instead as servants or slaves. And some have Poseidon's sickness. It is not helpful that overseers constantly accuse them of being lazy, incompetent, and only good for the most menial tasks."

"Kephtorians know that if they don't work, they don't receive rations. Impress that on your Therans."

"I will, but you need to inform your priests and all Kephtorians that Therans are to be treated with consideration."

"Our problems were bad enough with what Poseidon did to us," Jenora retorted, "and you Therans weakened us even more. Can you not understand that?"

"We still need to be treated with justice."

Jenora waved a dismissive hand at Cavanila. "Tell your Therans to complain to their local priests when they have problems."

"They will, but if matters are not resolved, they will bring them to my council and to me. I will then bring them to you, since you are the high priestess. If you don't resolve them, I will go to the king, or to his chamberlain, if he has one."

"That won't be necessary. "I am the one to deal with people's behavior."

Cavanila rose from her seat. "I also hope it won't be necessary."

"Yes, you may go. I am on my way to speak to the king." And then, with a self-satisfied smirk, she added: "I know you have a close relationship with Bardok, but don't expect much help from him. He is only a naval commander. Minos has him building an army. We never needed one before your Therans began arriving".

"Thank you," Cavanila said as she walked from the room, pondering the implications of their conversation yet delighted to think of the shock Jenora would soon suffer.

Jenora entered the king's throne room, her head up, her shoulders back, her arms bent at their elbows, displaying her most spiritual, enticing form. She felt and looked triumphant until she saw Bardok in Handoro's seat next to Minos.

"You look nice," Minos said. "I am glad you have come. I have something important to tell you. I decided to make Toran my next chamberlain. He is now in the northern islands, so Bardok will perform his duties until he returns."

Jenora froze. Red splotches broke out all over her face and chest. Her chin thrust forward, her nipples hardened.

"When did you decide that?"

"I told Bardok about it yesterday so he could arrange for boats to summon Toran." Jenora looked angrily at Bardok. "I hope you and your father will have more respect for the gods than Handoro did."

"Did you want to speak about something?" Minos asked.

"It was not important," she replied as she stormed from the room.

That whore, she fumed on her way back to her rooms. She spent the night with Bardok and while I was telling her she couldn't depend on him for help, she knew he and his father would be the new chamberlains. She already knows how to use her body to get power. And that Minos, he never asked me what I thought about a replacement for Handoro, and he never told me what he was going to do. First he stopped making love to me when he found I was with child. Then he appointed Cavanila to her position over my objections. Now he ignores me when he makes important decisions. He trifles with me. He will be sorry.

Cavanila had just left her own room when she saw Jenora crossing the central court and could tell by her stride that she was an angry woman. Cavanila smiled to herself as she thought about why.

"I'm glad you have come, Cavanila," Minos said when she arrived at the throne room. "We have things to discuss. Have some refreshment while we talk."

"Thank you, Sire. Just a little milk and some fruit."

"As I said yesterday, Handoro managed everything so well for Minoa. Bardok and Toran will not easily replace him." He paused for an instant and looked into Cavanila's eyes. "I assume you already know I ordered Bardok to act as chamberlain until Toran gets here."

Cavanila's felt her face grow warmer as she glanced at Bardok who sat to the right of the king. "Yes, Sire, I know."

"Then you two should be able to work together. You should also know that your father came to me after we buried Handoro and asked to be appointed chamberlain or, if not, that I give your position to him. I told him I would not go back on my word so long as you do as I ordered. Your father would not be unhappy if you were to fail."

Cavanila took a deep breath and nodded. "I know my father. I will do my best."

"Then how do you propose to begin?"

"I will start with Theran craftsmen here in Knossos; the potters, the artists, and others who labor in workshops. I will ask each group to choose one person to be its leader, someone who can bring problems to me and pass my advice and orders on to his group. I will then do the same with other groups like the bronze workers, goldsmiths and stonecutters. I will eventually include scribes and others who work for merchants. After that is done, I will get to those working on farms and roads outside Knossos."

"What will you tell them?" Bardok asked.

"I will tell them to be patient, to work as hard as they can, and to realize their presence here is also a hardship for Kephtorians. I will also tell them that they are not to resort to violence or disobedience when problems arise. Instead, they must bring them to their group leaders, who will bring them to me if necessary."

"That means your leaders will often be away from their work," Bardok said. "How will they eat?"

"You and the king will have to help. Those who serve as leaders will have to be recognized for what they do and earn their rations accordingly. In a way, they will be acting like priests and should be compensated like priests."

"Another important thing," she continued, addressing Minos, "is that you let everyone know that Bardok is your new chamberlain and that I am the leader of the Therans. People must understand that you approve of my actions."

"So as long as Therans act as they should," Minos answered.

But Bardok was skeptical. "It seems to me you are setting up a new priesthood, like the one we already have except that it will ignore the gods, and your group leaders won't be called priests. Aren't you worried about problems with the high priestess?"

"Once I have the councils organized, I will invite her to appoint priests to them. I think she is not very happy today, especially about me, so I will wait some days before I talk to her again."

"We will help you," Minos said, "but don't forget, I brought you here to stop disobedience among Therans."

"That's true, Cavanila," Bardok added. "I will also help you as much as I can, but Minoa is having a difficult time. If you can't pacify the Therans, we will have to find another way."

She avoided responding to their implied threats. "I understand. I will keep you informed."

Bardok is just starting his duties as chamberlain, she thought to herself, and he already sounds like the king.

Over the next seven days, Cavanila organized Theran craftsmen in and around Knossos and formed her councils, each of which included a priest appointed by the high priestess. But despite her attempts, the situation only worsened. Kephtorians, under pressure to be more hospitable, found other ways to express their resentment against Therans.

"Some Kephtorians are now trying to evict Therans from their homes or farms, saying they need the rooms," Cavanila told Bardok. "Some are even forcing Theran families to sleep on straw with no roof over their heads. They are feeding their own families in secret while claiming that short rations require them to skimp on food. We can't allow that."

"Rations are short for everyone," he replied. "Maybe people shouldn't complain so much."

"But we can't ignore what's happening."

"What would you have me do, send guards to make people like each other? That's your job, yours and Jenora's. Maybe you should speak to her again."

Surprised by Bardok's attitude, Cavanila let her anger get the best of her. "Thank you for your deep concern, Bardok."

Stung by her sarcasm, he changed the subject. "There is another matter for you to consider. The last arrivals from Thera say the fires there have cooled. Your father thinks it's time to return, but I disagree. I heard the animals there are all dead or dying, the storehouses are nearly empty, and there will be no harvest, except maybe in the north. Even water could be a problem. I advised the king to keep Therans here until after the rains of the cold season wash the ash away and provide fresh water. Then perhaps a few can return."

"We also have to be concerned about the people on Nios," Cavanila said. "There aren't many left, but if ships can continue to supply them, it might be best for them to remain where they are until they can return to Thera."

"I'll suggest it to the king, but that might not be possible. Remember, the seas become too rough for boats during the cold season."

"I was thinking the same thing," Minos said when Bardok brought the suggestion to him. "I tried to convince Rhadamantis to become the regent at Nios once the weather turns warmer, but he refused. He said he was a prince, not a man who rules lean-tos on a beach."

"Then I suggest you send a message on the next boat appointing Lendor regent of Nios, and order Zardik to come here to help me build and train your army. I also think Zardik should sail around Thera on his way here to assess the situation, particularly in the north, and to bring my father here if he isn't already on his way."

While Bardok was conferring with Minos, Cavanila went to see Jenora. She found her on her throne, formally dressed, a familiar smirk on her face.

"I hear you have a problem, Cavanila, and you want my help."

"I have many problems, but the problems are yours too. Despite the king's decree, Kephtorians continue to make difficulties for Therans, who sometimes retaliate. Road building has slowed down, farm work isn't getting done, and even craftsmen are not producing as they should. Your priests do nothing to improve matters, and some seem to want to cause problems. Their only response to any complaint is that everything is in the hands of the gods. If we want conditions to improve, we must make more sacrifices and offerings."

"Do not criticize my priests. They serve the gods as they should. You were once a priestess. You should understand that. But, of course, you no longer have faith in the powers of the gods. What do you think I can do?"

"You must order your priests to work for better relations between our peoples."

"Cavanila, there may be some truth in what you say, but don't keep telling me what I must do."

"You asked for suggestions."

"I didn't ask you to give me orders."

"Unless your priests begin to behave differently, I will have no need for them on my councils. I need people who can be helpful."

"Cavanila, there seems to be little else to say now. It may be best for you to leave."

"Yes, I think it may be."

"Many of my people want to return to Nios," one of Cavanila's councilors said at her next meeting with them. "They say they would prefer the hardships there, where they could live in peace."

Others nodded in agreement. Another said, "I'd even go back to Thera if the fires and spewing have ended. Maybe the ash will be washed away once the rains begin."

"Until we know people can live there again, you must continue to tell everyone to be patient. And you must convince the priests in your areas to do the same with the Kephtorians. Otherwise, our situation here will only get worse."

Her eyes fell on two men who had been sitting quietly.

"Rhitori, what do you have to say?"

"My overseer has Therans and Kephtorians working on separate parts of the road. He decreed that our rations will depend on how much of the road a crew completes each day. So the two crews work hard and do not speak to each other. It's better than fighting. Maybe things will get better with time."

"And what about you, Priest? What do you say?"

The hard edge to her voice surprised even herself. The priest was an elderly man, short, with a round face and a rounder belly. He had yet to speak since he joined her council.

His face flushed. "Cavanila, I would speak with you in private, if I may."

She looked at him, wondering what might be on his mind. "Very well, as soon as we are finished here."

He approached her after the others had gone. "Perhaps it would be better if I came to see you after your evening meal."

She saw sadness in his eyes and became more curious about the man whose gentleness she hadn't expected from one of Jenora's priests.

"I will sup alone tonight," she said. "Come when you think best."

It was dark by the time her servant ushered the priest into her inner room. Even in the subdued light of her oil lamps, he seemed bent with worry. He ignored her offer of a seat and refreshment.

"I'm an old man, Cavanila," he said after a deep breath. "I have served the gods and the people of Minoa for many years. We are a good people. I do not like to see the difficulties that have arisen between Therans and Kephtorians. I serve on your council because the high priestess ordered me to do so. She also ordered me to inform her of everything you say and do. Please forgive me, but I am sorry to say that I have mostly done what she demanded. What disturbs me just as much is that the high priestess ordered me and the other priests on your councils to appear to cooperate but to do little to make things easier between us. Cavanila, I don't want people to be enemies. The high priestess seems to prefer otherwise."

He paused again, his head hanging low for a few moments, as though he were trying to deal with his own internal conflicts. But he soon straightened up, as if he had finally unburdened himself of a heavy weight.

"Be well, Cavanila, and do your best for all our people."

Before she could reply, he turned and walked back out into the darkness.

Cavanila spent the night alone, sleeping little. The next morning, she went to tell Bardok what the old priest had said. Bardok was surrounded by several of Handoro's scribes and asked her to return later to have her midday meal with him.

As they ate, she told him about her meeting with the priest. "And now I cannot even discuss the most important matters with my councils without her learning about everything I say."

"What would you have me do?"

"You can't do anything about the priests on my councils, but you could persuade the king to forcefully decree that he won't tolerate the kinds of behavior my people have been subjected to. I will speak to him too, but he probably won't listen to me despite his promise."

"I don't know if he will listen to me either. I assume you know your father took two longboats to Akrotiri this morning. He said he had to see if it could be made livable again. The winds turned around to the south yesterday, and he decided to take advantage of them. He ignored the fact that such winds can bring bad weather."

"Could Thera be made livable again? Why did you let him have those boats if you thought that trip would be so dangerous?"

"Minos and I both warned him about going there now, especially with the cold season approaching, but he wouldn't listen. Actually the king seemed happy to see him go. As far as Thera is concerned, a captain who returned from there said the lagoon is quiet, no spewing of ash or fire. He also said that some of the buildings in Akrotiri are still standing and could be made livable again. No one lives in Akrotiri now, but they did find small settlements on the northern and western sides of the island. My father left there to join the Therans on Nios. Zardik is on his way to bring him back here. I'll be happy to see him."

Later that day, a young priest Cavanila hadn't seen before appeared at her council meeting. He told her that he was replacing the older priest who previously sat on her council.

"The high priestess thought he was too old to serve properly," he said.

PART II

CATACLYSM

CHAPTER 22

RETURN TO AKROTIRI

The mountaintops were already aglow although the sun had yet to brighten the beach at Poros, where two longboats sat waiting. Their mission, under the command of Kodamta, was to take Rhadamantis and his cargo to Akrotiri and to remain there to help rebuild that town.

"If the south winds hold, we should have a fast run to Akrotiri," Kodamta told Parik, his second-in-command.

"But those winds could bring heavy storms," Parik replied.

"I know, but if we sail soon, we should get there before they develop."

Parik nodded his curly head toward the road from Knossos. "Maybe, but there he is. Look what he's bringing."

Kodamta spun around to see Rhadamantis in a chariot leading four wagons filled with amphoras and clay storage jars half as tall as a man. "I see 'em," Kodamta said with a frown.

Rhadamantis's driver pulled his chariot up next to the boats. Behind him, drovers whipped the oxen to keep the wagons moving despite the deep ruts they were carving in the sand.

"We can be off as soon as you get these loaded," he told Kodamta.

But Kodamta shook his head. "It's too much, more than we can carry."

"Then remove some of your ballast."

"We'll still be too top-heavy for rough seas. Send those jars on supply ships. They'll get to Akrotiri only a few days later."

"It is all coming with us," Rhadamantis demanded. "There is not a cloud in the sky and the winds are favorable. I am paying you well in gold. Load them and let us depart."

Kodamta and Parik looked at each other, shrugged their shoulders, and ordered their crews to lighten their boats.

Five of the jars, filled with grains, beans and chickpeas were lashed in place along the center lines of each boat. The conical amphoras containing olive oil, wine, or water were stacked along the walls of their hulls. Rhadamantis stowed four bags of his personal possessions under his stern seat. His manservant sat on skins atop the remaining rock ballast.

The boats had barely pushed off from the beach, their oars poised for their first stroke, when Kodamta, at the bow of his ship, raised his arms and ordered both crews to stop.

"We're too low in the water," he yelled across to Parik. And then to Rhadamantis, "Sire, we have to offload some of those jars. We can put them ashore, or we can dump them right here. But I'm not going to sea with overloaded, top-heavy boats."

Rhadamantis glared at Kodamta, a powerfully built sailor whose face bore the scars of many battles, and dropped his eyes.

"Don't unload any more than you have to," he said.

He then looked up and added, "I am the Prince of Minoa. Don't ever speak to me like that again."

On Kodamta's command, the boats backwatered to shore where they each unloaded two storage jars and half of their amphoras. Rhadamantis left orders with the harbormaster to send them later by supply boat.

Like all sailors whose lives and livelihood depend on the weather, Kodamta continually scanned the skies. By midday, the wispy clouds he saw earlier had grown into distinct, dense puffs. He knew they could billow higher as the day progressed, and the taller they grew, the greater the likelihood they would develop into thunderstorms. He waved to Parik and pointed skyward. Parik nodded his head and pointed skyward himself.

Kodamta made his way to the stern. "Sire, look at those clouds. We could get caught is some bad storms. We need to turn back."

Rhadamantis, lost in his own thoughts about returning Akrotiri to its previous grandeur, looked up at him. "Why are you so worried?

We see clouds like those all the time. It is a beautiful day, and we have strong winds behind us. We will make Akrotiri in good time. It makes no sense to head back to Kephtor against these winds."

"We don't have to go all the way to Kephtor. We could shelter at Dhia. I don't want to get caught out here in a storm."

"Everything frightens you, Kodamta. I was told you were one of Minos's best captains, but you act more like a coward. Have your balls shriveled up in your old age? We are going to Akrotiri. Do not defy me. You did that once already today."

Kodamta shook his head, disgusted with himself for agreeing to make this journey and frustrated because he couldn't convince Rhadamantis of the dangers they might face.

"More speed!" he yelled to his rowers. "Up the beat!"

By late afternoon, the clouds had coalesced and grew into a menacing blue-gray mantle. The two captains could see Thera ahead, but it was still far off. Strengthening stern winds drove Kodamta's bow deeper into the water and threatened his mast and sail. The sea became a mass of whitecaps. Kodamta continually strummed the lines that ran from stern to masthead, like strings of a lyre, to test their tautness. If they snapped, their masts and sails would go too.

When he decided their limit had been reached, he ordered his crew to lower the top boom and sail. Parik gave the same order to his crew. Despite the high winds, both crews managed to spill the wind from their sails and get them and their top booms down and lashed to the bottom booms.

Without the stabilizing effects of their sails, the still dangerously top-heavy boats pitched and rolled in the heavy seas. Synchronized rowing became impossible. On a steep roll, oars on one side had nothing but air to pull against while rowers on the other side fought to keep their oars from becoming too deeply submerged. Control of the boats' heading became another problem because their pitching and rolling made it too dangerous for the steersmen to stand at their positions on the rear decks. Water splashed over their gunwales each time the boats rolled too far over, increasing their load and causing them to ride even lower in the water.

Kodamta made his way from the bow to amidships, his feet spread apart to maintain his balance. He slashed the lines that secured a grain-filled jar and, with the help of two crewmen, toppled it overboard. He looked over at Rhadamantis expecting a tirade, but that Minoan prince, finally understanding that he shouldn't have ignored his captain's warnings, kept his eyes averted and said nothing. Kodamta then ordered a second jar jettisoned.

The rain began with a few, large, splattering drops that quickly became a wind-driven torrent. Lightning lit the clouds and struck at Ascania and the more distant Thera. Thunderclaps punctuated a continuously rolling thunder. Thera first and then Ascania disappeared in the downpour. Kodamta lost sight of Parik's boat.

His boat took on more water and rode still lower in the sea. He ordered more of the crew to ship their oars and help with the bailing, despite his need for rowers to maintain way. He ordered another storage jar jettisoned. With water dripping from his beard, he yelled for Rhadamantis, and his servant to help bail. At first, Rhadamantis only ordered his servant to bail while he remained in his seat. But he soon realized his life was at stake and left his shelter to help. Finding nothing to bail with, he scooped water with his hands.

"That's no good," yelled Kodamta. "Break one of those amphoras and use a piece to throw water."

"We need them," Rhadamantis shouted back.

Kodamta emptied a wine-containing amphora over the side, broke it with a bronze hammer, and pushed a large curved fragment into Rhadamantis's hands. Rhadamantis, who had shunned physical labor his entire life, discarded his rain-heavy, woolen robe and, though struggling to keep his balance, shoveled water over the side until his arms and back ached. Naked except for his codpiece, gasping for air and hardly able to see in the downpour, he found himself exhilarated, even aroused, as he struggled with the others for survival.

But water continued to accumulate. Kodamta's boat was almost to the point of foundering when he ordered the crew to throw the last of the storage jars and most of the amphoras overboard.

Eventually, the winds lessened. The downpour tapered off to a more gentle rain and then stopped. The seas calmed and visibility increased. Sun beamed through holes in the overcast, lending a silvery sheen to spotty areas on an otherwise nearly black sea. The boat was still afloat, though just barely. Kodamta could see he was to the east of Ascania, but he saw no sign of Parik's boat.

By the time Kodamta's crew ran the stern of his boat onto Akrotiri's shore, only the top of Profitis Ilias, the highest peak on Thera, remained hidden in cloud. For a few moments, no one aboard moved. The crew, soaked, cold, and exhausted, sat motionless, savoring their survival. Only the waves lapping the shore broke the silence. The caustic stench of rain-soaked ash permeated the air. Rhadamantis, looking seaward from his stern seat, kept his back to the city. Kodamta stood next to him, absorbing the bleakness of that once vibrant harbor.

"We're here," Kodamta said to no one in particular.

Rhadamantis rose and turned to look toward the ruined city. He let himself down into ankle-deep water and trudged across the beach through the sticky mud of wet ash and pumice. He ignored the mound that covered Gridawi's body. The rain had left the bones of one leg exposed to the elements.

He stopped, turned toward the boat, and with a wave signaled the others to follow him. He led them to what was once Serevida's house, the one whose stone façade fell on her during the first earth shaking, They picked their way through its ruins, wary of unstable walls and the roof that might still collapse. Some of its rooms remained undamaged, though ash nearly filled those that faced the lagoon.

"This will be our quarters," Rhadamantis told Kodamta. "Have the men clean out these rooms. My room will be the one that looks out to the sea."

Kodamta and his crew supped that night around a fire in a scavenged clay brazier, their shadows dark against the firelit walls. Rhadamantis sat brooding.

It will be more difficult than I thought to get this town livable again and the markets working. But if I don't, I will rule over an empty, ruined city. I cannot let that happen. I will not let that happen.

He called Kodamta to him. "Since you threw all our storage jars overboard, your crew will search town in the morning for any food they can find. And send some to the north to see what they can find up there."

"I can spare a few for that," Kodamta replied, "but I'm going to search for Parik's boat as soon as mine is seaworthy again."

"A few men will not be enough. You will do as I say, Captain. Parik and his crew may not have survived. But if they did, they must have spent the night someplace safe and should arrive here in the morning. Either way, you don't have to go looking for them."

"Sire, those are my men. Even if they all drowned, we must recover their bodies and send them to the gods properly. We cannot do otherwise."

"Be careful how you speak to me, Kodamta. Repair your boat but use most of your men as I command. They are to report back to me by midday."

But Kodamta wouldn't be put off. "Sire, I need to search for my men as soon as my boat is ready."

"Then come to me when it is. I will decide what to do next." Rhadamantis rose and went to his room without looking at his captain or waiting for a reply.

Kodamta had his men out and working by first light the next morning. He assigned some to Rhadamantis's tasks but kept most at work on his boat. Thankful to find his ship's rigging intact, he ordered the men to empty the hull. They formed two lines to pass the ballast rocks and stack them on the beach. Then they bailed the remaining water and replaced the ballast, adding more rocks from a pile maintained in the harbor for that purpose.

Later that morning, Kodamta found Rhadamantis sitting under a light well in the largest room in the house, admiring the paintings on its walls.

"Look at that girl on the rock, Kodamta," Rhadamantis said before the captain could speak. "You can see the pain in her face, even in her body, as she examines a wound in her foot. And look at that priestess high up on the wall, sitting grandly as younger women offer her the sacred crocus. She's elegant and beautiful, but that picture should have been of me. I am the high priest of Thera."

"Sire, my boat is ready. I need to go look for my men."

Without taking his eyes off the paintings, Rhadamantis said, "You defied me, Captain. I won't forget that. Go, but be back by midday. Your scouts should be back by then."

"Doesn't give me much time to search."

Rhadamantis, his jaw set and his brows furrowed, turned to face Kodamta. "You will be here when I say. I decide what you do."

As he approached the beach, Kodamta saw his crew had stopped working and were looking seaward. Then he saw it too. Parik's boat, riding low in the calm morning sea. The crews greeted each other with shouts and waving arms as the boat pulled up onto the beach. But Rhadamantis, alerted to their arrival by his servant, stood back, waiting for Parik to come and explain why he failed to arrive there the night before.

"That storm nearly swamped us," Parik told him, "but we stayed afloat by dumping ballast, all but one of the storage jars and some amphoras. We also threw the anchor stones overboard but kept them tied to the stern to protect us from running onto rocks in case we got blown into shallow water. That helped steady us. By the time the storm ended, we were to the west of Ascania. We found a small bay to spend the night. We bailed what we could this morning and unloaded more ballast so we could make our way here."

"You acted like a brave and competent captain, Parik," Rhadamantis said while leering at Kodamta. "You managed to save a storage jar, which is more than Kodamta did. As a reward, you will now command both boats."

To Kodamta he said, "You will direct the cleaning and rebuilding of the town. Perhaps in that work you will not defy me."

Kodamta stared into Rhadamantis's eyes for several moments, muttered, "Yes, Sire," and turned to walk alone into the town.

By midday, scouts back from the hill to the northwest of Akrotiri reported seeing no smoke or vapors rising from the lagoon and no signs of people, only the remains of dead goats. The leader of the men who climbed the flank of Profitis Ilias to the northeast said they saw human footprints in the ash leading into and out of the town, but no people or animals.

"They came to steal from our storehouses," Rhadamantis said. "Kodamta, take some armed men to the north. Order everyone you see to come here and bring any animals or food you find with you. They will work here if they want to eat."

People trickled into Akrotiri over the next several days. Crews collected and stacked usable furniture like beds and chairs and cleaned out still livable houses. They rebuilt and plastered walls and roofs, piled ash and rubble out of the way, and began to put down a new surface of flat stones atop the thick layer of ash on the main street. They even started raising doorways of some houses to compensate for the rise in street level.

The work was quite far along when Zardik's boat, with Toran aboard, entered the harbor.

"Welcome," Rhadamantis said when they came ashore. "I am surprised but pleased to see you. Why have you come?"

"We are on our way to Kephtor," Toran replied, "and decided to stop here to rest and examine the condition of the town and my house. We didn't know you were here."

"Well, we are. You must see the great progress I have made. Walk with me and I will show you."

A few steps beyond the beach he stopped and pointed to the house he now occupied.

"My first task was to make the houses closest to the harbor habitable," he said. "My throne room and living quarters are now there."

Then he directed their attention to a large building on the other side of the street. "Most of my workers are housed in there, and we are using its storerooms for our food and drink. A supply ship stopped here two days ago, so we have enough food for a while."

He walked them through the main square where many of the unstable walls had been torn down, then to the northern part of the town where they stopped in front of Toran's house.

"Yours is one of the few that survived the earth shakings," Rhadamantis said.

Toran and Zardik left Rhadamantis in the street and walked through drifts of ash and pumice to look into his house.

"Except for ash that came in through the north windows, my house is in good condition," Toran told Rhadamantis after they returned to the street. "Even the pictures of the boat procession high on my walls are undamaged. I will have Zardik's crew clean it out so we can spend the night here."

"No, no," protested Rhadamantis. "Stay with me. Your crew can stay with my crews. There is no need for you to clean your house for just one night."

But Toran declined the invitation. "No, we will do it. It contains much I must attend to myself."

"All right, but I trust you and Zardik will sup with me tonight." Toran reluctantly agreed, despite his disdain for the man.

Zardik, however, said he would eat with his crew. "I want to be sure they'll be prepared to leave for Kephtor at first light," he told Rhadamantis.

As they ate, Rhadamantis told Toran how he was going to make Akrotiri grander and more successful than ever. "Minos will be proud of my accomplishments and my contributions to Minoa."

Toran tried to change the subject. "Do you know what happened to Reda, my housekeeper?" he asked.

Rhadamantis said he didn't and continued on with his chatter. Toran listened but said little. Rhadamantis kept his eyes moving as he continued to talk, seldom looking at Toran. He bragged about Cavanila's accomplishments, and talked about the difficulties that arose between Therans and Kephtorians.

"Most Therans are Islanders, not Minoans," he said. "They do little to please the gods. They won't listen to our priests and they cause problems for those who do. And they are ill-suited for the kinds of work they must do to earn their food. To make matters worse, Jenora doesn't understand how to deal with them. Besides, she is with child. She says it is a child of the gods, but everyone knows she enjoys Minos's bed. Minos thinks it's his, but it might not be. He should replace her. Cavanila would be a good high priestess if she would change her ways. Bardok has done well since Handoro went to the gods, but Minoa needs an older and more experienced chamberlain like you to direct its fortunes."

When Toran could no longer tolerate Rhadamantis's ranting, he rose from his seat. "It is late. I suffer from good food and a long day at sea. And I have another long day tomorrow. I must retire."

"Sleep well," Rhadamantis replied, knowing he tried too hard—and failed—to make an impression on Toran.

CHAPTER 23

A MAN WHO SUDDENLY UNDERSTOOD HE HAD BEEN SENTENCED TO DEATH

Toran had hoped for a dawn departure but, in deference to Rhadamantis's position, couldn't avoid joining him for an early morning meal. He ate but, like the night before, said little while Rhadamantis bragged about his successes and dreams for Akrotiri. Toran rose to his feet when he could no longer tolerate the man's harangue.

"Please excuse me, but I must go. We should have been at sea by now."

Rhadamantis persisted. "I will walk to the harbor with you."

Zardik's longboat, already afloat, stood waiting for Toran. But even then Rhadamantis continued to urge him to deliver his boastful message to Minos. Toran, no longer listening, waded into the shallow water and climbed aboard. He looked at Zardik with a grimace, shrugged his shoulders, and with a wave of his hand, pleaded for Zardik to depart.

Zardik set a sustainable pace for the rowers whose oars, dipping and pulling in perfect synchrony, propelled the boat southward out of the harbor. By then, the sun was well above the horizon.

"Not much wind, now," Zardik told Toran, "but it will get stronger. I think we should row westerly until midday, and then turn southeast and run for Poros with the wind at our back."

"Whatever you think best. I'm sorry I couldn't get out sooner."

Zardik smiled and nodded his head to indicate he understood. "We'll still get to Poros before dark."

Once past the Ascania islands, Zardik ordered the steersman to turn southwestward and to keep the white mountains of western Kephtor on the boat's port quarter.

That morning at Akrotiri began like many before it. Some men worked to repair the house Rhadamantis occupied, rebuilding the collapsed outer wall and plastering its inside surfaces. Rhadamantis insisted that the walls be perfectly smooth because he planned to have artists cover them with paintings of himself surrounded by goddesses and female supplicants. Others worked to ready harbor-side warehouses for the ships Rhadamantis hoped would soon arrive with goods for its revived markets.

Two teenage boys had the easiest task. Rhadamantis sent them to the cliffs every day to watch over Thera's lagoon and report back if the volcanic island in its middle began spewing fire or black smoke again. Bored by having to sit there with nothing to report, they amused themselves by practicing swordsmanship with wooden weapons and by challenging each other to contests with spears and slings.

They had just begun their midday meal when they noticed a white cloud rising over the island. They had seen vapors rising from it for several days, but when they reported this to Rhadamantis, he said, "They are nothing new. I want you to watch for black smoke."

But this cloud was denser and drifted higher than before. They stared at each other, wondering what to do when a puff of brown smoke shot up.

"It's not black," said the younger of the two.

"It's not just white vapors, either," the other said. "We need to tell the prince!"

They jumped up, spilling their food, and scrambled down the hill with their news. But it was already too late. The eruption announced itself to the town before the boys arrived.

Rhadamantis was in the great room when it began. He often took his midday meal there because the sun, beaming down through the light well at that time of day, brightened the scenes on its walls and made their colors even more vibrant. His servant had just brought his meal when he heard the low rumble and saw ripples in his wine cup. Like everyone else in the town, he rushed into the street and stared up at the cloud drifting over them. Ash had already begun to fall. He hadn't been there long when Kodamta tapped him on his shoulder to get his attention. Parik stood behind him.

"It could get bad," Kodamta said. "I think we should leave, now. Our boats are ready."

"It does not seem as serious as it once did," Rhadamantis replied, "but perhaps you are right. Come with me."

He led them into his sleeping room where he took the time to pack two cloth bags with his possessions and told Parik to take them to the boats. And while Kodamta nervously waited, he wrapped his jewelry and his favorite chalice, carved from soft stone, in his best robes and stuffed them into two other bags. He gave one to Kodamta and carried the other as they returned to the street and rushed to the harbor.

By then, the cloud, thicker and darker, covered the town like a brown shroud. Frightened people milled around in the streets, not knowing what to do. Noxious odors filled the air and the rain of ash grew heavier. Hot, glassy pellets of pumice began to fall, a flurry at first that soon grew into a blizzard. It was like an ice storm, except the hailstones were hot, not cold, and would never melt. They covered the ground that, like sun-heated sand, burned the soles of those who walked barefoot upon it.

People streamed toward the harbor. They covered their heads and faces as best they could, but the foul-smelling vapors irritated their eyes and throats, and had some gasping for air.

Parik's boat was already under way when Rhadamantis and Kodamta reached the beach. Kodamta's boat stood in shallow water, its crew fending off people with their weapons to avoid becoming overloaded.

Kodamta climbed aboard and ordered his crew to row while he helped Rhadamantis up over the side. Rhadamantis stuffed his bags under his seat and only then glanced back to see his servant watching from the beach, fear in his eyes, his posture rigid, the look of a man who suddenly understood he had been sentenced to death.

The rumble grew louder as the inferno intensified. The cloud thickened and billowed higher, propelled by intermittent blasts.

The falling particles were now larger, some the size of olives, and hotter than before. Some had pink and orange hues. Showers of hot, black stones—molten fire only moments earlier—rained down.

Panic gripped those left behind. Some knew that the greatest ash fall from the earlier eruption had occurred along a path that went directly through the town. To escape what they thought its track would be this time, men and women, some with children in their arms or in tow, ran either east toward the hills or west, where they hoped to find protection in the lee of the steep-sloped red mountain. Some managed to get beyond the edge of town. But blinded by the falling ash, pelted by the hot, solid rain, and laboring for air, their pace soon slowed. Some staggered on, dragging their feet through the hot, mounting detritus. Others fell to their knees and tried to crawl. But eventually, all reached their limit and collapsed in exhaustion. Soon, only mounds in the deepening fallout showed where their bodies lay.

The pumice, light enough to float on water, formed a continuous layer that extended out to sea. It was like a floating blanket that dampened the waves. The shoreline disappeared.

The crews of the two boats struggled to row through the layer that deepened with every stroke. The falling ash turned everything and everyone to a ghostly gray. Pumice piled up in the boats. Kodamta kept all his men at their oars. He knew their only hope was to get to the open sea. He called to Rhadamantis to help dump the accumulating pumice, but Rhadamantis refused to leave his little shelter.

Inundated by the deadly rain and pelted by the hot stones, all aboard gasped for air that, with its foul-smelling vapors, had lost much of its life giving essence. One by one, the crewmen grew weaker. Some dropped their oars in fits of coughing. A few who were still able stood at their seats and, in desperation, tried to paddle. But they made little headway.

Despite the heat, Rhadamantis sat shivering in his paltry stern shelter, skins draped over his head and around his body. The cloth he held to his face filtered most of the ash and pumice, but not the fumes. Like everyone else, his eyes stung and his throat burned as he fought for air. He sat weak and helpless, watching crewmen falter and collapse, a horror that foretold his own fate.

"Save me, Poseidon," he tried to shout. But he had little voice, and the cloth over his face muffled his raspy words. "I am Rhadamantis, Prince of Minoa. I have always worshipped you. I made sacrifices and prayed to you. Please great god, let me live."

Those were his final words.

The last thing he saw before he too collapsed was Kodamta standing at a rower's seat, staring at him, an oar in his hands but no longer paddling, his chest heaving, his tearing eyes filled with hate and contempt.

As the roar grew louder, the blasts became more frequent and more violent until an enormous explosion shot lava, ash, pumice, even huge boulders in all directions. A dense, searing cloud rolled over the lower hills that surrounded Thera's lagoon, incinerating everyone and everything in its path.

Like a huge stone falling into water, that surge, when it hit the pumice-covered water, drove waves outward from Thera's shores. Except for a few creatures high up on Profitis Ilias, all life on Thera ended. Even fish far beyond the shore soon suffocated in the pumice-covered sea. As Rhadamantis once predicted, Thera had met its doom.

Zardik's boat was still on a southwesterly course when a rower pointed rearward at the brown smoke rising over Thera. Zardik left the bow to confer with Toran, who had risen from his stern seat to study the cloud.

"It's the island in the lagoon again," Zardik said. "Maybe we should turn back. We could take some people off that island."

"We can't," Toran replied. "Look at it. That fire must be huge. We would be rowing right into that cloud."

All aboard watched as the cloud rose higher and leaned eastward in the prevailing winds. What sounded at first like a far off storm grew into a loud roar punctuated by violent thunderclaps. Even at such a distance from Thera, it hurt their ears and shook their bodies. Zardik tried to call for a course change, but the din drowned out his voice. He had to wave and point to get his steersman to turn the boat southward, directly away from Thera. He mimed increasingly rapid rowing motions to demand maximum speed from his crew.

A sudden look of awe on his rower's faces caused him to look back at Thera again. He saw that the plume had expanded as the volcano shot its contents both horizontally and higher into the air. Thera, except for its highest elevations, disappeared in a hot, expanding, opaque cloud that rolled over the island at high velocity.

They hadn't rowed many more strokes when a shockwave and an even louder blast hit them. It threw Zardik, Toran, and the steersman on the stern forward into the boat. Stern lines to the mast snapped. The mast with its attached booms and sail, crashed forward, decimating everyone in its path. Oarsmen in the aft part of the boat slammed against the seats behind them. The few still surviving sat agape at the approaching cloud—an avalanche of still searing ash, bits of pumice, and poisonous, suffocating fumes—until it engulfed them. They perished in an instant.

Not long afterward, a speeding swell raised the battered, foundering boat half the height of a man as it passed beneath it on its southward journey.

At Poros, the roar and intermittent blasts, magnified by echoes from the mountains to the south, grew louder and more frequent. Craftsmen left their shops and villagers ran from their houses. They gathered in groups on the bluffs above the beach, staring at the cloud rising over Thera. They stood close to each other, parents hugging their children, couples with their arms around each other, until the fury that struck Zardik's boat hit Poros as well.

The blast and accompanying shockwave, attenuated because of Poros' greater distance from Thera, still threw a few frail men and women to the ground. The fetid vapors were cooler and less toxic, but they sickened many and left everyone coughing and struggling to breathe. Many ran back to their houses to try to escape the storm.

Waters receded from the beach. Sands, rocks, and even long submerged, ancient stone walls became exposed, a strange phenomenon where tidal shifts are minimal. Curious adults and children ventured onto the wet sands to pick up flopping fish and other stranded sea creatures. They didn't see the approaching swell and couldn't hear warning shouts from those who did. It wasn't until they saw others running that they turned to see the threat and joined in the race back to the beach and to higher ground. Even those who had remained on the beach realized they had to run. Parents and other adults snatched up children as they went, or tried to help the more elderly along. For some, even that small delay was fatal.

The wave, already as high as the bluffs, rose even higher as it came in over the shallows. And as it grew, its velocity slowed until its crest curled over and crashed down on people, animals, houses, boats, storage sheds, and everything else along that coast. The surging water tumbled and battered people and animals. It tore children from their mothers' arms as it carried them along.

A few managed to stay afloat, clinging to debris as the surge raced inland and washed up against the lower hills. With its forward energy spent, the flood slowed and seemed to hesitate until it reversed direction, sweeping everything it gripped, drowned bodies, animal carcasses, floating debris, and even crops and the soils on which they grew, along with it.

People who managed to reach safety beyond the water's high mark could only watch as those still trying to swim or clinging to floating debris were carried out to sea.

CHAPTER 24

THE SECOND BLAST

"No!" Cavanila cried as soon as she climbed out onto the palace rooftop, four stories above the central court. Like everyone else there, she was stunned by the reverberating thunder and the growing cloud on the northern horizon. She knew it had to be from Thera and that this upheaval was far more violent and destructive than the quakes and eruptions she had witnessed at Akrotiri.

She felt an arm around her waist and turned to see Bardok.

"My father...What's happening there?" she asked, more a plea than a question.

"It looks bad, Cavanila. I'm worried about my father too. I think he is safe on Nios. Maybe your father is with him. Or they might be on their way here. All we can do is wait."

"We can't wait! We must do something!"

"I know how you feel, but what can we do?"

Cavanila went into his consoling arms, her cheek against his chest. "I don't know," her voice not much above a whisper.

He held her for a while, searching for words to comfort her. But she soon stepped back and with a stronger voice said, "I want to go to Thera. I have to find my father."

Bardok shook his head. "You can't, at least not until those fires cool. If your father left Thera before they started, he could be here by tonight or tomorrow morning. We could go to the harbor to see if any ships have arrived from that direction. Their captains might know something."

"Yes, let's go. Please."

"Why are the gods doing this?" Minos shouted at Jenora when she entered the throne room. "I thought we had soothed their anger. What have you been doing?"

"I have done as you ordered. I always do. What have *you* been doing? A moon has passed since I last saw you at our shrine. Or maybe there are other reasons for Poseidon's anger."

"What other reasons?"

"Your brother. A cloud appears over Thera whenever he is there. Or perhaps the gods are angry because you appoint nonbelievers to high positions. But the fault is not mine."

"High Priestess, I am Minos," he said, pointing his finger at her. "You will not criticize me or what I do. Gather your priests and pray to the gods. Make more sacrifices."

Jenora stared at him, forcing what she hoped was an alluring smile.

"Maybe we should go to the sacred mountain again," she said. "We could perform our rituals while closer to the gods...as we did before."

His eyes traveled over her enlarged breasts and thickening belly for what to her seemed an eternity. "Perhaps. I will consider it."

In the past, she welcomed his attention to her body. But seeing distaste rather than lust on his face, she turned away and rushed from the room.

He blames me for everything, she thought. And now that I grow large with his child, he treats me like I'm an ugly servant girl. He will be sorry.

Cavanila and Bardok had hardly started down the Royal Road when they heard the blast. Soon after they felt the gust and the still-warm, foul air. Bardok's favorite horse, a mottled gray and white stallion, its mane tied up into tufts, bobbed its head, pulled back its ears, and began to run. Cavanila held on to the chariot's side rails while Bardok fought to control the frightened animal. As a last resort, he put all his strength into his left rein and turned the horse toward the high, stone retaining wall that lined the road. The horse, larger than most at Knossos, barely avoided slamming its head against the wall but hit it hard enough to scrape layers of skin off its shoulder.

Frightened and in pain, the animal whinnied and rose up on its hind legs. Once down on all fours, it pawed the earth with one leg, snorting and rotating its head from side to side. It finally stood still, its muscles twitching, while Bardok tried to calm it with soothing words. He waited until the horse settled down, then coaxed the limping animal farther along the road until his way was blocked by people running toward them.

"Go back!" a man yelled. "Everyone's drowned. Nothing's left."

A second blast, as powerful as the first, then struck them.

The horse reared up and began to run again. Cavanila managed to hold on while Bardok turned the horse toward the stone wall as before. This time it stopped short of colliding with it. Bardok let it rest until it appeared calmer and then, with gentle use of his whip, he prodded it to continue toward the shore. He brought it to a halt when they reached the level of the last wave's farthest advance.

Cavanila and Bardok stared open-mouthed at the bodies of people and animals among the debris, the broken boats high up on land, washed out earth where there had once been cultivated fields, and only piles of stones where there had once been workshops and houses.

"Take this chariot back to Knossos," Bardok yelled as he handed Cavanila the reins and jumped to the ground. "Tell Minos what you have seen. Tell him to send help."

Cavanila wasn't sure she could control the animal, but knew she had to try. After seeing her off, Bardok organized the people he could find to search for survivors among the masses of debris. They found many bodies but few people still alive.

Their frantic search ended when a man yelled, "Another one's coming! Run!"

A glance out to sea sent everyone scurrying for higher ground. A few tried to carry or help injured people along. Bardok scrambled back up the road with an old woman in his arms. But he couldn't outrun the wave. It hit the back of his legs and threw him off balance. He fell over and lost his grip on the woman. He fought to keep his head above the surface as the surge carried him along, tumbling him over and over. He became disoriented could see little in the debris-filled water, and sometimes found himself scraping against the bottom.

When the surge slowed, he got to his knees in chest-high water, coughing and gasping for breath. He wiped water from his face and was surprised to see blood on his hands. He managed to stand but was caught by the backflow. He leaned into it to keep his balance, but the water washed the ground out from under his feet and threw him down again. The receding current tossed him about as it carried him along until it slammed him against the multiple trunks of an old olive tree where he held on against the rush until the waters left him behind.

Limp and battered, he lay on the muddy ground beneath that lifesaving tree, his chest heaving as he tried to catch his breath. He felt sore all over but experienced no sharp pains when he tried to move. He used the tree to pull himself up to a sitting position.

He looked around and saw nothing but desolation. And the woman he tried to save was nowhere in sight.

Chapter 25

THE GREATEST WAVE

"I must see the King," Cavanila told Torulus, Minos's manservant, when she rushed into his quarters.

"Priestess," he replied with a condescending bow, "the king said he does not wish to be disturbed."

"There has been a disaster. I must see him...now!"

With an obedient nod, he waved her to a seat and entered the king's sleeping room. But she couldn't sit. She paced the room from one wall to the other, her mind on the destructions, until Minos finally appeared, unkempt hair, no jewelry or makeup, holding his robe closed with both hands.

"You were told I was not to be disturbed. What is this about a disaster?"

"Huge waves hit our harbor and washed people, animals, and everything else away. They destroyed all the houses and boats. Bardok said he needs workers down there to search for survivors and help the injured. Didn't you hear the thunder? It's from fires on Thera. My father and his men might be there, maybe Bardok's father too. Maybe they were all killed."

"Be calm, Cavanila. What were you doing down there anyway?"

Before she could reply, Jenora burst into the room. "Sire, there has been a..." She stopped short when she saw Cavanila. "Oh, I see your brother's daughter is here. Do you know what happened in the harbor?"

"Cavanila just informed me."

"There is much to do," she said. "Why isn't your new chamberlain here when we need him?"

"He is down on the lowlands helping people," Cavanila answered.

Jenora ignored her and spoke directly to Minos. "What are you going to do about it?"

"If Cavanila is right, many have been killed. Send priests and anyone else who can help to all the villages along the shore. Send messengers to find out how bad the destructions really are."

"What about Therans?" Jenora demanded. "They should go help too."

"Everyone," Minos replied.

He turned to Torulus. "Find the captain of my guard. Tell him I want him here immediately."

"What else can you tell me?" he asked Cavanila.

"Only what I said before. The waves swept almost all the people and animals near Poros away. All of the ships in the harbor were destroyed. All the shops and houses too. Everything is gone."

Minos turned to his captain, who had just entered the room.

"Everything at the harbor has been destroyed. Take all your men there to provide whatever help you can. Send food and water, and have the wagons bring back anyone who needs care or shelter. And send messengers to find Bardok. I want him here as soon as possible."

"As you command, Sire," the captain said as he backed away and departed.

"Jenora," Minos said, "find shelter for the survivors until their homes can be rebuilt."

"We have no free rooms," she replied. "Therans have filled them all. We should move them out of Knossos to make room for our own people."

"But there are many empty rooms here," Cavanila insisted. "And you can shelter people in your large shrines as well."

"I will not have our sacred places defiled by mobs," Jenora said. "I say move the Therans out."

"Cavanila's ideas have merit," Minos replied without looking at Jenora. "We will first use empty living quarters here in the palace and then decide what other spaces are needed. Give the necessary orders to your priests. And you, Cavanila, be sure all available Therans go to help at the shore."

Minos's servants had already placed lamps around his rooms and provided refreshments for him when Bardok arrived, tired and dirty, his tunic torn. Blood still oozed from his face.

"You look awful," Minos told him. "Sit. Have some wine. What happened to your face? What about the damage in the harbor?"

Bardok eased himself into a seat and emptied the cup Minos handed him. He described the destructions he saw at the harbor and added, "The water washed our crops away and even much of the soil. And what is left has been ruined by the seawater. We will have no harvests from those lowlands, maybe for years. What have you heard from other places?"

"Nothing besides what you and Cavanila told me. How could this happen? I thought the gods looked favorably on us. How will we feed our people?"

"We won't know until we find out how widespread the damage is, and that will take time."

Minos fumbled for words for a few moments. He looked down at the floor. "Since we can't do anything more tonight, I am going to retire. We will decide what to do in the morning."

Without wishing Bardok a restful night, Minos returned to his sleeping quarters, where servants waited to bathe and prepare him for his bed.

Bardok remained seated, still in shock over the enormity of the disaster, while he gathered strength to lift himself from his chair. Cavanila met him as he emerged from the king's quarters.

"I heard you were here. What happened to you?"

"I got caught in a wave, but I am well, just tired. I walked halfway here before I found someone with a wagon and donkey."

"Then come to my rooms," she said. "My maid will help you wash and get you to bed."

They were halfway across the central court when the thunder began again. They stopped, looked at each other for a moment, and climbed four flights of torch-lit stairs, a struggle for the nearly exhausted Bardok. The rooftop was already crowded with people staring northward toward a red glow and white lightning in the sky. Like earlier in the day, the thunderclaps became louder and more frequent until they merged into a continuous roar.

Some on the rooftop fled. Those who remained saw a huge burst of fire. A deafening blast, the most powerful of the day, followed many moments later, nearly throwing Cavanila off her feet. Hot, foul-smelling air had every one choking and racing for shelter. Bardok held her close while he guided her down the stairs, knowing that the greatest wave of all must be on its way. He tried to talk to her but she couldn't hear him over the noise and the ringing in her ears. He could barely hear his own voice.

They found Torulus sitting on the floor in a corner of the king's anteroom, hugging his legs to his chest, his forehead on his knees. With barely a glance, he waved them into the king's bedroom.

Minos was in his chair drinking from his chalice while a young serving girl combed his hair and another arranged the pillows on his bed.

"I heard the thunder," Minos said when he saw them. "What is that terrible smell?"

"It's from Thera," Bardok replied. "We saw a great fire and were hit by a wind so strong it almost knocked Cavanila down. Another wave could be its way, maybe bigger than the last one."

Minos's eyes widened. "What can we do about it?"

"Nothing, right now. I'll return to the lowlands at first light."

"Then you may leave me," Minos replied as he put an arm around the waist of the girl. "But bring me whatever news you receive."

Bardok reached for Cavanila's arm.

"Yes, Sire. I will do that. Sleep well."

The blast also shook Jenora, who stood on another rooftop. She grabbed the arm of one of her priests to keep from falling. They walked her back to her rooms and helped her to her throne. A servant handed her a gold cup filled with watered wine, but she took only a mouthful before throwing the rest on the floor.

"I want wine, not water," she screamed, her voice sounding to her like her ears were clogged or full of water. She saw the mouths of her servants and priests moving but heard little of what they were saying.

"Leave me!" she shouted, sending everyone from the room.

She stared at the gold bull, frightened and confused. Its eyes, reflecting the fire in the brazier near her feet, stared back at her. She spoke to it in her thoughts.

"I understand your anger because of the nonbelievers, but why have you hurt me? What more could I have done? What else must I do? Tell me."

She waited for an answer, but none came.

She rose, as if in a trance, and walked to the middle of her sleeping room. She stood motionless while her chambermaids removed her gown, anointed her body with scented oils from a tiny ewer, and helped her into her bed.

CHAPTER 26

WE NEED THAT FOOD

Cavanila awoke the next morning when she felt Bardok roll over and leave her bed.

"Must you go now? It's still night."

"No, it's morning," he replied as he donned his tunic. "Smoke is blocking the sun. I need to see what happened in the lowlands."

He bent over and kissed her cheek. "I wish I could stay, but I can't."

After Jenora awoke that morning, she thanked her gods that she could hear her servants' chatter as they dressed and fed her. Her four senior-most priests were already in her throne room, deep in conversation when she entered. They stopped talking and turned away from each other as soon they saw her.

"What are you whispering about?" she asked as she took her seat. But none answered or would look her in the eye.

She stared at each of them in turn. "Speak!" she ordered.

One elderly, nearly bald priest stepped forward.

"High Priestess, Poseidon continues his punishments despite our prayers and sacrifices. Now it is darkness. And we have news that another great wave hit our shores last night."

"Why shouldn't the gods be angry?" she replied. "Our king has turned Minoa into a godless state. I warned Minos, but he ignores me. You see what has happened."

They all nodded in agreement.

"Drastic action is required," another priest said.

"What kind of drastic action?" she asked, though she thought she knew what they were thinking.

"We don't know," two of them said in unison.

Yet their faces suggested otherwise.

Angered to think her priests were concealing something from her, she dismissed them. "I am going to Minos. Have your advice ready for me when I return."

"Where is he," Minos demanded when he found Jenora and Cavanila but not Bardok waiting for him in his throne room.

"He went back to the lowlands," Cavanila replied.

Her words brought a smirk to Jenora's face. They must have enjoyed their night together despite the fire and blasts in the sky, she thought. I expect he had her seeing stars of more colors than what we saw over Thera.

"He must have been very worried about the people down there to leave a comfortable bed so early in the morning. Why is he never here when we need him?" She looked at Cavanila and added, "Though it seems he is always there when you want him."

"He went to see to the safety of his people," Cavanila answered, "what any concerned leader would do. Have you thought to inquire about the people down there?"

Minos held up his hand, swallowed the cheese he had in his mouth and said, "Enough. We have important matters to discuss. What, High Priestess, have you been doing to appeal to the gods?"

"We have done everything you ordered. More sacrifices are planned for today and tomorrow. What else would you have me do? Perhaps you should ask the nonbelievers what they are doing to calm the gods."

She was about to leave the room when Bardok entered.

"I thought you were on your way to the harbor," Minos said.

"I was," he replied, "but I didn't get far. Another big wave hit our shores last night. One of the survivors said everyone down there ran for higher ground when they saw the red flash and heard the blast, the same one we heard. They thought they'd be safe once they got above the high water level of the previous wave. But this one came in even higher. He said he saw many workers washed away."

He stopped for a moment to collect himself, his voice filled with grief. "I fear most of my crew were among them. Some were men I sailed with for many years."

"I am sorry for the loss of your men," Jenora said, "but you do not sanctify your ships or dedicate them to the gods. Are you surprised that the god of the seas destroyed your ships and punished you and your crew?"

She began to leave but then looked back at Bardok and said, "You should be glad you survived."

Cavanila and Bardok stared at each other in disbelief. No one spoke, not even Minos, until Cavanila broke the silence.

"Sire, with all our real problems, all she can do is blame others for everything. Hasn't she any better sense than that?"

"She is upset," Minos replied, "I am, too, because we believed we served the gods well. She thinks they are punishing us because the Islanders who came here care little for them, and because I appointed you to your positions." And with a downcast look he added, "Perhaps there is something in what she says. I don't know. I must think about it."

"Sire," Bardok said, "I have served you and Minoa all my life, and I think I have served well. But if you no longer want my services, I will leave Knossos and go elsewhere."

Minos looked up at Bardok. "No, no, I need you. Ignore Jenora's words. I will talk more with her."

"What about me?" Cavanila asked, "Do you still want me to look after Therans?"

"I suppose so," Minos replied, "There is no one else I can trust to do that."

"Do you have orders for us?" Bardok asked, trying to direct Minos's attention to the problems before them.

"What orders can I give? Find out how badly we have been hurt and what we must do to rebuild Minoa. Handoro helped my father do it after the great shaking that once destroyed this palace. You are the chamberlain now. You must do the same. Begin your work and return here in the evening to tell me what actions you are taking."

"What's happened to his good sense?" Cavanila asked as she and Bardok walked back to her rooms. "He acts like my father did."

"I don't know," Bardok replied. "I have never seen him like that. I think Jenora has weakened his spirit and turned him into a blind zealot. He is our king, so we must help him. But if he won't act, we must do what's necessary without him. I am going down to the lowlands now and should return by tomorrow night. Until then, you will have to work with Minos and Jenora to see that everyone here does what is needed."

"But what about Jenora?"

Bardok looked grave. "You will have to do what you can."

"I don't want more bad news," Minos told Bardok the next night at their evening meal with Cavanila and Jenora. "Just tell me how we are going to survive."

"I'm sorry, Sire," Bardok replied, "but you have to know what happened. As I told you before, all of our crops and animals near the coast have been destroyed. All we have left are the animals that had been grazing on higher grounds. We can live off them for a while, but we'll need their meat to get through the winter, and we have to maintain breeding stocks for next year too. Our grain supplies have been shrinking, and we have no boats to send elsewhere for more food.

"Messengers I sent to our other ports have not returned yet, but I doubt their news will be good. I know Malia has been destroyed, and expect Zakros and Kydonia were too, though places away from the coast should be untouched and able to help. I also sent messengers to inform the regents at Phaestos and Arcanes about the great waves and the damage they did. I asked them to double their usual tribute and send it as soon as they could."

Minos sat straight up in his chair.

"You *asked* them? You should have *ordered* them to send what we need?

"Sire, a request from you is an order."

"Suppose they refuse?"

"Then our problems will get worse. I don't know what else we can do. They must comply."

"We won't survive the cold season unless we get more food," Minos said. "Send messengers back to those places. Tell those regents I will tolerate no delays. They must send their tributes immediately or we will take action."

"Are you suggesting we can send armed men to take what we want?"

"I am."

"Sire, we lost most of our fighters to the waves. The few we have left are still searching for survivors and trying to deal with all the destruction. It will be difficult to raise an army."

"We need that food, Bardok."

After Bardok bowed out of the room, Minos turned to Cavanila.

"And what have you been doing?"

"Sire, I ordered my councils to send all able Therans to the lowlands to help, but from what Bardok said, they may have all been killed. We won't know for a while. I also tried to find places here in the palace for needy survivors, but your servants refused to cooperate. They said they only take orders from the priests."

"What do you say about that, Jenora?"

Jenora jumped up from her seat to stand within an arm's length of him, her face as fiery as he had ever seen it.

"I am responsible for what happens in this palace. Not her."

Minos averted his eyes. "Don't be angry, Jenora. We need to find shelter for those who have none."

"I will do it," she replied. "I am the high priestess. Let Cavanila worry about her Islanders."

Minos turned to Cavanila, apology in his voice.

"The high priestess will tend to things here in the palace."

"Then what do you want me to do?" she asked.

"I will tell you when I need your help."

Cavanila took a deep breath and said, "Thank you, Sire. Since you do not need me, I will go."

"What about you?" Minos asked Jenora after he watched Cavanila walk away. "What have you been doing?"

"I told you, we prayed to the gods and made sacrifices, but few attended our ceremonies. My priests say people are too frightened to leave their houses in the strange darkness. You didn't come either."

"I had other things to do. Continue with your prayers and sacrifices."

"I will, but before I go, you should know that when your brother's daughter talks about speaking to her council, she really means she will confer with her handsome assistant, Rhitori. She has been very close to him. Maybe too close. And he is an Islander, someone we cannot trust."

"Don't question my actions, Jenora. I told you before, I am Minos. You will speak to me with respect."

Jenora bowed deeply.

"Yes, Sire, as you wish King Minos. I will do as you say."

CHAPTER 27

I HAVE SPOKEN

It's darker today than yesterday, Cavanila thought when she awoke. She donned her robe and called for Leroma, an elderly maid provided to her when she arrived from Nios. She heard movement in her outer room but no reply.

"Leroma," she called again, "bring me my meal."

Leroma appeared at her doorway. The lamp in her shaking hand lit her face, a mosaic of amber highlights in a sea of blackness.

"Priestess, the darkness...What is happening?"

"Don't be frightened. Smoke is blocking the sun. It's still spewing from Thera. Put the lamp down and bring me my food. And stop calling me Priestess."

"Yes, Cavanila."

Leroma left and soon returned with a tray of cheeses, olives, barley bread, and a ewer of water.

"No milk this morning?" Cavanila asked.

"The man who brings it didn't come."

"Why didn't you go to his house?"

"I couldn't, Priestess, the darkness...I was afraid. Why?"

Cavanila tore a piece of bread from a large slice.

"I don't know why," she replied, "but we have things to do. Go to Rhitori's house. Tell him I need to see him."

Leroma covered her face with her hands and began to cry.

"Why are you crying?"

"Please don't make me go outside."

Cavanila rose from her seat and pulled Leroma's hands from her face.

"Stop it, Leroma. It will soon be lighter."

"I am frightened, Priestess. Please don't make me go."

"Send a servant."

"They all went to the lowlands."

"Then we will go together as soon as I've eaten a little more."

With Leroma trailing behind her in the semidarkness, Cavanila made her way out the east portal of the palace and along a path that went downhill toward the river. Rhitori's house, a single room like the others around it, stood on a winding, unpaved street that paralleled the river. Once in front of it, she called through the curtain that covered its door.

"Rhitori, I must speak to you."

She heard movements inside and a female voice that said something she didn't understand.

Rhitori came through the curtain a moment later, his hair askew, pulling the cloth belt of his apron tight. A young woman dressed only in a blue kilt darted out of the door behind him and ran down the street.

"Yes, Cavanila?"

She glared at him. "Go to my quarters and wait for me."

Cavanila also sent Leroma back to her apartment but didn't go with her. Instead, she walked northward through deserted streets that took her to the hill where Minos's father, Handoro, and others of the Minoan elite lay buried. It was a place where she could be alone to ponder her problems in the morning stillness.

But in her mind she saw the great waves approaching and the devastation they caused. She thought of her father who could not have survived the blasts of such magnitude. He was still her father and she mourned for him. She knew that enormous efforts would be needed for Minoa to recover from such appalling damage. And she worried that Minos seemed unable to provide the necessary leadership.

Bardok is right, she thought. If Minos won't act, we have to do what we can for Minoa despite Jenora's ill will and lack of cooperation.

She nodded her head, as though she agreed with her own thoughts, and in the solitude of that half-lit morning, she walked slowly at first, and then more resolutely back to her quarters. Once there, she rushed past Rhitori and ordered him to follow her into her inner room.

She turned to face him. "How are people reacting to what has happened?"

"Everyone is sad and mournful for those who were lost in the waves, and they are frightened and confused. Even priests are causing us problems."

"What kind of problems?"

"Yesterday morning, guards ordered everyone to help with the destruction down at the shore. But priests came and threatened to reduce our rations if we didn't attend their sacrifices and prayers here in Knossos every day. What are we to do?"

"Why didn't you tell me this before, or were you too busy satisfying your own pleasures?"

"I tried," he said pleading with his hands. "I came to tell you about it last night but you weren't here."

The look on Cavanila's face softened. "You could have left a message with my maid."

"I'm sorry. So much was happening. I knew it was too late for you to do anything about it. I planned to come here this morning to tell you."

"I wish to speak to my council. Have as many as you can find here at midday two days from now."

While Cavanila and Rhitori were speaking, Jenora arrived at Minos's anteroom.

"Tell the king I have important things to discuss," she ordered his manservant.

"Yes, High Priestess," he replied with a deep bow. "I will give the king your message."

Torulus raised an eyebrow when he saw Minos, still in bed, haggard and unkempt, flanked by two serving girls who were feeding him his morning meal. All three looked weary and joyless.

Torulus bowed and kept his eyes on the floor. "Sire, the high priestess wishes to speak to you."

Minos looked up at his servant. "What does she want?"

"She did not say, Sire"

"Tell her to come back later."

"The king is not well this morning," he told Jenora when he returned to her. "He asks that you return later today."

"Did you tell him I had important things to talk about?"

"Yes, High Priestess."

"Then tell him I will not return again until tomorrow."

"I will do so, High Priestess," he said with another deep bow.

Back at her throne room, Jenora summoned Negorti, her most senior priest. A tall gaunt man, his bony, ascetic-looking cheeks set him apart from most of her other priests who looked healthier and much better fed. His gnarled hands and fingers were those of a man in constant pain. The furrows between his brows and his fixed stare evinced a strange intensity. The black of his robe seemed a mirror of his persona.

"What have you to tell me?"

His voice was deep and resonant. "It is difficult to describe how fearful the people have become, and what it may mean for us."

"I want to know!"

"The fires on Thera, the darkness and the cold are driving our people from us. The last shocks and our losses to the waves made matters even worse. Many have shut themselves in their homes and refuse to pray to the gods. When a priest became angered and ordered a family to attend a shrine, two women pushed him out of their house. They were Therans, but many of our own people are acting the same way. Even some priests have lost their respect for the gods."

"We can't let that happen. Everyone must be made to understand that only the gods can save us, and only sacrifices and prayer can satisfy them. Have priests go to all houses with gifts of food to induce people to attend our shrines. I will conduct ceremonies in the central court in two days. Tell them we will have more food for them there and that they need not bring any for offerings."

After Negorti departed, Jenora sent for Alpada and ordered him to make many clay figurines of people, and to have them ready for use as offerings at her ceremony.

Jenora tried to see Minos early the next morning, but he still refused to see her. Instead he summoned Bardok.

"What have you to tell me?" Minos asked as soon as Bardok entered his throne room.

"Sire, I have no good news."

Minos frowned. "Then tell me if you must."

"We received two carts of grain and ten she-goats from Archanes and nothing from other farms and villages. Malia is devastated, and messengers say the same is true of Rhetimo and Kydonia, though in some places the waves were not as high as here. The lowlands around the Beautiful Bay have been destroyed, but Gournia, on higher ground, suffered little. So far as I know, all boats along our north shore have been destroyed. More ash has fallen in the east than here. In some places, it's thicker than a man's finger.

"We are still finding bodies in the wreckage left behind by the waves, and more wash up on the beaches every day. Dead animals are everywhere. Workers are burying people and digging trenches for the animals. The stench there is awful."

Minos took a deep breath but said nothing for a few moments.

"What about Phaestos?" he finally asked.

"Jawana said he will send help. If he does, it should be here in the next few days.

"And my army?"

"Sire, like I told you, we have no men to spare. We lost so many. Everyone is working as hard as they can."

Minos clenched his teeth in an effort to remain calm.

"Bardok, we have been friends since boyhood, but you have to remember that I am Minos. When I tell you I need an army, you are to build an army. We must guard our food stores and make farmers and overseers in the countryside provide what we need. If we don't get adequate supplies from Phaestos with its fertile Mesara, we must take what we need. Do you understand?"

"I understand, Sire."

"One more thing," Minos said. "Take only Minoans into the army. Let the Islanders do the work on the lowlands."

Bardok looked puzzled. "Why should I do that?"

"Because I don't want nonbelievers bearing arms. The gods have brought this destruction upon us. We must be served only by men who believe in them."

"I taught them how to fight while we were on Nios. They know how."

"I don't trust them."

"But we will lose the services of good men."

"Bardok, I have spoken."

"Yes, Sire."

PART III

CHOICES

CHAPTER 28

LET THE SUN SHINE

Only Rhitori and two others of her council attended Cavanila's meeting.

"Where are the others?" she asked.

"Some have been lost, and the rest are frightened," a potter from Knossos said. "They won't leave their houses."

Cavanila looked at Rhitori. "In the countryside, too?"

"It's the same, but there are other problems as well. Some farmers have stopped sending their tributes to the palace. They know it will upset the king, so they are forming small armies to protect themselves."

"That's not all," said a third councilor, a winemaker from a village south of Knossos. "Priests are causing more trouble. One of them threatened to take half of what I earn because I don't pray or make offerings to his gods. Everybody I know is scared, and nobody knows what to do."

"Do the king and high priestess know of those things?" Cavanila asked.

Rhitori shook his head. "If they don't, they soon will."

Minos can't deal with the problems he already has, she thought, and now he has more to worry about.

Aloud she asked, "Would it help if I went to speak to people, to try to calm their fears? Would they listen to me?"

"It would help, Cavanila," Rhitori answered. "They will listen."

"Then I shall. I will first speak to Therans near your shop," she said to the potter. "Tell as many as you can find to gather there at midday tomorrow. Be here before then, so we can walk there together."

"I didn't expect so many people," Cavanila told her three councilors as they neared the chosen square.

The potter moved closer to her and whispered, "I think many of them are Kephtorians, not Therans."

She nodded her head and turned to face the crowd. She saw fear and confusion in their faces. They just stand there, not even looking at me, she thought. They are like the people I saw at Akrotiri. This could be difficult, but I have to try.

"I understand how you feel," she began, her voice weaker than she had hoped, "because I feel the same way. Terrible things have happened. So many have died."

She lowered her eyes, and her voice softened even more. "I believe that includes my father and the men with him on Thera. They could not have survived those blasts."

She looked up at the crowd. Her gaze went from face to face and her voice strengthened. "But the blasts, the waves, and the darkness are not your fault. They are not punishments from the gods. They did not occur because of anything you did or did not do. They just happened, and you must not feel guilty because of them."

She paused for a moment to let them absorb her words, then continued. "Your lives are difficult now. They may be even more difficult in the coming days. But you will survive if you have the will, if you act in ways that are best for everyone, if you work together in fairness, if you share what can be shared in these difficult times. You must understand each other's problems and avoid confrontations. When problems that can't be avoided arise, and I know they will, bring them to your councilor or to understanding priests. If you do as I suggest, your lives will be easier, and Minoa will grow stronger."

She watched their eyes as she spoke about the help they could expect from her and Bardok, the king's new chamberlain, and from the king himself. She saw more of them looking up at her rather than at the ground. A few even smiled. But when she finished speaking, no one spoke out or asked any questions. They just silently drifted away. She had hoped for a more positive response and was left with an empty feeling when she didn't see one.

"What do you think?" she asked Rhitori and her councilors as they returned to the palace. "They seemed to listen but were so quiet. Was I of any help?"

"Cavanila," Rhitori answered, "you heard no complaints or arguments and no muttering in the crowd, despite everything. That wasn't like them. They understood what you said. I could tell. You should speak to more people. Word will spread."

"Then let's go to a country village tomorrow. I will talk to people there and see for myself what is happening outside Knossos."

As soon as it was light enough to travel the next morning, Cavanila and her three councilors visited two small villages to the south of Knossos. She was again surprised by the size of the crowds, which again included both Therans and Kephtorians. Many had obviously left their work to come listen to her.

She spoke as she did the day before, and again people listened quietly and politely and then dispersed with no overt response. Afterward, she walked among the houses, greeting villagers and offering encouragement. Despite their worries, people acted friendly and thanked her for coming but said little else.

On her return to the palace, she told Bardok about her talks and the ideas she tried to instill in those who heard her.

"I was surprised so many came to hear me. I hope I did some good."

"Do you think they will follow your advice?"

"I don't know. They seemed to understand what I was saying. And I saw a little of what life is like for people outside this palace."

But Bardok didn't share her enthusiasm. "You enjoyed it. I see it in your face. Minos won't be happy when he learns you left the palace. And Jenora will be furious because you spoke to Kephtorians as well."

Cavanila couldn't tell if Bardok's statement was a warning or a criticism. "I know, but I did the right thing. I will speak to more people, anyone who will listen. I hope you understand."

"I do, but you have to understand that I serve my king."

A worried look came over Cavanila's face. "Why do you say that?"

"Because if there are more disturbances, I will have to obey whatever orders Minos may give me, even if they make you unhappy."

"I hope that won't happen. But you have to understand that I must do what's best for my people, for all our people."

They glared at each other for a moment.

"I hope you won't interfere," Cavanila added as she walked from the room.

Several days later, Jenora met with Negorti, her oldest priest.

"High Priestess," he said, "the cloud over Thera is getting smaller, and light is coming earlier each day. If the winds don't change, we should see the sun rise over the Ailias hill in a few more days. It would be the first time since the great thunder. People will take it as a sign we have pleased the gods. That would be a favorable time for prayers and sacrifices."

"You are a clever man," Jenora replied. "Arrange for ceremonies to begin in all of the shrines and squares of the town just before dawn on that day. I will conduct the rites in the central square for the people of the palace."

Just before dawn on the appointed day, the residents of the palace and the richer houses outside its walls gathered around the altar in the palace's central square. The golden bull rhyton and the double axe were set in their holders on either side of it. Jenora and her senior priests stood on a roof on the west side of the palace, where they could look down on the altar and the crowds in the square. They were high enough to see the Ailias hill to the east of the residential quarters and the oxhorn-like sculptures that line its roof.

As the eastern sky began to brighten, Jenora, bejeweled in gold and wearing a white, gold-threaded gown, held her arms to the sky. Loudly enough to be heard below, she began her prayer:

Dear Great Goddess,
We thank you and Poseidon,
For ending the smoke and fire on Thera,
We ask now for the morning sun.
We beseech you to continue to look favorably upon us."

She paused until the moment the sun was almost high enough to illuminate the peak of the sacred mountain behind her, and then she shouted in a louder voice:

Great Goddess,
Hear our prayers,
Let the sun shine.

She turned her back to the central courtyard and looked out to that mountain until its top began to glow. She raised her arms again and proclaimed:

You are good to us, O gods,
We thank you again.

She turned to face the courtyard again and stood waiting, her arms in the air, mimicking the horn-like structures on the roofs of the palace, until the sun rose high enough to beam directly on her. She glowed in her radiant gown and sparkling jewelry. People, still in the shadows, gazed at her in awe. The gods had responded to their goddess. They stamped their feet on the paving stones and clapped their hands, rejoicing that better days lay ahead.

Soon afterward, Jenora went to Minos, jubilant and still attired as she was for the ceremony.

"You should have attended my ceremony this morning," she said before she even sat down. "We saw the sun rise again. The gods have accepted our offerings and prayers."

He took little notice of her dress and high spirits. He looked drawn and somber.

"I'm not feeling well this morning," he said.

"Perhaps those young girls are too much for you these days," she replied. Raising an eyebrow, she added "Or maybe they don't know how to treat you as you like."

"What do you know of my problems?"

"Servants talk, Sire."

His head perked up. "What do they say?"

"It seems that none of them can make you as happy as I used to," she said with a wry smile.

"Maybe I am just getting old."

Her smile didn't change. "That is what I heard."

"Tend to your duties, Jenora."

"I will because we still have problems, mostly with the non-believers. They refuse to worship properly and have even abused some of our priests. They are being led by your brother's daughter, who will soon have problems of her own."

"What kind of problems?"

"Bardok doesn't seem to be enough of a lover for her."

"Why do you say that?"

"I am told she visits her councilor, Rhitori, when Bardok is else-where. She has traveled to villages with him and has even admitted him into her sleeping room. I told you once before he was not to be trusted. She can enjoy herself as she wishes, but she doesn't have the sense to be discrete. What will happen when Bardok finds out?"

"Are you going to tell him?"

"No, but you should because of other things she is doing."

"Such as?"

"She has been making speeches against us and the gods, telling both Therans and Kephtorians to resist our priests. Some of our country priests are listening to her, as well. She is dangerous and must be stopped."

"How do you know all this?"

"One of my priests told me."

"Then leave her to me. Continue with your duties."

After she left him, Minos ordered a servant to bring him more wine.

Later that day he summoned Cavanila to his throne room. Jenora sat to his left, her self-satisfied smile made Cavanila think of someone who had just witnessed the punishment of her worst enemy. Bardok, unaware of what was happening, sat to the king's right.

Minos glared at Cavanila who stood in front of him.

"You still cause me great problems, Cavanila. I thought you were a wise person, but you have been telling people to disregard the gods and rise up against me. And you do this with your scribe with whom you have become too close."

"That is not true," she replied. "I have not told anyone to disobey you or disregard the gods. I only said that the gods are not responsible for what happened at Thera or for the cold and darkness."

"And is it not true that you went to your scribe's house early one morning and then invited him into your sleeping room?" Jenora asked.

Shocked to find that Jenora knew so much about her activities and offended by the implied accusation of her infidelity to Bardok, Cavanila responded angrily.

"I did, but only to learn how people are reacting to the darkness. Who has been telling you these things?"

"It matters little how we know," Minos said. "You will no longer represent me among Therans, you will have no council, and you will no longer have anything to do with your scribe. He is a troublemaker who should be punished. Confine yourself to this palace and make no speeches to anyone. If you defy me again, I will banish you from Kephtor. Return to your rooms."

Cavanila paced her floors until she could no longer contain herself. She rushed to Bardok's quarters, but he didn't wait for her to speak.

"I warned you, Cavanila. You were wrong to speak against the king and the gods, whether you believe in them or not."

"But Bardok..."

"You've changed Cavanila. You enjoy your powers too much and you have taken a new lover."

Cavanila scowled at him. Her body stiffened.

"I'm telling you again, Bardok, none of that is true. I have not spoken against the king or the gods, and I don't have a new lover. I love you and only you. Don't you know that? Didn't you believe me when I told Minos that? None of his accusations are true. Who told him all that?"

"I asked the same question after you left us. Jenora said it came from a priest who sat on your council."

"The one Jenora appointed?"

"Yes."

Cavanila tried to explain how that priest came to be on her council. In response, Bardok only said he would question that man himself. But she saw the look on his face and knew he still doubted her.

"I will not let myself be the victim of those lies," she yelled at him as she rushed from the room.

Cavanila realized someone close to her had reported her movements to Jenora's priests and that the only person who knew of her visit to Rhitori's house was her servant, Leroma.

"Why have you been spying on me?" Cavanila demanded as soon as she returned to her rooms.

Leroma slumped into a chair and began to cry.

Cavanila stood over her. "Stop your sobbing. Why did you do it?"

"I had to, Priestess. The priest said the king was worried about your actions. If I didn't tell him who you saw or where you went, he would reduce my family's rations. Please forgive me, Priestess. I meant you no harm."

"Who was that priest? The one who was on my council?"

"No, Priestess. It was no ordinary priest. It was Negorti, the old one who is always with the High Priestess. But the one I talked to most was the young one on your council."

"Leroma, it would be safest for me if I sent you away."

"Please don't," she pleaded. "I want to serve you. If you send me away, no one else will have me."

Cavanila searched Leroma's face for a few moments. "I will allow you to continue serving me, but only if you do as I say."

"Anything, Priestess."

"If you want to stay with me, you will continue to report my activities, but I will tell you what to report and what not to report. If

I find you doing otherwise, I will beat you and send you away. Do you understand?"

"Yes, Priestess."

For each of the next two days, mornings remained bright and sunny. The winds blew the clouds eastward as Negorti had promised. On the evening of the third day after Jenora's ceremony in the central court, a sunset marked by fiery red clouds was so striking that people stood in the streets, enchanted by its beauty. That night, the moon rose, a brilliant white as usual, but by the time it was overhead it had acquired a blue cast.

The sun that rose the next morning was deep red and provided little warmth. That evening it settled behind a curtain that was rising from the western horizon. And on each succeeding day, the mantle grew thicker, darker, and covered more of the sky. It was as though the dark clouds that had been blown eastward were now returning from the west. The days, for Kephtor and the world around it, were no brighter than late twilight. No sunrises or sunsets, no moon or stars, only darkness and cold.

CHAPTER 29

I WILL NOT TOLERATE DISOBEDIENCE

"I don't know how many there were, Sire," Bardok said as he and Drondak stood before Minos. "They pushed aside the guard and emptied the storehouse outside the west wall."

Despite the burning braziers that provided some heat against the unseasonal cold, Minos sat cloaked in sheepskins. Oil lamps lit the room.

"You are both responsible for our stores. How could you let that happen?"

"Three of my guards failed to appear," Drondak said. "Even so, they couldn't have stopped the looting without killing or injuring some people. And they too could have been hurt."

"What about our other storehouses?"

"The ones inside the palace are safe, but there were confrontations at others in the town," Drondak replied.

"I want those guards and everyone who stole from our stores punished."

"We tried to find those guards," Bardok replied, "but it seems they have left Knossos, like a lot of others. They are the only ones who might identify the thieves."

Minos looked surprised. "Why are so many leaving?"

"Life is difficult for people here," Bardok replied. "They get little food beside the meager amounts we dole out. Craftsmen can't barter their wares. Torches and oil for lamps are scarce. Thieves roam the streets or go to the countryside, sometimes in gangs, to steal what they can. Many think they can survive better in the countryside."

"I cannot provide more food because farmers are not paying their tributes," Minos said. "That must stop. I am sending priests to collect what farmers owe us, and I want your guards to go with them to enforce my demands."

"That might be difficult," Bardok replied. "Many farmers now have their own guards. Some have banded together to form small armies. We could have some serious fights."

"Why has no one told me this before?"

"Sire, we have just learned of it," Drondak replied.

"But those country people are not fighters, even if they do have weapons."

"They've been hiring Therans," Bardok replied. "As I once told you, many of them know how to use weapons."

A puzzled look came over Minos's face.

"I didn't know Rhadamantis had an army."

"He didn't. We were worried about pirates when we first started moving people to Nios. Cavanila and I ordered all able-bodied men to train with swords and spears."

"I will not allow every farmer in Minoa to have his own army. Order those farmers to disband their armies and have your guards collect their weapons."

"And if they refuse?"

Minos sat up straight on his throne. His hands gripped its armrests, his voice grew louder. "Don't you understand, Bardok? I will not tolerate disobedience! If they resist, take their flocks and food stores and burn their farms. If we do this in a few places, the others will obey me."

For a while, no one spoke until Minos asked, "What have we received from Phaestos and the Mesara?"

"Three carts of grain and ten goats," Bardok said. "And four of those were old males."

"That is an insult. Send guards. I want ten carts of grain and one hundred animals from them now and more later. If Jawana refuses, take what we need."

"Sire, we don't have enough men for that."

"No more excuses, Bardok, or I will get someone else to command my guards."

The two men, once good friends, faced each other with a degree of mutual antagonism that neither had experienced before.

A move against Phaestos like he wants would require a large force, Bardok thought. I don't have one and don't have enough men or time to train one. And burning farms will only hurt our food production. How could he possibly want me to so that?

Minos, for his part, felt that Bardok had failed him and was questioning his judgment. I have all these problems, with no one to help—not Bardok, not Jenora, not even the gods. I'm alone. My father would know what to do, but he can't help me either.

Bardok finally broke the silence. "I'll do my best. Please excuse me."

"Your servant said you wished to speak to me," Jenora said when she entered Minos's throne room.

"You claimed you appeased the gods. Why have we returned to darkness?"

"Sire, we pray and make offerings every day. I don't know what else to do."

"Then think of something."

"I have been thinking. My priests say there is one final offering we can make to the gods. Something that hasn't been done since the days of our grandfathers' grandfathers. And so serious that I will not do it unless you approve."

Without waiting for a reply, she went on to tell him about her meeting with Negorti and her other priests.

That meeting occurred two nights earlier while twilight was turning into real darkness.

"High Priestess," Negorti said as he stood in the light from candles and oil lamps that lit her throne room, "our prayers and sacrifices remain unanswered."

Behind him, the other priests shook their heads and murmured their assent.

"There is only one more thing we can do," he continued, "something we have never before considered, the greatest offering we could make to the gods—the sacrifice of a living person."

Jenora pretended surprise. She suspected they had been thinking about this since the day after the great explosions. And she had been considering it herself.

"It would be the final thing we could offer," she said. "How would we choose a proper victim, and where could we do it? Who would the gods be happiest to receive?"

"As I once told you, High Priestess, stories from our grandfathers say that the shrine on the side of the sacred mountain was built for that purpose. You passed it on your way to its top. It has never been used for anything else, so far as I can remember, and few even know of its existence. We think a nonbeliever should be sacrificed. It would be just punishment and demonstrate our servility to the gods. But you must choose who it will be."

Jenora suppressed a smile. She had already decided who it would be.

"The king will have to approve of such a drastic thing," she replied. "I will speak to him about it."

"Sire," she said after she finished her story, "my priests say we have no choice if Minoa is to survive."

"I know such things occur in far off lands, but not here," he replied. We don't sacrifice humans."

"Our ancestors did," she said, and they built a special shrine for that purpose. I know it's a dire and fearsome step, but Minoa has never been so threatened. It is the only thing we have left to offer. If you know a better way to appease the gods, tell me what it is."

Minos looked down at the floor. "You decide. I have other things to worry about."

He looked up again to meet her eyes. "But the reason I summoned you is to talk about the tribute our farmers owe us. Why are we not getting more?"

"Because farmers know their products become more valuable every day and that you will do nothing to punish them if they refuse to pay. Why shouldn't they try to keep what they have?"

"You are supposed to be collecting those tributes."

"Sire, their only concern is to feed themselves and see to their wealth. They barter for gold and silver or for workers in exchange for miserly amounts of food. They get richer by keeping what they owe us. They no longer believe in the gods and don't respect my priests, or even you as high priest. I perform my duties as I should, but you are the one most responsible. If you made everyone worship the gods as they should, we wouldn't have all these problems. It all started with the Therans."

"It's not my fault, Jenora, I made you my high priestess because I thought you could deal with the gods. You boasted about your successes when we saw a little sun, but Minoa still suffers. Tell people I have ordered Bardok to send guards with your priests to collect our tribute and punish those who would deny us. I will be respected"

"Priestess," Leroma called to awaken Cavanila from the doorway of her sleeping room. She entered the room and placed a lamp on the low table next to Cavanila's bed.

"Priestess," she said again to be sure she was awake. "Rhitori is here to speak to you. Shall I have him enter?"

Cavanila sat up and reached for her robe.

"Of course," she said.

Rhitori's hunched shoulders and nervous hands told her he had something serious to say. There must be, she thought, for him to risk Minos punishing both of us if he knew of our meeting.

"Cavanila," he said, "there is trouble in the countryside. Two days ago, a wagon with a priest and driver and several shepherds appeared in a village near Archanes. They were accompanied by four guards who demanded everyone's weapons and half of every farmer's animals. When the villagers refused, the guards became abusive. There was some pushing and shoving, and a fight broke out. The guards became frightened because they were so few among so many people. They wounded several villagers with their spears. The priest was also frightened and ordered his group to turn around and come back here. The villagers thought that would be the end of it, but it wasn't."

"They should have known better," Cavanila said.

"They should have," Rhitori continued. "More guards arrived the next day. They burned all of the farm buildings and took everyone they could find—men, women and children—as servants. Farmers have now formed large armies of their own. They have people watching the roads and pathways to the villages to warn of approaching guards. It's like a war. Where will it end?"

"I will see Bardok in the morning," she replied. "He has to stop this. Whatever happens, we must tell farmers to pay their tributes and avoid senseless confrontations. And don't get into any fights yourself."

"Those were your guards, Bardok," Cavanila charged after she told him what Rhitori said. "How could you let that happen?"

But Bardok lashed back at her. "The king said you were to have nothing to do with Rhitori. He would banish you if he knew. Don't say you were not warned. Those villagers got what they deserved for holding back their tribute and arming themselves in secret. I do not like what is happening but I will obey the king's commands. I have told you before, and I am telling you again, do not defy the king. Do not have anything to do with Rhitori. And stay out of things that no longer concern you. I leave on a mission in the morning, but if you force me, I will place a guard near your quarters to see that you remain in the palace and receive no forbidden visitors."

Too upset to reply, Cavanila rushed back to her rooms. *He's treating me like a prisoner because I don't want people to get hurt. I won't tolerate guards watching everything I do and everyone I talk to. I won't.*

CHAPTER 30

A BROAD SMILE ON HIS FACE

The next morning, Bardok led a band of forty men, each with a spear and short sword, and ten oxcarts south toward Phaestos. The wagons contained food and supplies for his men and large empty storage jars to be exchanged for similar ones filled with grain at their destination. A drover walked beside each animal.

The route from Knossos followed a mountain stream before turning uphill and crossing a low ridge on the north end of the sacred mountain. After another half-day on the lowlands beyond, their path turned uphill again, into the mountains that form the spine of Kephtor.

Even before the Theran eruption, this would have been a difficult march at this time of year. The weather would be turning cooler and windier, especially at higher elevations, and the rains would have just begun. But that catastrophe made conditions far worse. Kephtor was now fixed in daylong twilight. The rains began earlier than usual. A mist obscured the highlands and snow already covered the high passes through the mountains.

The road, the only direct route between Knossos and Phaestos, was wide enough in places to allow carts moving in opposite directions to pass each other. And thanks to Handoro's foresight, a center strip along much of it was paved with flat stones so wagons and people on foot could avoid slogging through deep, sticky mud.

Bardok and his troop encountered only light, intermittent rain since they left Knossos, but it left them wet and cold. His men walked with their heads down and spoke little to each other except in hushed, complaining tones. Bardok saw their downcast expressions and sensed their mood, but he maintained a forceful pace. Vactor, who was posted at the rear of the group, had no need to prod them to keep moving. Walking faster helped them stay warm.

Bardok had his own misgivings. Not much of an army, he thought. They could have used a lot more training. I don't know how many fighters Jawana can muster, but I hope I can convince him it would be better to satisfy Minos's demands than to start a deadly fight.

Two days later, on their way out of the mountains, they came to a turn in the road that gave them an expansive view, despite the semidarkness, of what lay ahead of them: the fertile Mesara plain with its cultivated fields, groves of olive, fruit, and nut trees, grazing sheep, goats, even a few hogs and oxen, and the palace of Phaestos beyond.

"That's why we've come," Bardok told his men. "We will go back up the road and camp there for the night. Light no fires, and be careful to make no sound. We don't want Phaestians to know yet that we are coming."

By the middle of the next day, they had come down out of the mountains and begun their march through olive groves and fields of barley and lentils that seemed healthy despite the near darkness. They surprised the shepherds and farmers, a few of whom raced to the Phaestos palace with news of Bardok's approaching band.

That palace, a smaller version of Knossos, sat on a high, steepsided ridge. It commanded a view of the fields and groves to the north, where Bardok's force now openly moved. To its south, it looked over another fertile plain and the sea beyond. A well-used road led from the palace south to its harbor, a trading site for vessels sailing west along Kephtora's southern coast on their way from Egypt to the mainland. Another winding road climbed the west slope of the ridge. A more direct but steeper footpath with occasional steps cut into the hill provided the only other access to the palace.

As Bardok's group approached the palace, the captain of Phaestos' guard came down the path to welcome them and offer to take Bardok to Jawana, Phaestos's regent. Before leaving his men under Vactor's command, Bardok settled them into a defensive formation with his fighters encircling the wagons and animals in an open field. He then accompanied Jawana's captain back up the path, through a pillared portico lined by craftsmen's workshops, and around the side of a large, multistoried building. They climbed more stairs to a courtyard laid out like the one at Knossos, and across it to a reception room where Jawana sat under a large light well. He was smiling, but with malice in his eyes and disdain in his voice.

"You must be Bardok," he said. "My lookouts told me you were coming. We have heard of you and your exploits. I knew your father and am sorry to hear he is missing. I can understand your coming with many carts. We know Knossos needs food, but why so many armed men? Surely you don't think gangs of marauders will try to steal what little we can give you for your return trip across the mountains."

"Thank you for your thoughts about my father. King Minos sent me to demand that you pay your full tribute to Knossos. My armed men are just a token of our army. We have come to uphold King Minos's demands."

"I see. Of course, you realize we know how weak Knossos has become since the great waves destroyed so much of your land and killed so many of your people. My men who brought you our last contribution were not blind, they heard what was being said in your marketplaces. We can talk more about your king's wishes, but it will soon be time for our evening meal, and your men must be tired and hungry. Why don't you bring them up to our court yard? I will provide refreshments, and we can discuss your King's demands in greater detail."

But Bardok didn't want his fighters in an enclosed space or separated from his wagons and drovers.

"Thank you for your offer. I am sure my men would appreciate your food and drink. But I think it best if they remain where they are and that I stay with them. I could send men for the food you offer."

Jawana smiled. He understood Bardok's caution. "That will be fine, but you need not send your men. Please just enjoy my hospitality. My servants will bring you food."

"Thank you. I will now rejoin my men."

By the time he returned to the top of the stairs, Bardok could see his troop in the same formation in which he had left them, except now they had their body-length ox-hide shields up and were surrounded by Phaestians, who far outnumbered them. Most were armed with spears, short swords, and axes but none, Bardok noted, were archers or carried shields. To his relief, no fighting had yet occurred. He passed through them with no difficulty and went directly to Vactor to review defensive tactics.

Soon afterward, three carts of food and drink came down to them via the circuitous road on the south side of the palace. The sword hanging from the leader's belt identified him as a soldier, not a servant.

"I have a message for you, Chamberlain," he said when he stopped the carts within the circle of Bardok's men. "The regent is ready to sup and he invites you to join him."

"Please tell the regent that I thank him for his food and hospitality, but I will remain with my men. Tell him I would be pleased if he could sup with me here."

A little later, with the skies even darker, Jawana followed torchbearers down the path and approached Bardok.

"I hope you are pleased with the food I sent," he said." I have already eaten so let us discuss your demands over some wine before I return to my quarters."

They sat on skins and waited silently until servants handed them cups of wine.

"With the darkness and cold weather," Jawana began, "we have little food to spare. However, I am willing to send the king three carts of grain and a herd of goats, perhaps thirty, but no more for now."

"That is not enough," Bardok replied. "King Minos demands at least ten carts of grain and one hundred animals."

"Bardok, I understand that Knossos is in need. I want to help you, but we are in need too. You lost many of your best men in the great waves, and I would not like to see you lose those you brought with you as well. So I will make you a final offer. I will let you have five wagons of grain and fifty animals. If you insist on more, you had better prepare your men to fight."

Bardok took a long drink from his cup while he considered his options. *If I return to Knossos with only half of what Minos wants, he'll accuse me of cowardice and another failure. Yet Jawana's men far outnumber mine. Even if some of us survived I would lose valuable men and return to Knossos with nothing.*

"Very well," he finally said. "I will take what you offer, so long as you agree to send your allotted tribute to Knossos each moon."

"The grain will be ready for you in the morning and the animals will be waiting for you along your path back to the mountains." was all Jawana said as he rose and climbed the path back to his palace.

The day after Bardok left for Phaestos, Cavanila went to his rooms to talk to him. She had left him so abruptly when they last spoke that she never learned about his mission or how long he would be away. She was surprised and angered to find him gone.

Too agitated to return to her quarters, she walked out to the central court and visited the shops of craftsmen who practiced their trades within the palace. She didn't stay out long, but the short respite helped clear her mind.

"I must get a message to Rhitori," she told Leroma when she got back to her rooms, "but you have to avoid Bardok's guards. Leave the palace through the north portal as if you are going into the town to barter for something. If you are sure you are not being followed, turn toward the river and go to Rhitori's house. Tell him I must speak to him but that he should come during the darkest part of the night. If anyone questions you, tell them I sent you to get more cloths. I am having a severe case of moon sickness with stomach aches and much bleeding, and I have to remain in my bed for several days."

"Priestess, are you ill?"

"No. I haven't bled in two moons. Just do as I say. And call me Cavanila"

"Cavanila," Leroma said after she returned, "I gave Rhitori your message. He said he will come late tonight. I don't think there will be any problem with guards because I saw none when I was leaving or when I returned."

"Thank you, Leroma. You did well."

Cavanila waited most of the night, but Rhitori didn't appear. Eventually, she fell asleep and awoke the next morning wondering what had happened. Perhaps he saw guards and was afraid to come, she thought, or maybe guards stopped him. Or maybe Leroma was untruthful and didn't see him at all.

While she was still eating her morning meal, Leroma rushed into her room and said, "Rhitori's girl wishes to speak to you. Something bad has happened."

"Bring her in."

It was the same girl Cavanila saw leaving Rhitori's house the morning she went there. She was hysterical.

"Priestess," she blurted out, "they took Rhitori away."

CHAPTER 31

HE KNOWS

"Who took him away?" Cavanila demanded. "Where did they take him?

"Priests. We were asleep. They tied him with ropes and took him away."

"Are you sure they were priests?"

"One of them had a lamp. They wore priest's robes and carried no weapons. I woke when two of them grabbed me. I tried to scream, but they put a cloth in my mouth. They put a cloth in his mouth, too. They tied a blanket over him and took him away. A tall priest with a deep voice said they'd take me too if I told anyone. What will they do to him? I shouldn't have come. What will happen to me?"

Cavanila took hold of the woman's hands. "What is your name?"

"Dorella."

"Dorella, I don't know what is happening but I will find out. Stay here with Leroma. I will return soon."

Unable to find Bardok, Cavanila rushed to Jenora's throne room.

"She bathes," a young priestess said, "but I will tell her you are here."

The wait seemed interminable to Cavanila. Jenora, when she finally appeared, looked dressed and made up as though prepared for an important ceremony.

"What is so urgent, Cavanila?" she asked.

"What have you've done with Rhitori. I want him freed."

"Has something happened to your lover?" Jenora asked with no attempt to hide the same smirk Cavanila had seen before.

"He is not my lover. And you know very well your priests took him during the night."

"I know no such thing. If you cannot find him perhaps you should search houses where widowed ladies sleep."

"Where is he?" Cavanila shouted.

"You unbelievers are the cause of all our problems. Do not interfere with the will of the gods."

Cavanila's eyes widened, a shudder went through her body. Jenora had confirmed her suspicions. Realizing she would get no more information from her, she rushed to see the king. Minos's servant said the king was occupied and would not see her.

She ran back to her own rooms.

"Dorella," she said, "do you know the people who sat on my council with Rhitori?"

"I know some."

"Then find them. Tell them I want them to meet me at Rhitori's house tonight."

Cavanila turned to Leroma.

"Go to your priest and talk to anyone else you know. Try to find out what happened to Rhitori. Someone must know something."

Cavanila then ran back to Minos's throne room. This time he agreed to see her.

"I know nothing about Rhitori," he told her after she repeated Dorella's story. "Talk to the high priestess if you think he was taken by priests."

"I did. She knows what happened but she won't tell me."

Minos didn't reply. He remembered the conversation he had with Jenora about a sacrifice. His face reddened and his eyes went down to the floor, but he said nothing.

He knows, Cavanila said to herself as she watched him grapple with his guilt, but he won't tell me.

"Where is Bardok? When will he return?"

"I sent him to Phaestos to claim the tribute we are due. He should return in a few days. I warned you to have nothing to do with Rhitori. If you had listened to me, perhaps Rhitori would still be here. You and your Therans have brought this down on us. Leave me. I have nothing more to say to you."

Cavanila then ran back to Jenora's rooms.

"She is not here," her servant told Cavanila. "She left the palace after she spoke to you. I do not know where she went."

Cavanila found Dorella waiting for her back at her own rooms. "I found two of your council members," she said. "They will come to Rhitori's house after full darkness."

Leroma appeared shortly afterward. She said she had talked to many people but learned nothing about Rhitori.

Rhitori lay tied up and gagged on the floor of an oxcart headed south into the hills. A priest sat next to him. Four others walked alongside. Once out of hearing distance from Knossos, the priests stopped the wagon. Two of them climbed up onto it, uncovered Rhitori, and pulled the gag from his mouth. One held his nose despite his attempts to shake free while another poured wine laced with juice of the poppy into his mouth whenever he opened it to breathe. He choked but had to swallow as he struggled for air. They repeated the treatment each time he tried to breathe until they thought they had forced enough into him. They then replaced the gag and watched over him until he descended into sleep.

Rhitori next awoke deep into the night, naked and cold, his hands and feet bound, shocked to find himself lying on a stone altar. His blindfold was off but the gag remained in his mouth. He saw he was in a large room lit by numerous candles. Pictures of bulls, goats, and sheep in the midst of trees and blooming lilies covered most of its walls. In one corner, a ewe was pictured on an altar like the one on which he lay.

The two priests who watched over him saw he had awakened and forced more wine into him until he slept again.

Bardok returned to Knossos the next morning and went directly to Minos.

"You only got half of what I demanded," Minos said. "Why didn't you take what we need? You had armed men with you."

"Sire, we were surrounded by a much larger force. With my untrained men, I saw little chance of overcoming them in battle. We would have lost many good men, maybe all of them, and gained nothing. I decided to take what Jawana offered and avoid the fighting. He promised to send more at each moon."

"I thought you were a fighter, Bardok, not a coward. And why didn't you take a larger force with you."

Bardok glared at Minos. "I am *not* a coward. I told you how many people we lost in the waves. I told you how weak we are. I took every man I could find who had ever carried a weapon. I could have taken more if you had allowed Therans into our army."

Minos refused to listen.

"You failed me again, Bardok. You didn't protect our storehouses, and now you refused to fight for our food. I have so many problems and no one I can depend on for help, not even you. You think you can decide which of my orders you will obey and which you will not. I don't need a chamberlain or army commander like you. I am the king. And now I will also be my own chamberlain. Vactor will command my army."

Bardok straightened his shoulders.

"Then you no longer need me. I will leave Knossos, maybe go to the harbor to help build some new boats."

"No, I have another mission for you, something you refused to do before. Maybe this time you will obey me. Take guards to outlying farms and villages. Begin with one or two. Take their food and whatever valuables they have and burn their houses. Make examples of them. Maybe others..."

But before he could finish his statement, the room began to shake. Both men and everyone else in the palace fled into the central court. As the noise grew, rising dust reduced visibility to the length of one or two strides. Everyone used cloths or part of their garments to protect their faces. They heard crashing sounds but couldn't see their source. Only after the shaking ended and the dust settled did they see that the roof over the fourth story of the living quarters had collapsed. Bardok didn't wait for orders. He quickly organized a search of the rooms below the damage and found no one had been hurt. He returned to the courtyard to report his findings to the king.

Thankful for Bardok's information, Minos returned to his throne room and again tried to summon Jenora, but his messenger returned with news that neither she nor Negorti could be found.

She must have done what she said she would, Minos thought, but where are they? Could Therans have found out about it and retaliated?

"Have guards bring Cavanila here," he told a messenger.

Cavanila went willingly, walking faster than the two guards who trailed behind her.

"Jenora cannot be found," Minos said as soon as she entered his room. "What have you done with her? You and all your Therans will be severely punished if she isn't returned."

"Sire, don't you remember me telling you that it was Jenora and her priests who took Rhitori away? I want him back."

"I don't care what you want. What did Jenora tell you when you spoke to her?"

"She said she knew nothing about Rhitori. But I know she had him taken away."

"Return to your rooms, Cavanila. I am tired of your accusations."

"Sire, we can help search for both Jenora and Rhitori. Let me use my people."

"Very well, but you will remain restricted to the palace once they are found."

At about the time Minos was charging Bardok with cowardice, Rhitori, lying on the stone altar, wasn't sure if he was awake or having a frightful nightmare. He tried to move but could not. Menacing figures stood over him. The one behind him grasped his hair and pinched his nose. As before, another one poured wine laced with juice of the poppy into his mouth when he tried to breathe. He coughed and swallowed hard as he again gasped for air. When they decided he'd had enough, they let him rest. His chest stopped heaving and his breathing slowed. His eyes closed but he remained half-awake.

He felt his body being shifted toward the edge of the altar. He opened his eyes to see the high priestess in her sacred gown bending over him, a jeweled dagger in her hands, her breasts close to his face, her nipples hardened with excitement. She stared at him through widened eyes made deeper by their outline of kohl. He saw her reddened lips moving and heard her chanting, but didn't understand her words. His eyes closed again as if on their own accord. Though still in a trance, he felt something hit his chest, and the altar begin to shake. He heard the roar and her screams and the shouts of a deep-voiced man. He forced his eyes to open and saw Jenora staring up, terror on her face. He looked up too just as the ceiling collapsed on them.

CHAPTER 32

THERE IS SOMETHING ELSE
I NEED TO TELL YOU

"Bardok, did you hear what happened?" Cavanila asked when she finally found him.

"Yes. It was good no one was injured when that roof collapsed."

"That's not what I meant. Some priests took Rhitori away, and Jenora can't be found."

"I didn't know."

"We have to find him. She is going to hurt him."

"Why would she do that?"

"I don't know, maybe just to punish me. She once caused one of her priests to disappear because he wanted Therans and Kephtorians to live together in peace. We need to find Rhitori."

"Cavanila, I am no longer chamberlain or the commander of Minos's army. He was angry with me because I did what I thought best for Minoa. He said I was disobedient and a coward. Now he wants me to take food from farmers and burn their farms. I don't know what to do. I hope Jenora and Rhitori will soon appear, but there is little I can do to help."

"I am so sorry," she said as she went into his arms.

After a long embrace she pulled back and said, "You have been loyal to him since you were boys. To have him treat you that way must really hurt. And to give you such an awful task. Please be careful whatever you decide."

She took his hands before he could reply. "There is something else I need to tell you."

"What?"

"I think I am with child."

His face lit up, and he smiled for the first time in many days. "That's wonderful." He gave her another hug that had her gasping for air.

"Are you sure? Are you feeling well?"

"Yes, I am sure, and I do feel well."

"This is not a good time for you to be in Knossos. You must go to the countryside where there is more food, someplace where you will be welcomed and safe."

"I can't go. I can't leave Knossos until we find Rhitori."

"That could take a long time. You have to think about our child."

After a short pause, she said, "I will go at the proper time. But you must come with me."

"I can't, Cavanila. If I refuse Minos's orders, the next person he appoints might be more brutal with the farmers than I would be. But I will find a place for you."

"Someplace where I have friends, where I can meet with more of my people, despite what Minos says. They need me."

"I think Minos will approve, but it must be safe."

"Then find me such a place. I'm going to talk to my councilors now. Minos said I could until Rhitori and Jenora are found. Come to my rooms when you can."

"I will be there," he replied with another big smile.

On her way to her quarters, Cavanila passed a small flock of sheep and goats that had been wandering around the central court, but she paid little attention to them. Her mind was a mixture of happiness, her own and what she had brought to Bardok, and dread over Rhitori's safety. She found her councilors waiting for her in her outer room. None had any news about Rhitori or Jenora.

"We must find him before she harms him."

"Cavanila," one of them said, there is something else you should know."

She stared at him, wary of the look on his face and the ominous tone of his voice.

"What's happening?"

"Since the riots at the storehouses, people have been stealing everything they can. The grain in the king's storehouses is now more heavily guarded and is being doled out in tiny amounts. Some who have a sheep or two or a goat are keeping them inside their houses, especially at night. Our only other food is what hunters bring from the forests, and that won't last long. You saw the goats and sheep in the courtyard."

"I did. Why are they there?"

"Because it is the only place where they can be protected. They are the animals Bardok brought from Phaestos. But they won't last long either."

"Many have gone outside the town to barter what they have for food but return with little," another added. "Some tried to move their families to the countryside, but farmers won't let them stay."

"What about fishing?" she asked.

"Priestess, the sea is poisoned. Dead people and animals still wash up on the shore; dead fish too. People won't eat anything from those waters."

Cavanila took a deep breath and said, "I do not know what we can do about food, but we have to keep searching for Rhitori."

"My councilors are searching for Rhitori everywhere they can think of," Cavanila told Bardok later that day as they sat at a low table in her sleeping room. "What else we can do?"

"There are tales that people have become lost in tunnels under this palace," Bardok replied, "but I don't know where they are and neither does Minos. We ordered a search for them because he is as upset about Jenora's disappearance as we are about Rhitori. We searched all the tunnels we know of, but found nothing."

"What if we don't find them?"

"I don't know, Cavanila, but I hope we do and that Rhitori is not hurt. I don't know what Jenora will tell Minos when she returns."

Before Cavanila could answer, they heard a loud pounding on the outer door to her quarters. Leroma came to announce that one of Bardok's officers had a message for him.

"King Minos wants you in his throne room," he said. "There's fighting in the streets."

"Tell Drondak to assemble guards in the courtyard," he told the messenger. And to Cavanila he said, "I must go, but be prepared to leave Knossos as soon as we find a place for you."

Eight days later, Cavanila saw Bardok approaching the farm where she had been staying. He was alone except for one of the lookout who escorted him in.

They kissed and hugged for a long time until Bardok stepped back to look at her.

"You don't look like a woman with child."

"Maybe not but I've missed my blood for the third time. You might not see it yet, but I can feel the changes."

"Actually I do see it. It's in your face. It glows."

Cavanila's face broke out into a sunny smile and her whole body relaxed. She gave him another hug.

"I'm so happy to see you, but why have you come?"

"Much has happened since you left Knossos."

Cavanila saw sadness in his face and uneasiness in his posture, a demeanor she had never witnessed in him before. He seemed like a dispirited man.

"Let's go someplace where we can be alone," she suggested.

They walked out into a nearby forest and sat among oaks and pines on sheepskins they brought with them. Bardok took her hands in his.

"I don't know where to start. I should first tell you that Rhitori and Jenora have still not been found. They must be well hidden wherever they are. Could they be lovers?"

"That's not possible. My people have no word of them either. I am so worried about him. But you look like something else has happened. What is it?"

"The riots we had before you left were just the beginning. We put them down with only a few injuries, but as the days passed and with food even more scarce, there was more violence. A crowd attacked another of our storehouses. Many on both sides were injured and a few were killed. But Minos still refuses to release any food. And there have been riots at other towns like Malia and Zakros. Buildings have been burned. It made me sick inside, but I had to send guards to more farms, to take their food and destroy their buildings, like Minos ordered. The farmers fought back, and you can imagine the deaths and injuries on both sides. Some survivors ran into the forests.

"Cavanila, I didn't mind using force to take tribute owed to the king. But to take everything and destroy those farms is wrong and senseless. Minos got angry with me again when I told him how I felt. He said Knossos needed that food more than it needed me. He said if that was how I felt, he could do without me."

Cavanila moved closer to him, put an arm around his waist, and took hold of his hand. "I am so sorry. You and your father served Minoa for so long. Minos was your friend. Can't he understand how you feel? How can he turn against you like that? And what will happen now? Will other farms will be raided?"

With sorrow on his face and in his voice he said, "I think so."

"Then we need you to tell us what to do if we are attacked here. Our headman is out in the fields and won't return before our evening meal. In the meantime," she said as she laid back on the skins and pulled him down to her, "no one can see us, dear Bardok, and I have missed you so."

"Do you think it wise? What about the baby?"

"You will have to be very gentle."

"I will be, dear Cavanila."

While supping that evening, Bardok outlined defensive strategies for the farm's headman and for Cavanila. The next morning Bardok dispatched messengers to inform other villages and farms of his instructions. He also spent time teaching more men about the use of arms.

Several days later, around midmorning, a breathless runner appeared at the farmhouse.

"An unarmed man is approaching," he said. "He might be alone, but our lookout remained in place to be certain he is not just a scout for guards who might follow."

When the visitor arrived, he sought out the headman and said, "We have been ordered to inform all farms that the commander of King Minos's army is looking for Bardok, who was once the king's chamberlain. He ordered us to say that Bardok's help is needed at Knossos."

Bardok stepped forward and said, "I am Bardok. Have some food and drink, and we will return to Knossos together."

"I'm glad you came," Vactor said as soon as he saw Bardok. "Everything here is in shambles. Minos pays little attention to anything except his wine. Not even his women. He can't even decide how food should be doled out. The goats and sheep you brought from Phaestos are still in the courtyard. Servants bring them fodder, and they are being milked, but people clamor for their meat. The place reeks with droppings. There are a few old males that could be slaughtered, but Minos can't bring himself to do it. I told him several times that he needed you back, but all he does is cry that he misses Handoro and Jenora. Late yesterday he finally said he wished you would return. So I sent messengers to find you. Let's go to him now."

CHAPTER 33

YOU CALL ME A FAILURE?

Bardok watched Minos walk to his throne. His red eyes and unsteady gait verified what Vactor told him about the king's drinking. A golden goblet already sat on the small table in front of his throne.

"What is it?" the king asked without looking directly at either of them.

"Sire, Vactor said you wanted my help."

"He thinks you should be my chamberlain again, "but I don't know. Can you do better than you did before?"

"If you are asking whether I can deal with all of Minoa's problems and calm the people, the answer is no, at least not by myself."

Minos looked up. "Then what?"

"I can manage some of our problems, but I am not the person to end the unrest here. Only one person can do that."

"But we cannot find Jenora."

"I am speaking of Cavanila, not Jenora. You know how she succeeded on Nios. Her people love and respect her. She is respected by Kephtorians as well. You need a high priestess. Appoint Cavanila. She could bring peace to Knossos."

"I have said it over and over. She has been a problem for me since the day you brought her here. She defies me constantly and is not a believer. How can I make her my high priestess? I will not have her."

"Then you will not have me, either."

Bardok's voice was calm, but Minos understood the ultimatum. He reached for his goblet steadied it with both hands as he drank.

"What can she possibly do?

"She has a rare ability to induce people to work together. She can bring order and calm."

Minos hesitated again, turned his reddened eyes away from Bardok.

"Have her come," he said.

"He finally realizes he needs our help," Bardok told Cavanila when he returned to her. "He asked me to be chamberlain again, but I told him I would only do so if he made you his high priestess."

"Why did you say that? You know I no longer believe in the gods."

"Cavanila, we have serious problems. I can deal with some of them, but you are the one people will listen to. As high priestess you could bring big changes to Minoa."

"What would I do with all those priests?"

"That would be for you to decide."

She paused for a few moments, overwhelmed by Bardok's proposal, and shocked to think that Minos would even consider it.

"I will speak to him, but I will not become his high priestess unless he lets us rule as we did on Nios."

"I understand.

"And you will have to help me do what I think best."

"I know," Bardok said as his face broke into a broad smile. "And one more thing."

He opened the small bag that always hung from his belt. "This is for you." He handed her a gold pin, the one he didn't get to give to Lovanna before she died.

"It's beautiful. But why?"

"It is something I have treasured for a long time. I want you to have it."

"So you want to be my new high priestess," Minos said when Cavanila and Bardok stood before him the next morning.

"No, Sire, I do not. At least not like Jenora was."

"Then why have you come?"

"I came because our people, all our people, need help."

Minos's head snapped back. "Are you accusing me of ignoring my people?"

"Sire, I know you want what is best for Minoa, but our new problems mean we have to change how we govern Minoa."

"And you think you can cure all our problems."

"I think Bardok and I together can govern as we did on Nios."

"But why should you be the high priestess? You are not even a believer."

"Because priests rule in towns and villages. They know their people and their people know them. I don't want to interfere with that. They can retain whatever beliefs they have in their gods and perform religious ceremonies as they wish. But they will not use their gods or beliefs to control how people live."

"What about me? I am the king and the high priest."

"Sire, you will still be king and high priest. You can still revere your gods and direct Minoans in worship as you wish. Bardok and I will deal with the practical needs of our people."

"And if you fail?"

"Then Minoa won't be any worse off than it is now."

Minos sat up straight. His eyes widened and his voice grew louder.

"You call me a failure?"

"No, Sire. Only that our problems require a different way of dealing with them."

"So you think the ways of my father and his fathers before him can no longer be followed. You think we can no longer rule according to the gods. You think you can risk their wrath. Haven't you seen what happens when they become angered? Don't you understand their power?"

Cavanila tried to keep her voice soft and gentle. She understood how difficult the situation was for Minos.

"If you are pleased with what is now happening in Knossos and elsewhere in Kephtor, Bardok and I will return to the countryside and not interfere. But if you want to stop the bloodshed and help your people, let us try our way."

Minos took another long drink from his goblet and began to shout.

"If you think you can make the sun shine again, if you can end hunger and restore the power of Minoa, then go ahead. I give you my authority."

He tore his necklace with its seal ring from his neck and threw it at Cavanila who, in her surprise, failed to catch it.

"Do as you wish," he continued, "but if you fail, the gods will see to your punishment."

He rose to his feet, took up the goblet, and walked on unsteady legs to his sleeping room.

Cavanila picked up Minos's necklace and looked at Bardok.

"This is a small ring, but it's a great weight we must bear," she said. "Can we really do as we said?"

"I don't know, but I think we can do better than what Minos has done."

"Oh, Bardok," she said as she went into his arms, "I hope you are right."

A young priest hurried toward Cavanila when she entered what was now her throne room.

"The high priestess is not here," he said.

She held Minos's ring for him to see.

"I am now the high priestess. This is my throne and these are my quarters. Inform the elder priests that I want to see them here. And send Jenora's personal maid to me."

It took him a moment to recover from his surprise. "Yes, High Priestess," he finally replied as he bowed and left the room.

Cavanila sat on the throne for the first time, her shoulders against its back, her arms on its rests. Images of her father and of Minos ruling from their thrones, and of Jenora from the seat Cavanila now occupied, ran through her mind. She realized the power it symbolized and wondered at the burdens she had now assumed.

"Leroma will continue to be my personal maid," she told the woman who had served in that position for Jenora. "You may remain here as her helper if you wish to serve me. Do you?"

"Yes, High Priestess."

"What is your name?"

"I am called Tuma, High Priestess."

"Tuma, go to my old quarters and inform Leroma that I want her here. The two of you will bring my personal possessions with you."

What had been Jenora's inner circle of priests remained silent as they stood before her, hostility and contempt on their faces.

"Jenora is missing and can't be found..." she began to say when one of them blurted out, "Some of our priests are missing too!"

Cavanila paused. Her instinct told her that she had just heard something important, though she didn't understand why.

"Who is missing?" she asked. "What happened?"

"Negorti and four others," one of them replied.

"Have you looked for them?"

Again, silence.

"Then send word throughout Kephtor that Negorti and the others have disappeared and need to be found."

She held up Minos's seal-ring for them to see and said, "What I started to say is that King Minos has appointed me high priestess in Jenora's place."

She heard their muttering and saw their agitated movements but she ignored them.

"We have serious problems, but with your help I intend to see to it that Minoa and its people survive and return to prosperity and greatness. To do so, we need to change the way we rule Minoa."

"What changes, High Priestess?" one of them asked while his eyes were on the other priests rather than on her. The smirk on his face showed his disdain. "It is the gods who tell us how we must act."

"You will look directly at me when you speak," she replied. "I will tolerate no disrespect. If you wish to remain priests, you will do as I order. I understand the gods are important to you and most other Minoans. I do not wish to change that. You and your priests may follow your beliefs, perform your ceremonies, and counsel people regarding their beliefs. But you will no longer indulge yourselves at the expense of the people or threaten their well-being in the name of your gods."

"Then how do we control people or collect tributes?" one of them asked. "And how will you govern without the gods to direct you?"

"Those of you who agree to serve and others I appoint will act as a council to oversee the activities of priests and priestesses in ways I have just said. But people's daily lives will be governed by a separate council. I will send runners to all outlying areas and into all the neighborhoods of the towns to tell everyone that they are to choose people to represent them on that council. Those council members will make my orders known to everyone and keep me informed of what is happening in their regions. They will see to the distribution of food and collection of tributes."

"But that is what we do," one of them said.

"Not anymore," she replied. "You must each make a choice. Those who wish to be part of our new way may stay. Any who do not may leave."

The priests looked around at each other, thinking about their options. Three, who had established their wealth through years of service as part of the ruling aristocracy, turned away and walked from the room. The others, still unsure about what to do, remained standing in front of her, silent, even sullen.

"Fine," she said. "Choose one from among you to speak for you and select more priests for your council from towns and villages. I will meet with your council in three days."

"We have so many problems," Cavanila told Bardok at their evening meal.

"But the most immediate ones are to stop the violence and find more food," he replied.

"Actually, they are the same problem," she said. "We could slaughter most of our male goats and sheep and distribute their meat. We can also open our grain stores a little more."

"Cavanila, our food won't last long that way. What will you do if you distribute what we have and little comes in from the farms? How will we survive through the cold season?"

"I think I am well enough respected so farmers will provide us with what they can."

As a military commander, Bardok's life was built around a constant concern for contingencies. It frightened him that Cavanila was willing to risk the depletion of their food stores on just the hope that farmers would replenish them because of their goodwill toward her.

"Suppose they don't have much to send? All the farms along the coast have been destroyed. The darkness and ash are ruining what crops we still have. Our flocks have suffered too."

She looked at him, surprised by his critical tone. "Then we might have to take more drastic actions."

"What kind of drastic actions?" he asked. He saw her squirm in her chair and was sorry he upset her with his challenging question. Yet he knew it was a critical one she needed to consider more seriously.

Cavanila was indeed upset with him because of his persistent questioning, but mostly with herself. I shouldn't have been so quick to answer without first considering what it meant, she thought. Is that how kings and people like me come to terrible decisions, saying things or making decisions without understanding their consequences? How could I be like that? Am I really a fit guide for Minoa?

When she replied, her voice had softened to a level that Bardok could barely hear. "I need to think about it."

CHAPTER 34

I WILL MAKE YOU A A TRADE

The next morning, Bardok took Cavanila on a tour of the palace's storage rooms. Each contained one or more rows of person-high storage jars for grains, beans, and lentils, but many were already empty. She finally understood why Bardok was so concerned about husbanding their food supplies and why she had to be more frugal with them. But that led to other difficulties. The people of Knossos soon became disillusioned when they found she provided them with little additional food. Crowds again gathered around the entrances to the palace to clamor for larger distributions. Confrontations with guards at storerooms outside the palace became more frequent, and, like before, some turned violent.

Despite her sickness each morning, Cavanila spent days traveling with Bardok to nearby farms and villages. At each place, people came to greet her as soon as she stepped from Bardok's chariot. Farmers and village headmen offered her refreshments and acted pleased to see her, until she told them she came to insist they provide Knossos with the tributes they owed. They nearly all said they could afford to send little but would try to comply with her wishes. But few actually did. And those who did sent only a few goats or sheep or a single waist-high clay jar of beans or grain.

"Only Phaestos has rich-enough lands to provide us with enough food to get us through the cold season," Bardok told her. But Jawana sends only trifling amounts. We have to back our demands with force, like Minos said."

"I think there is a better way," she replied, "especially since you don't yet have enough of an army. I will go to Phaestos myself as soon as my sickness ends."

"What can you do there that I could not?"

"We still make the finest quality of woolen cloth, jewelry, and painted vases. I will offer Jawana everything we can produce in trade for enough food to last us until the warm season begins. I will tell him that Knossos remains the largest city in Minoa and will again become the strongest and most powerful—powerful enough to depose him if he fails to comply with our demands."

"Cavanila, he considers Phaestos to be an independent kingdom, strong enough to defy Minos, and himself to be an all-powerful ruler. I will go with you and bring as many soldiers as I can."

"No, Bardok. I will just take an escort. Remember, my father was once regent of Phaestos. I will be welcomed there."

"I am not so sure of that, Cavanila. Jawana is a strange man who could do strange things."

Cavanila sent Jawana a message saying she wished to visit him to discuss important matters. Two days after receiving his reply that he would be most pleased to receive her, she departed for Phaestos with Leroma and Tuma in a horse-drawn cart. Vactor commanded her escort, which followed on foot. When they arrived late on the second day of travel, Jawana met them on the road where it crested the ridge just outside his palace. He was a tall and broad-shouldered man, but what stood out for Cavanila were his high cheekbones, prominent brows, and deep-set eyes. They projected an intensity she had never before experienced in a man, not even with Bardok or Minos.

"Welcome back to Phaestos, High Priestess," he said with an exaggerated bow and a broad smile. "You must be pleased to be returning to the home of your childhood, though I see you are no longer a child. You have developed into a beautiful woman. We have prepared rooms for you in the best part of the palace. From your window you will be able to look out to the north, over our fertile Mesara plain."

"Thank you, Regent," she replied, "I trust my escort will be housed nearby."

"Actually, High Priestess, I planned to provide them with rooms on the south side of the palace."

"That puts them too far away from me. I will order them to camp on the grounds just to the north of the palace."

"If that is what you prefer," he replied. "Tonight we will feast in the great hall. I will have a servant call you when we are ready to begin."

The stairway that descended to the narrow corridor through which Jawana's servant led her looked familiar to Cavanila. Once she saw the square pillars and the paintings on the walls of her room, she realized that this had once been her mother's bedroom, where she had played when she was a little girl.

After bathing and a brief rest, Cavanila considered her dress for the banquet. She knew Jenora considered herself the embodiment of the Mother Goddess and the Goddess of Fertility and would normally choose her ceremonial, open-bodiced gown to emphasize her personification of those roles. She also understood that she was expected to dress similarly and that her pregnancy would only enhance her status as a symbol of those goddesses. Yet Jawana's manner made her uncomfortable about exposing her growing breasts in his presence. In the end, she settled on her Minoan gown but wore a diaphanous veil over it. Her condition also required her to leave the gown's constrictive belt tied loosely around her already expanding waist.

Jawana met her at the door to his banquet hall. He had dressed the way Minos often did for formal occasions, a sleeveless purple jacket that left his chest exposed and a knee-length blue apron with gold threads running through it. His hair hung loosely down his back and he wore no hat or makeup. His only jewelry was the gold seal ring he wore on a gold chain around his neck. The elites of the palace, including a few elderly priests and wealthy merchants were also there to welcome her, the first high priestess of Minoa to visit Phaestos in many years. They stood in front of their stone seats that ran along the walls of the hall and bowed to Cavanila as Jawana walked her to her seat. They were fascinated by her youthfulness and beauty, but her somewhat unconventional dress raised eyebrows among several of them.

"Fashions must have changed at Knossos," the wife of one of the merchants whispered to her neighbor. "Maybe we should start wearing veils like that too."

Without taking her eyes off Cavanila's torso, the second one leaned toward the first and replied, "If mine were like hers, I certainly would not."

Before the meal began, Jawana's priestess stood and prayed to Poseidon, asking for his forgiveness and begging him to let the sun shine again. She poured a libation from her wine cup into a depression in the offering table in front of her and sat down.

Compelled by her role as high priestess, though not a believer, Cavanila rose to her feet.

"May the sun shine and may Minoa prosper again," she said as she poured a libation of her own, sipped from her cup, and sat again. The others in the room repeated Cavanila's actions, all except Jawana. Though he was the high priest of Phaestos, he poured no libation and made no appeal to the gods. He only ordered the food to be served.

The meal was the most sumptuous Cavanila had witnessed since the darkness began: roasted lamb, a variety of cheeses, fresh fish baked in olive oil, dried figs, olives, bread still warm from the ovens, and much wine. But with her starving people always on her mind, she ate very little.

Several times, Jawana stood to propose toasts to Cavanila and Minoa, but he never mentioned Minos or Rhadamantis.

Throughout most of the banquet, Cavanila and Jawana conversed quietly. He noted how little she ate but said nothing about it. He asked if she was pleased with her accommodations and whether she recognized the room that had once been her mother's. They also talked about Jenora's disappearance, about trade, and the problems of living and raising food in perpetual twilight. She told him Knossos needed more food and reminded him that he had not paid the tributes he owed.

When she offered to exchange Knossos' products for more food, he ignored what she said. Instead, he told her that Mycenaeans had taken over many islands to the north and seemed to be spreading their empire southward toward Kephtor.

"Be wary," he said. "They wish to extend their power all the way to Egypt. They know you are weak and want your harbor for their ships. Fortunately, we here at Phaestos are protected by the mountains and will survive long after Knossos has been sacked. You would do well to join me here and leave your beloved chamberlain and his useless king to preside over the final destruction of Knossos."

"You underestimate Knossos," she replied. "We are a strong and gifted people. We will recover and again rule the northern seas."

She is beautiful and spirited, he thought, but she is young and innocent. It is time she learned a lesson. He rose and offered her his hand to help her rise.

"We must speak more about Knossos's problems," he said, "but in private."

While others continued with their feast, he walked her to the room across the corridor from her mother's where they sat on piles of sheep skins in the light from a single oil lamp.

"Do you remember this room?' he asked.

"I do."

"So it must have some special memories for you. It has some special memories for me too, but they are not as pleasant as yours. I will soon tell you about them. I am glad Thera did well while your father was regent there. That trading center made all Minoa stronger, including Phaestos. It also brought more ships to our port here at Komo and provided us with many trading opportunities. Ships continue to stop here on their way from Egypt to the mainland. And our trade with them remains strong and profitable despite everything that has happened. You see, we don't need your products."

He paused to let her consider his statements and then asked, "Do you know why Minos moved your father from here to Thera?"

But Cavanila wasn't listening. A sudden feeling of weakness had passed through her body when she realized he had swept aside the only inducement she could offer for more food. She felt confused and demoralized, unsure of what she could still accomplish with him.

When he received no reply, Jawana asked his question again.

"No, I do not," she answered this time, wondering why he raised the subject.

"Then I will tell you. It was because of the scandals he caused here. His final act was to bed the wife of the captain of his guard, and he didn't care enough to be discrete about it."

Cavanila stared at him but said nothing.

"It wasn't the first time he did such a thing," he continued, "but in that case the husband rebelled. He took his objections to the priests and rallied his troops around him. He made speeches condemning Rhadamantis's behavior and sent word to Minos that Rhadamantis had to be removed from Phaestos or he would take strong action on his own. Minos appreciated Rhadamantis's help in setting up rules of trade, but he couldn't tolerate an uprising here at Phaestos. That is why you and your family were sent to Thera."

His eyes narrowed, a deep furrow appeared between his brows. "You didn't know about that, did you?"

"No. I did not, but it has nothing to do with why I am here."

"Oh, but it does," he replied. "You see, I was that captain, and the lady was my wife. She claimed he raped her but could never explain what she was doing in his quarters, in this very room, across the corridor from your mother's room. My wife was a comely woman, as lovely as you. I divorced her and sold her in exchange for a beautiful, young horse. I have waited many years for a more fitting revenge."

"My father is dead."

"No matter. You came to trade. I will make you a trade. Spend one night in my bed, and I will see to it that Knossos gets all the food it needs to survive through the cold season. If you refuse, Knossos will get nothing. I will not force you. It is up to you to decide. But think about your children who are already starving."

Cavanila jumped up from her seat and glared at him. Her hand went to Minos's seal ring on its chain around her neck.

"I am the high priestess of Minoa, not a servant. I will not be treated with such insolence. I regret my father's behavior but I will not pay for it with my body. And you will regret your behavior."

As she turned to go, he said, "I don't usually sleep here but I will tonight. Come if you should change your mind."

Cavanila hurried back to her room and sent Leroma to tell Vactor to have her escorts ready to leave for Knossos at first light. She ordered both her maids to sleep on her floor and went to bed with a dagger at her side. But her anger refused to let her sleep.

That cur! How dare he? He wants my body to avenge my father's misdeeds. He even thinks I might let him have it. I am a princess and the high priestess of Minoa. I am not a settlement to redress a dead man's wrongs, even my father's. I am not a wench who sells herself for a price.

She turned onto her side and sobbed into a woolen blanket. But I have to keep my people from starving. How could I face seeing chidren die if I might have been able to get them the food they need? Should I go to his room? It would be a small sacrifice and a meaningless act. But if I did, he might just use me like one of his servants and discard me in the morning. I would have to trust him to keep his promise. But would he?

As the night wore on, her anger and worries rolled continually through her mind. Her thoughts grew darker and more frightening. If he wished, he could kill my guards and keep me here as his servant or even do to me what he did to his wife. And what about my baby? Bardok was right. How foolish I was to ignore his warnings.

Sleep finally came to her just before dawn, but her troubled mind allowed her no rest. She saw herself stepping over her maids and walking across the corridor. She stood in the doorway to his room.

In the soft light from a single candle, she saw him lying there, wide awake, eyeing her, a lurid grin on his face.

"How do I know you will do as you say?" she heard herself ask.

"You will have to trust me."

She leaned against the doorjamb for a moment and then stepped into the room.

"I am with child. You will have to be very gentle."

"I will be, dear Cavanila," he replied just as Leroma shook her awake.

"There's trouble," the maid said.

Cavanila jumped up, pulled on her robe, and rushed outside. Her escorts, drawn into a tight circle, swords drawn, shields up, and spears at the ready, were surrounded by Jawana's much larger forces. She stood terrified, thinking that the worst of her fears was about to occur.

Jawana approached her closely, a broad but cold smile on his face.

"Don't look so frightened, High Priestess," he said in a voice low enough so no one else could hear. "There will be no fighting. Just remember that you could have enjoyed the night with me and returned to Knossos with all the food your people need. Instead, you chose to remain virtuous. Now you will return with nothing. But I could not let the high priestess of Minoa depart without some tribute. So I have brought you a gift."

At his signal, a shepherd came forward with a single male goat on a tether.

"Please accept my small contribution to Knossos as a symbol of what you could have had. And remember the opportunity I offered when you see your children dying."

He signaled his troops to clear a path for Cavanila and her guard and walked back to his palace.

She looked at Vactor, hoping he was not close enough to hear Jawana's words.

"Let us go," she said.

Empty handed and dejected, Cavanila led her group to the road back to Knossos. Jawana's troops followed as far as the mountains to make sure her men took no more animals or food as they passed through the Mesara.

Bardok listened as Cavanila told him about the dinner and Jawana's rejection of her offers. But she did not tell him about her father and Jawana's wife or the exchange Jawana offered her. She feared he would react too violently and attempt some kind of action before his forces were really ready for it.

Even so, when he heard about the goat, he jumped up from his seat. "I warned you about him. He's no better than that goat. He will pay, Cavanila. He will regret that insult."

"I am angry too, but we have to concentrate on surviving."

"Just until the mountain passes are open again. By then, my army will be strong enough so we can take what we need and punish him as he deserves.

"But that's a long way off. How do we feed our people until then?"

"We have few possibilities and none are good. The forests will provide some meat, but they will soon be depleted. We could also harvest fish, eels, and crabs from the river, but that won't amount to much, either."

"What about the seas?"

"Bodies of people and animals have stopped washing up on the beaches, but the waves are now so high that fishermen can't go out in their boats. Some try to cast their nets from shore, but even that's risky this time of year, and their yields are small."

"So what else is there?"

"Nothing, Cavanila. Nothing."

CHAPTER 35

PLEASE, NOT AGAIN

As the dark, frigid winter progressed, Cavanila saw fewer people in the streets and desperation on the faces of those who did venture out. She attended increasingly frequent funeral processions, always in anguish, castigating herself with thoughts of how she might have prevented them. When she could no longer tolerate it, she let her priests represent her and seldom left her rooms. Yet the faces of hungry children tormented her night after sleepless night.

Over and over, she compared herself to her father. Am I any different? I hated that he cared so little for others, not even for my mother. His own wants always came first. Maybe I am worse. I might have prevented much suffering with a single act, but I refused to try. I served myself ahead of my people—just like him.

Her remorse made it difficult for her to eat, to take food away from others, as she perceived it.

"You must eat more," Leroma kept telling her. "You are getting too thin. Think of your baby."

But she could not eat more, and the healthy glow of her early pregnancy disappeared.

Bardok spent most of that winter devising a plan for an attack on Phaestos. He, too, spent sleepless nights brooding about the Phaestos palace atop its hill, about its walls, and its few easily defended entrances. He knew a direct attack by the kind of army he could raise had little chance of succeeding. He had to find another way.

He saw how important archers had become for hunting and how valuable they would be for his nascent army. He provided them with new types of bows and arrows. In addition to the simple bow of cypress wood, his workshops built composite bows made of wood and the horns of wild goats, something he had learned about on one of his trips to Egypt. They required much more strength to draw, but the speed, distance, and accuracy of arrow flight were all increased.

He also designed bronze arrowheads that had broader, chisel-shaped points. They had less penetrating power than the simple points but were better for severing structures closer to an animal's surface, such as its arteries and tendons.

With the help of Vactor and Gantaros, he schooled the archers in the new weapons and organized contests. With prizes of increased rations, they provided incentives for men to improve their skills. The contests also helped him identify the strongest, most accurate marksmen and the most productive hunters.

He had other problems, too. He had to wait until the mountain snows melted and the roads across them became passable again. But he couldn't delay his assault too long because almost nothing remained of Knossos' stores. And the warmer weather would bring calmer seas and increase the likelihood of the Mycenaean invasion about which Jawana warned Cavanila. Knossos would be nearly defenseless with Bardok and his forces over the mountains.

"There are always risks," Minos said one morning when Bardok went to him with his concerns. "Come back in a few days, and we will talk more about it."

When he returned, Bardok found Minos conferring with Drondak.

"One moment, Bardok," Minos said when he saw him. Turning back to the captain, he said, "You know what I want done. Proceed with the preparations."

Bardok stood bemused by the unexpected changes he saw in Minos. He looked stronger and more alert than Bardok had seen him in a long time. He sat upright on his throne, his attitude was more positive, and his voice more resonant. He wore a short-sleeved jacket that left his chest exposed instead of a dirty robe, and his long hair had been combed smooth. He was even clean-shaven.

He's like his old self again, Bardok thought. Dealing with a threat he feels he can handle seems to have restored his confidence. I like it.

"Concentrate on your mission to Phaestos and let me worry about the Mycenaeans," Minos told Bardok after the captain had gone. "They are not likely to come during the few days you are away. But if they do, I think I can hold them off until you return. Just leave me a few good archers."

Neither man considered the possibility that Bardok and his men might not return at all.

When Bardok discussed his intentions with Cavanila, she said, "We need that food, but remember, the people of Phaestos are our people too. I don't want anyone killed or injured unnecessarily. Not even Jawana. He needs to be punished for refusing to send us our rightful tribute and for the way he insulted me, but I don't want him killed because of it. I don't want you hurt either."

"It's hard to know what might happen once we are there," he replied. "I can make no promises."

Yet something else she said stuck in the back of his mind. That was the first time I've heard her say that Jawana had insulted her. Something serious must have happened that she hasn't told me about. But if she wants revenge, she will have it.

As winter progressed, the light-absorbing clouds thinned and the sun on some days could be seen as a bright orb. Even so, it was a cold, wet winter. Snow blanketed the mountains and sometimes even the lowlands. The weather was particularly harsh for Knossos and the lands on the north side of Kephtor's mountains. At the same time, breezes off the great deserts across the seas to the south helped temper the weather at Phaestos and other areas along Kephtor's south coast.

Spring came late and offered little relief. Sheep and goats dropped fewer live young and olive trees produced little fruit. Barley and beans, planted in fields untouched by the waves with the last of the seeds showed some green above the soil, but the plants were stunted. To put even greater demand on the already meagre food supply, large numbers of women became pregnant that winter. Normally a cause for celebration, that by-product of the dark and cold only worsened an already serious situation.

By the time mountain roads became passable, Cavanila's pregnancy was far advanced. Bardok wanted her and her unborn baby safely away from Knossos during his absence. He knew she would refuse to leave if he suggested it, so he went to Minos for help.

In response to Minos's summons, Cavanila went to the throne room, where she found Bardok seated to the king's right. Something about the looks on their faces made her wary. When the king tried to usher her to her usual seat on his left, she declined. She stood in front of him instead and waited for him to speak.

"Bardok will soon leave for Phaestos," Minos said. "If the Mycenaeans attack us before he returns, we could be forced to abandon this palace or perhaps suffer worse consequences. For your safety and your baby's, and for the good of Minoa, you will leave Knossos until Bardok and his forces return and the danger of a Mycenaean invasion is over."

"What do you mean for the good of Minoa? I can't leave my people while they are in danger. Where would I go?"

"Let me worry about the danger. There is an old settlement called Trapeza in the mountains to the east, where you can be safe and well cared for. Just above it is an ancient cave. It overlooks a huge, flat, and swampy land surrounded by mountains. If we have to abandon this palace, we could live up there until we regain our strength. If necessary, we could also build a new town higher up those mountains, in a small valley below a peak that looks like the head of a pin. It is too far from the sea to attract sea raiders, and visibility from that peak is so good that no raiders could approach it without being seen. Its steep walls make it defensible if they should try. Our ancestors once built a shrine up there. You will direct the people in that region to be ready to receive us should we need a refuge."

"Can I travel there in my condition?" she asked as she put her arms around her protruding belly.

"I'll take you in my chariot," Bardok said. "A runner could make it there in less than a day, but we will go slower, take two or three days if we must. And there are villages along the way where you can rest. Your maids can follow in carts."

"I will go," Cavanila said after a brief pause, "but I need time to get ready and to give my people instructions."

"While you are doing that, order the priests to hide our valuable possessions in the hidden compartments under the floors of their shrines. Take whatever they cannot hide with you to the mountains."

"I will, Sire," she replied.

"One final thing, Cavanila, the name of your baby. If it is a boy, I would like him to be called Staphylos. It is a happy name that refers to our vines. I once had a son by that name, but he died soon after he was born."

Cavanila nodded. "It is a good name. Do you agree, Bardok?"

"I think it is a very good name," he replied.

Cavanila and Bardok departed Knossos on his chariot two mornings later. Ass-drawn carts carrying Leroma, Tuma, Cavanila's possessions, and numerous gold pieces followed behind. Cavanila placed a bundle at her feet when she stepped up onto the chariot.

"What's that?" Bardok asked. "Why don't you put it in one of the wagons with your other things?"

Cavanila gave him a shy look and opened the skin wrappings to show him the gold bull.

"Have you become a believer again? Are you going to pray to Poseidon while we travel?"

"I have not become a believer again, and I will not be praying. I think this bull is beautiful. I love the sparkle in its eyes. We will find a safe place for it in the mountains."

Their route that day took them down the Royal Road toward the harbor and then eastward along the devastated coast. They hadn't gone very far before Cavanila realized that standing in Bardok's bumping chariot was too difficult for her. She changed places with Leroma so she could continue the trip sitting or even reclining in one of the carts. Before they reached Malia, they turned north into the mountains. Two days later, they arrived at their destination on a high plateau. By then, Bardok and her maids had to help Cavanila from the cart. They settled her into one of the houses below the cave entrance.

The next morning, Bardok buried most of the valuable objects they brought with them in the back of the cave that, according to legend, had been used for living quarters and burial grounds since long before the days of their ancestors.

However, Cavanila asked Bardok to bury the bull rhyton at the top of the peak that Minos had described. "I love the way it points to the skies," she said. "It's a much more suitable place for that beautiful animal."

"It's a long way off, and I need to leave for Knossos tomorrow, but I will do as you wish."

The sun was at its zenith by the time he found the wide path an elderly villager had described to him. He followed it until he came to the goat track he was told about. He left his horse and chariot there and began his climb on foot until he reached a spring, where he refreshed himself.

From there, the path upward was steep, ill-defined, and rocky in most places. Footing was difficult and he sometimes had to hold onto a shrub to avoid sliding backward. He eventually reached a plateau that contained only a small shepherd's shelter. He walked on nearly level ground for a few steps before again having to work his way up an even steeper hillside to the peak.

At the summit, out of breath from exertion in the rarified air he was unaccustomed to, he searched for a place to bury the rhyton. The ground in most places was too rocky for digging with his short sword, but he eventually found a spot on the north side of some ancient ruins that was mostly soft earth. He dug as quickly as he could, laid the skin-covered rhyton in the hole, and refilled it. He smoothed the earth, scattered some rocks around it to disguise the site, and immediately began his descent. By then, the sun was already on the horizon.

He moved as quickly as he could, sometimes working himself down over rocks in a sitting position, sometimes sliding down them almost uncontrollably. It was nearly dark by the time he made it back to the spring. From there on, the terrain was less steep and he followed the path easily in the light of a partial moon.

"I'll be leaving in the morning," Bardok said to Cavanila as they lay in bed that night. "Our raid on Phaestos should take about seven days. If everything goes well, I'll return here in eleven or twelve days."

He gently stroked her bulging belly. "I don't think Staphylos is going to give you any problems until after I return."

"I hope you are right," she replied as she cuddled next to him.

Five days later, Bardok led his army out of Knossos in three groups of one hundred men each, mostly archers and spearmen. Vactor commanded one group, Gantaros another, and Bardok the third. Oxcarts with their drivers and shepherds made up a fourth group. They camped that first night under a full, blue-tinted moon near the first way station on the road across the mountains.

Cavanila's pains began late that same night. They were mild at first with long intervals between them. As the night passed into morning, they came more frequently and were more intense. Messengers were sent to Minos and Bardok at first light to announce the impending birth.

On the second morning of his army's march, Bardok sent fighters ahead to control the guard stations along the route and to interdict any lookouts Jawana might have posted along the road. But they found none. They reached the edge of the great plain by nightfall and camped in the forest just above it. They lit no fires and maintained strict silence.

Early the next morning, Bardok's forces separated into three groups. Vactor's group circled the plain to the east, remaining out of sight in the forests. Gantaros' group did the same to the west. While Bardok waited for those units to get into position, a messenger arrived from his rear to tell him Cavanila's birthing pains had begun. The men around him slapped his back and congratulated him.

He thanked them for their good wishes and walked a few paces away to be alone with his thoughts and forebodings.

Not again. Please, not again. It's coming early like Lovanna's baby. And she died. Be strong, Cavanila, don't let it happen to you. Please Cavanila, don't die.

Arriving runners forced him to refocus his attention. They told him his encircling units were in position. He mounted his chariot and led his own group of one hundred men and his oxcarts openly down the road toward Phaestos. Most of his cohort wore the tunics of craftsmen. His best archers, dressed in animal skins, looked more like farmers. He led them to a point about halfway across the plain and stopped to await Jawana's response. When none came, he ordered his men to begin rounding up animals from nearby fields and take any food stores they could find in nearby farms. Except for some minor resistance, they avoided violence. He also sent a local farmer to the palace with the message that he was taking all of the tribute that was owed to King Minos.

Jawana's men, a few archers but mostly swordsmen and spearmen, soon spilled out of the palace. Jawana, at their head, drove a chariot drawn by a powerful and spirited black stallion. When close to Bardok's position, Jawana drew up his horse to examine the forces in front of him. Bardok's forces, he thought, were no larger than his own. He drove his chariot closer to Bardok and stopped again.

"What is it, Bardok?" he shouted. "I see you have a few more farmers with you than you had last time. Do you think I am going to let you take whatever you want?"

Bardok didn't reply and ordered his men to remain motionless.

"Can't make up your mind, Bardok? Or are you afraid? I would be too with the bunch of potters you have around you. Unless you want to see them slaughtered, turn around and return to Knossos."

With still no reply from Bardok, Jawana shouted again, "I appreciate you giving my men more time to rest. What are you going to do?"

Bardok turned to speak softly to his group. At his signal, his spearmen formed two rows behind him while his archers circled around to shooting positions on both of his flanks. In response, Jawana ordered his own troops to draw their swords and be prepared to charge.

"I see your men are better trained this time," Jawana shouted, "but they are still no match for my men. Go home before I get angry."

"Jawana," Bardok replied, "before you do anything, let me teach you some things about tactics. For one thing you have made one of the greatest errors a commander can make. You underestimated your adversary. You and your men concentrated on me and the troops I have behind me. But you failed to watch your rear."

Jawana and his men whirled around to see Vactor's and Gantaros' groups in position behind them. Their archers had their bows drawn and spearmen were poised to protect the archers if Jawana's swordsmen should charge.

"You outnumber us," Jawana admitted, "But your farmers are still no match for my fighters."

Bardok turned, spoke to his archers, and turned back to Jawana.

"Then it's time you learned another thing."

At his signal, four of his archers let chisel-pointed arrows fly. All lodged in the throat of Jawana's prized horse. It reared up and, after a brief struggle, collapsed, upsetting Jawana's chariot and forcing him to jump clear.

Enraged, he drew his sword.

"Hold!" Bardok shouted. "My men are better trained than you thought. My archers may be no match for your swordsmen in a hand-to-hand fight, but your men will all take arrows before they are close enough to use their swords. And you will too."

Jawana's men drew back into a defensive circle.

"It is I who will now dictate conditions, Jawana. You and your men will drop your weapons and, as you put it to me, turn around and go home. If you do not, on my next signal, my archers will let loose their arrows. They are now aimed at all your throats. You can send a wagon later for your horse's carcass. His meat could feed many people for a while. So drop your spears and swords, now!"

In disgust, Jawana threw his sword to the ground and signaled his men to do likewise.

"You will be sorry, Bardok," he yelled as he began walking back toward his palace.

After a few steps, he turned and yelled again. "Bardok, ask your beautiful darling if she enjoyed my hospitality."

Bardok sensed something sinister in Jawana's words, but he only replied, "Jawana, thank your gods that I let you live."

Bardok's men gathered up the abandoned weapons and continued their raids on the local farms. They filled their carts with containers of grain, cheeses, and any other stores they could find while his shepherds drove hundreds of sheep and goats back up the road toward Knossos.

Bardok longed to race back to Cavanila, but the animals and loaded carts slowed the army's advance. He thought about leaving the force under Vactor's command and driving to Cavanila as rapidly as he could. But he knew he couldn't abandon his men to any contingencies that might occur.

Since their slow progress made them vulnerable to retaliation, he ordered a rear guard to remain behind to warn him if large numbers of soldiers left the palace and began moving in his direction. He also maintained forward guards and pickets along his flanks to guard against surprise attacks from any direction. To his relief, none came.

The army camped for the night in a small glade along the trail and resumed its march the next morning.

CHAPTER 36

THE BABY...BOY OR GIRL?

Around the time Bardok's forces were breaking camp the next morning, a scout Minos had stationed on a hill north of Knossos raced to the palace to tell him that six ships were approaching Poros from the west.

"Four longboats and two merchant ships. They had big animals painted on their sails."

"Lions?"

"Could be."

"They are Mycenaeans," Minos told Drondak when he too rushed into the room.

"Send a messenger to Bardok. "Tell him the Mycenaeans have come and to return here immediately with as many fighters as he can bring. Are all lookouts and runners in place?"

"Yes, Sire, they are."

"Then put our plan into effect and prepare our chariots. I want to get as close to what is happening down there as I can."

Minos and a small contingent of his guards and messengers were about halfway down to the harbor when another messenger reached them.

"Sire," he said, "Men from the longboats have disembarked and spread out along the shore. Some climbed to the tops of the bluffs. Then the two larger ships landed."

"How many men?" the king asked.

"Maybe two hundred."

"And from the larger ships?"

"We only saw their crews."

"Could they have more fighters aboard them?"

"I don't know. There could be more hidden in their holds."

Minos turned to Drondak. "They are well disciplined. Send runners to remind everyone that we want the Mycenaeans to think we are unprepared for their landing. No one is to engage in any fighting without a command from me. Have your men circle around behind the invaders as they make their way here but be careful to remain out of sight."

Kori, the commander of the Mycenaeans, conferred with his captains as soon as they reached shore. "Looks like the waves did more damage here than to the mainland. There doesn't seem to be anyone here, not even fishermen. Search the town and its surroundings and let me know what you find."

"There is no one in the town," a scout reported on his return. "It's strange. Houses are being rebuilt but there's no one working there."

Kori's other captains reported similar findings. One said he found two longboats under construction farther up the shore, but no builders.

"Either this whole shore has been abandoned or people ran when they saw us approaching," Kori said.

"They fled," another said. "We found hot ashes in the hearth of one of the houses."

Kori pointed to two of his captains. "You and your men remain here. Protect our ships and keep the beach secured. The rest of us will move up the road toward the palace.

Farther up the road, a runner found Minos and Drondak. "Many Mycenaeans are headed this way. The others are staying with their ships."

A little while later, another runner informed Minos that the Mycenaeans had divided their approaching army. "Most of them are camped along the road, but a small group is moving toward us."

"How many?"

"I counted ten."

"How are they armed?"

"They left their spearmen and archers at their camp. The men coming this way only carry long swords."

"What do you think of that?" Minos asked Drondak. "That group is too big to be a scouting party, yet much too small for an attack force. And why would the larger group be camping along the road this time of day unless they are preparing for an early morning attack? But if they were going to attack, why would they leave so many men down at the harbor? I don't understand what they are doing."

To the messengers still standing next to him, he said, "Remind all groups to remain unseen and avoid all contact with the invaders unless I order otherwise."

To his captain he said, "It's time we returned to the palace to see to its defense."

Later that afternoon, Drondak entered Minos's throne room to tell him that the small group of Mycenaeans had arrived at the north entrance to the palace and asked to confer with the king.

"Let them in but only their commander is to enter this room. Offer the others wine, but guard them well in the central court."

Minos sat with a spear-carrying guard on each side of his throne as he waited. He wore a long dagger in place of his jeweled, ceremonial knife on his belt. A naked gold-handled sword stood beside him.

To Minos, the Mycenaean seemed to be an older, taller version of Zardik—the same bronzed skin, powerful chest and shoulders, and the muscular thighs of a man who must have spent years pulling an oar. His beard, though, was whiter than Zardik's. He wore only a small dagger on his belt, having left his sword in the anteroom. His eyes took note of everything in the room and he didn't bow. A servant placed some wine and a bit of cheese on a low table in front of him but he ignored them and waited for Minos to speak first.

"Who are you and why are you here?" Minos asked.

"I am called Kori. I come from Mycenae. Our mission is peaceful. We have come to see what damage you suffered from the great waves and to offer our help. I am sorry to see what happened to your harbor and its town."

"Thank you for your concern. "But how can you say you are on a peaceful mission when you enter our harbor with so many long-boats and who knows how many warriors hidden in your merchant ships? And why have you camped so many of your fighters so close to my palace?"

Kori smiled. "I see you have been watching us. I understand your concern, but we have no warriors in the merchant ships, only their crews. Those ships are laden with grain and other foods I expect you need. My fighters are camped along the road only to protect me."

"What will you take in return for your grain and foods?"

"We can trade for gold and silver or for your craftsmen's wool-ens, painted vases, or jewelry. But what we prefer in exchange is the use of your harbors where our ships bound for Egypt can rest their crews and replenish their supplies. We know your trading port at Akrotiri no longer exists. We can help you rebuild your harbors to replace it."

"That would be profitable for both of us if what you say is true, but we have been warned that your intentions might be otherwise."

"What do you mean by otherwise?"

"We heard you invaded several islands north of Thera and that you intend to sack Knossos and eventually control all of Kephtor. How can we be sure you are not really here to probe our weak-nesses in preparation for a later invasion?"

"Who said that about us?"

"That information came from Phaestos."

Kori smiled.

"I see. It was Jawana."

"Yes, it was."

"I am not surprised. We had some unpleasant dealings with him at his harbor that he will someday regret. So far as you are concerned, you have little alternative but to trust us. It is true I can see your weaknesses. You could not defend yourselves against the kind of invasion we could mount. But why would we want to do that? The best thing for both our kingdoms is for you to help us with our trade to the east while we help you rebuild your kingdom."

"Your offer is tempting. I suggest we discuss it in greater detail in the morning. If you wish, you can spend the night here."

"Thank you for your hospitality, but I will rejoin my men for the night."

A messenger reached Bardok the second night while he and his small army with their captured horde of animals were on their way back to Knossos.

"Lookouts reported the approach of Mycenaeans ships early this morning. King Minos wants you to hurry back with as many fighters as you can bring."

"How many?"

"Four longboats and two merchant ships."

"How many men?"

"I don't know. They had not yet landed when the king sent me."

Later that evening, a second messenger appeared out of the twilight while Bardok was organizing his best fighters for an early morning dash to Knossos.

"I come from Trapeza. I am sorry to tell you that the high priestess's baby was born dead and she is very weak."

"What do you mean *weak?*" Bardok demanded. "Will she survive?"

"She has suffered much but she still lives. She sleeps."

"Why do you say 'still lives'?"

"She gave up much blood."

"What else?"

"I can tell you nothing more."

"When did you leave Trapeza?"

"At first light this morning."

"And she was alive then?"

"Yes, Sire. They placed her on a bed under a tree where the cool breezes might comfort her."

"And the ladies were still with her when you left?"

"Yes, Sire."

Bardok turned away from the messenger, took a few steps, then turned back to him.

"The baby...boy or girl?"

"A boy, Sire."

Bardok turned away again and sat on the stone retaining wall that lined the road. Vactor and Gantaros tried to console him, but he waved them away.

Why do the women I love suffer because I give them sons, he thought, dead sons that tear their bodies. It's me and my seed. And with Knossos under attack, I can't even go to her. Live, Cavanila, please live.

The next morning, with his fighters straining to keep up with him, Bardok drove his chariot as fast as he could toward the palace. He saw no evidence of an invading force as he approached its south entrance and no one there to defend it. He ran up the stairs to the central court with his sword drawn, but found it as peaceful as always. He rushed into the throne room and was surprised to see Minos in conversation with the Mycenaean. Both men looked up at the breathless Bardok and smiled.

"Bardok, this is Kori," Minos said. "He is the commander of the Mycenaeans. His ships brought us some food and other things. He says he wants to help us rebuild our ports."

Bardok stopped and let out a deep breath. "My father once told me about you, Kori. He said you were a great warrior."

"I knew your father. I heard what happened. I am sorry he can't be found."

"Thank you for your thoughts. I would like to know more about your mission but I have another important concern."

He then turned to Minos. "Last night a messenger said that Cavanila's baby was born dead and that she was near death. Have you heard more?"

"She still lives," Minos replied, "but she has not awakened. Tell me what happened at Phaestos. I will have a chariot and fresh horse readied for you while we speak"

Kori rose from his seat. "I can leave if you wish to speak in private."

"No, stay and hear about Bardok's mission," Minos replied.

After Bardok described his encounter with Jawana, Kori interrupted him. "You did well. Your tactics were those of a good commander. You handled your groups like ships closing in on a pirate. Jawana got what he deserved. It would have been no loss if you had killed him."

Without replying, Bardok hastily told Minos about the flocks and other foods Vactor and Gantaros were bringing and asked to be excused so he could go to Cavanila.

"Yes, go. Kori and I will see to things here," Minos said. "I am pleased with what you have done. I hope Cavanila will be well. Keep me informed."

CHAPTER 37

I HAVE MADE MY DECISION

Cavanila blinked her eyes as she came awake and tried to focus on Leroma and Tuma standing stood over her.

"My baby?" she asked.

They helped her sit up and offered her a cup of warm goat's milk. But neither looked directly into her eyes or answered her question. She took barely enough to wet her dry mouth and parched lips, and pushed it away. Their silence frightened her.

"Where is my baby?" she demanded as she laid back in her bed.

Leroma took Cavanila's hand. "We are so sorry, Cavanila. Your son did not live."

Cavanila's gaze went from one woman to the other. "My baby died? I had a son?"

They both nodded. "You bled so much we thought you were going to the gods too," Tuma replied.

Then Cavanila remembered—the pain, the ladies holding her as she kneeled, their shouts of "breathe" and "push," their hands pressing her belly, their fingers trying to pull her open, her screams, and, finally, release.

She searched Leroma's face again, took a deep breath, and then another. "Where is he?"

"Up in the cave, High Priestess," Leroma answered. "We prepared him for his journey but haven't buried him yet. We thought you would want to be there."

Cavanila heard Leroma's words but didn't reply. Her eyes closed and she drifted back into sleep. She next awoke long after the sun had set. In the light from the single oil lamp, she saw Leroma asleep in her chair.

"Water," Cavanila said, bringing Leroma to instant wakefulness.

Leroma poured water into Cavanila's cup and helped her sit up to drink. She offered her a piece of cheese, but Cavanila took only a single bite before lying back again.

A beam of morning sun lit the foot of her bed when Cavanila next awoke. Alone, she lay quietly until she came to a decision. She sat up, drank more water, and struggled to stand. She leaned on the nearby table until her head cleared. When she felt confident her legs would support her, she picked her robe from a chair and made her way to her doorway. She leaned on the doorpost, surprised to find herself already out of breath and so weak. Her heart hammered. She stood there for several moments and then walked, stiff-legged, with her arms outstretched for balance, onto the path that led uphill.

She moved slowly from one house to next, leaning against their walls whenever she could. Beyond them, she found no support, and in places, not even a real path, only rock outcroppings she had to crawl over. She tried to protect her knees with the bottom of her robe that had become bloody, not from her knees, but from a trickle that ran down her thighs. At the cave entrance, a vertical cleft in the rocks, she stopped to rest again.

It's like me, she thought. It opens into a place of death.

She paused after her first two steps into the cave to let her eyes adapt to the darkness. An oil lamp burned beside the inverted clay urn. She stepped down a series of flat, wet boulders to reach the cave floor and sat next to the urn. She held it to her, lay her head on her arms, and wept until sleep overtook her.

She awoke, hot and sweaty, when she felt the urn begin to tremble. A rumble echoed through the cavern and the floor beneath her shook. She remembered her dream on Bardok's boat in which she struggled on leaden legs to reach the cave entrance. She knew what the shaking meant. She turned the urn upright, clutched it to her aching breasts, and hurried toward the cave's entrance. But her rear foot slid out from under her when she took a second step on the slippery rock. She twisted her body as she fell to protect the urn and landed on her back. She hit her head and slid back down to the cave floor.

She found herself in her bed when she next opened her eyes. Bardok held her hand in both of his. She looked into his eyes.

"Our son," she whispered.

He gripped her hand even more tightly. "I know."

"His urn?

"It didn't break. It's in the cave."

"Oh, Bardok. I'm so sorry,"

He leaned to embrace her, close to tears himself.

"It's all right. You are going to recover. We will have other sons."

They held each other until her sobbing stopped.

"You have to tell Minos what happened to Staphylos," she said.

"He already knows. I sent a messenger after we got you out of that cave. We were frightened because we couldn't find you until one of your maids found your trail of blood. Leroma said you are still bleeding a little. You need to stay in bed. Let me get you some food."

"Yes, please."

She ate a little cheese and a small piece of brown bread, drank some milk, and slept again. She next awoke to see Bardok eating his evening meal. She ate more too, and they talked until it was dark. He told her about his mission to Phaestos and what had happened at Knossos.

By the next day, her bleeding had nearly stopped and some color returned to her face. Her breasts hurt in the tight bandages Leroma had tied around her, but she knew that would end as soon as her milk stopped flowing.

"We have to bury him," she told Bardok during their morning meal, "but I don't want him in that cave."

"Then where?"

"On that mountain peak, next to the gold bull."

Bardok blinked in surprise. "You are in no condition to make that climb," he said. "He needs to be buried today."

"You can bury him. I will visit him later."

Bardok's climb to that peak was less difficult than before because he knew the path better. He dug a hole next to the one in which he had buried the golden bull. With loving care, he lowered the urn into the hole and covered it with rocks and dirt. As he worked, he thought about Lovanna and Cavanila and their sons that never survived. And he knew he had his own doubts when he told Cavanila they could have other sons. With each son he lost, he also lost or nearly lost the woman he loved. He shuddered to think of what could happen again.

When he finished, he took some time to look around. Cavanila was right, he thought. With the seas to the north, the long slope down to the coastal plain, and the mountain peaks all around, this was a fitting place for his son.

As Cavanila grew stronger, her daily walks with Bardok became progressively longer. During one of them, with her arm through his, she told him she now understood how Hekton, the old priest, felt when he held onto her arm the day of the first destruction. She told him more about that day and how unhappy she was with her father's actions—things she hadn't told him before. And she told him how badly she felt because she could not respect her father the way she would have wished.

On a subsequent walk, Bardok tried to get her to talk about her experience at Phaestos and Jawana's refusal to provide the food Knossos needed. He hadn't forgotten Cavanila's comment about Jawana's insult that she had yet to explain.

"It was a painful time," she replied. "Thanks to you, I expect it will never happen again." But she said no more about that mission for the rest of that walk.

As they approached her house, a messenger came to meet them.

"The king ordered me to tell the high priestess that he is saddened by the loss of her baby but is happy to hear she is recovering. He also said he has important things to discuss with her as soon as she can return to Knossos."

"What does he want to talk about?" Bardok asked.

"I was not told."

"Tell him we will come when Cavanila is well enough to travel."

A second messenger arrived two days later.

"The king sends you his greetings, High Priestess. He said you must come to Knossos as soon as you are able to travel." He paused, and then added, "I can also tell you that the king seemed ill when I left him."

Cavanila nodded to Bardok who replied to the messenger. "Tell the king that unless we need to stop to let the high priestess rest, we will arrive at the palace by dark, tomorrow.

Bardok chose a road that went past the tiny villages of Kera and Krasi and then downhill along a winding road to what the waves had left of Malia. The route was longer than the one he took when he first brought Cavanila to Trapeza, but he went slowly. At many breaks in the terrain, Cavanila looked back up into the mountains to see the peak where her son lay, where she hadn't been able to go before their departure for Knossos, and she grieved some more.

They arrived at Knossos late in the afternoon of the next day. Cavanila held Bardok's arm as they climbed the stairs to the palace's central court. Minos greeted them from his throne and didn't look happy. Without waiting for permission from Minos, Bardok escorted Cavanila to her seat at the king's left and took his own on Minos's right.

"You look ill, Devterex," he said. "What's wrong?"

Minos glanced away. "Just some strange pains in my side and back. But that's not why I sent for you two."

He turned to Cavanila. "Staphylos was to be my heir, but you lost him."

"I did my best, Sire," she replied in a soft but firm voice, disturbed by his accusation.

"I am sure you did. But now I am getting old and have no one to succeed me. I could name you the next Minos since you are my brother's daughter, but you have caused me so many problems. And you are not a believer."

"Sire…" Cavanila started to reply.

"Don't interrupt. It seems the people favor you and your way of doing things, but they may not be so happy to have you as Minos after another cold season."

"Sire…" she tried to say again.

He pointed his finger at her. "I said don't interrupt me."

This time she refused to be silenced. "Who said I will be the next Minos?"

"I did, unless you don't want to be. But if you do, you will have to follow my instructions. Do you want to help your people or don't you?"

"I want to help my people, but I do not want to be the next Minos. I am not ready to rule all Minoa."

"I don't think so either, but I can teach you things while I am still here. And with a competent chamberlain, Minoa might survive under your reign."

"What about Bardok? Make him your successor. He could deal with regents elsewhere and with the Mycenaeans better than me. I know nothing about trading or military matters."

"Bardok will be your chamberlain and command your army. He will know how to deal with those people."

"Sire, I am honored you want me to succeed you, but there is so much to consider."

"There is nothing to think about. Your people need you. Do you want to help them or not?"

"Sire," Bardok broke in, "Cavanila is still not well. Perhaps you could order some refreshment for her."

"Yes, of course, I am sorry."

Neither Minos nor Bardok spoke while Cavanila drank some milk but didn't touch the cheese or wine that was put in front of her. Its smell reminded her of the table full of food at Phaestos the night she rejected Jawana's ultimatum. Her stomach churned.

She got to her feet and paced the room from one end to the other. She tried to imagine herself on that throne, dealing with the kinds of problems she would have to face. Strength and wisdom, she thought. Do I have them? She stopped in front of Minos and looked up at him.

"Well," he said, "You've taken long enough. Will you be my heir and successor or not?"

"Sire," she said, "I need to be alone for a while."

The king's face reddened. "Why can't you decide?"

Cavanila's face hardened, she looked directly into his eyes. "I'm going for a walk, Sire. I will return soon."

Bardok rose from his seat. "I will go with you."

Cavanila held an open hand toward him, motioning him to remain in his seat.

"No," she said. "I have to be alone."

Bardok turned to look at Minos after Cavanila stepped from the room. For the first time since their boyhood days, he saw an impish smile on Minos's face.

From the throne room, Cavanila descended the narrow stairs to the north portal and then walked down the wide, tilted stairs where people sometimes sat to watch dancers perform. From there, she walked up the hill to the burial grounds, a tranquil place where she had gone before to ponder her problems and search for clarity. She sat next to the cave where Handoro lay. With the sea in the distance and the sun throwing long shadows, she felt calmed and composed.

I wonder what advice that dear man would give me, she thought. He said I have a way with people, that they loved and respected me. But is that enough? I am still so young. Can I really deal with Minoa's problems? Do I even know what they are? But Bardok does. He knows how to organize and command. He anticipates problems before they occur, like his warning about Jawana I wish I had listened to. And he is strong. He should be the next Minos, not me.

She sat for a while, enjoying her solitude and the peace that comes with having made a difficult decision, until she heard Bardok calling her name.

"You have been gone a long time," he said when he joined her. "We were worried about you. Are you well? Minos is waiting for your answer."

She smiled at him from her seat on the ground.

"I'm sorry. I had much to consider. But I have made my decision. I am not fit to be the next Minos. But you are. You can do what is necessary to govern Minoa and return it to its greatness. I will tell Minos you should be his successor, not me. I will be your wife and high priestess, if you want me. I will have sons for you, but I will not be the next Minos."

He knelt next to her, put his hands on her shoulders.

"Cavanila, I can help you do all those things as your chamberlain, the way I did on Nios. You were the regent there. You made the important decisions. You were the one who convinced people to work together and do what was needed. You were the one people loved, like they love you here. Minos is right to want you for his successor. No one else could do what you can."

"How could people still love me after I let them starve?"

He moved his hands to her upper arms. "You didn't let them starve. You did what you could, what anyone would have done."

Cavanila's most painful memories returned to her, but she only said, "I'm glad you think so, but I have made my decision. Please help me up."

Bardok held her hand as they retraced their steps back to the palace. The climb up the theatrical area was not difficult for her, but she took the steeper stairs to the central court more slowly, resting for a moment after every two or three. She gripped Bardok's hand, watched her steps, and tried to concentrate on how she would explain her decision to Minos.

When she reached the upper steps, close enough to be seen from the court, a chorus of cheers rang out. She looked up to see that the court was filled with people, broad smiles on their faces, waving their arms and calling her name.

Minos was there as well, in front of everyone, sitting on his throne, which his servants had moved out there. His frown she had seen so much of was gone, replaced by a fatherly, self-satisfied smile.

She stopped where she was, still several steps from the top. She looked up at Minos, at the crowd, and then at Bardok, his face a broad, encouraging smile. She wanted to speak but could find no words. She took a step closer to the top, stared again at Minos and the urging crowd, until something within her gave way. She gripped Bardok's hand even more tightly. Tears welled up in her eyes.

Her people left her no choice.

The End

Made in the USA
Lexington, KY
19 June 2014